DARK
DECEIVER
PAMELA PALMER

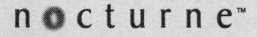

Silhouette Books

n⦾cturne™

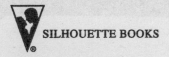

SILHOUETTE BOOKS

ISBN-13: 978-0-373-61789-0
ISBN-10:   0-373-61789-5

DARK DECEIVER

Copyright © 2008 by Pamela Poulsen

www.silhouettenocturne.com

Printed in U.S.A.

"It was just a dream, Autumn. It might be nothing."

But her laughter filled him with pleasure. "The dream of a Sitheen is nothing to take lightly. You saw them, Kade. I'm sure of it. I'll start researching as soon as I get home."

Sharp intelligence gleamed in her eyes as the excitement visibly bubbled within her, pleasing him immensely. What he wouldn't give to pull her into his arms and taste the happiness on her lips.

"You're an amazing woman, Autumn McGinn. If anyone can find the stones, you will." She wouldn't find them, of course. Ustanis's magical ability would lead him to the stones long before Autumn ever figured out where they were.

"Thank you." Her gaze turned soft and shy as she smiled at him.

Every intent flew out of his head as the need to taste her became too great to fight.

And all he could think was that he was just about to say goodbye to the woman he'd been waiting for all his life.

Books by Pamela Palmer

Silhouette Nocturne

*The Dark Gate #13
*Dark Deceiver #42

*The Esri

PAMELA PALMER

Pamela Palmer admits to a passion for all things paranormal, fed by years of *Star Trek, Buffy the Vampire Slayer* and Tolkien's classic *The Lord of the Rings*. Though she grew up wanting to be an astronaut (until she realized the space shuttle wasn't likely to get her beyond Earth's orbit), she became an industrial engineer for a major computer maker before surrendering to the romantic, exciting, otherworldly stories that crowded her head, demanding to be told. Her writing has won numerous awards including a prestigious Golden Heart. Pamela lives in Virginia with her husband and two kids and would love to hear from readers through her Web site, www.pamelapalmer.net.

Dear Reader,

My deepest thanks for your wonderful response to *The Dark Gate.* Your letters have meant more to me than you can imagine. This book, *Dark Deceiver,* is the sequel, the second book in what is now THE ESRI series. At the end of *The Dark Gate,* the humans feared that more of the inhuman Esri would infiltrate our world.

They were right.

I'm smiling as I write this, rubbing my hands together with devilish glee. I love conflict. Not in my real life. Like anyone, I want my days and my relationships to run smoothly. No, the conflict I love is the kind I create and direct through my stories. I adore throwing strong characters into impossible situations with no clue how I'm going to get them out. Or how they're going to get themselves out. As my characters and I plot and strategize, we often find that escape requires them to do something they never thought they would, or become someone they never thought they could. And in the process, they grow into the people they were meant to be—heroes and heroines capable of great love.

I hope you enjoy reading *Dark Deceiver* as much as I've enjoyed writing it. When you're through, I'd love to hear from you. You can reach me through my Web site, www.pamelapalmer.net, where you can also sign up for my newsletter and learn more about me, my books and the world and characters of THE ESRI series.

All the best,

Pamela Palmer

To my husband, Keith, for laughter, love and endless support. You really are my inspiration. More than you know.

Special thanks to Laurin Wittig, Anne Shaw Moran and Elizabeth Holcomb for keeping me on track and dropping everything to read for me when I needed you. Thanks also to my brilliant agent, Helen Breitwieser, and my wonderful editors, Ann Leslie Tuttle and Charles Griemsman. Working with you is a joy.

Prologue

The monster of the court had arrived.

Kaderil the Dark strode into the noisy and jubilant hall, half carrying, half dragging the captive at his side, turning gaiety into chaos with a single glower. Sweat dampened his tunic and rolled between his shoulder blades as he strode beneath the floating candles that lit the open hall. Kaderil demanded fear and knew how to get it. Seven tall feet of hard muscle, skin the color of coarse sand and hair as black as the king's stallion, his appearance alone was enough to strike terror into the breasts of the fair Esri. But it was the reputation for violence he'd carefully cultivated over the years that sent the court's finest scurrying for cover and had him nodding with grim satisfaction.

Above his head, yards of silk floated between the high marble columns, ribbons of color against the russet glow of the night sky. He'd traveled hard for seven days to the Banished Lands and back to fetch his captive for the king. Though he longed for a cool bath and a soft bed, both would have to wait. There were greater things afoot this night.

As he crossed the hall, one of the brightly dressed Esri lords—a man whose height reached nearly to Kaderil's chin—failed to clear his path quickly enough. Kaderil clamped his hand around the man's stark white neck and, with a flick of his wrist, he tossed him into the fleeing crowd. Frightened squeals filled the air, punctuated by the snap of bones and yells of pain.

The cries died almost as soon as they began, for the only injuries the immortal Esri could not heal within seconds were the scuffs and rips to their jewel-colored tunics or sheer, glimmering gowns.

With a satisfied grunt, Kaderil dragged his hairless and quaking captive across the hall. Furtive looks, sharp with terror, speared him from every direction, filling him with calm satisfaction. Their fear protected his secret. They dared not challenge him and therefore had never discovered that the unknown human ancestor whose blood tainted his veins had cursed him with more than his barbaric human looks. He'd left him with little magic—the true power of the Esri.

Kaderil the Dark, the one most feared, was the weakest of them all.

As he approached the throne, which was surrounded by an arc of guards in silver tunics, King Rith beckoned impatiently. "Come, come, Punisher. Bring me the slave." The king's white face was long and lean, the ethereal look at odds with the ambition that shone with a chiseled edge from his eyes. He wore a cloak of pure gold and in his straw-blond curls, a shimmer of emerald beads.

But it was not his king Kaderil watched with careful measure, but Zander, the captain of the royal guard, the only one in all of Esria who had the gift of sensing power...and lack of power...in others. The only one who knew Kaderil's secret.

Kaderil's blue gaze clashed with Zander's hated yellow, then broke away as he tossed the slave onto the low dais before the king. Behind him, he felt the throng of Esri fill the cleared path, pressing forward, their fear already forgotten in their growing excitement over the slave's arrival. He was tempted to whirl and fling another couple of bodies, but refrained, given the extraordinary nature of the gathering.

Around the hall, whispers darted from person to person like hummingbirds set loose on a garden of flowers. "The lost gate has been found!"

King Rith raised his hand, demanding silence, then speared the small man at his feet with an eager gaze. "Your master is dead."

It was not a question. All Esri knew the moment one of their own was killed, as well as the identities of both murdered and murderer. A month ago, the court had fallen silent, rocked by the knowledge that after fifteen hundred years, one of their own had been killed by humans.

"Aye, sire."

"And do you know the location of the lost gate?"

The slave touched the floor with his forehead, then lifted his bald head. "Aye. I have been through it myself."

Incredible, Kaderil thought, his mind racing even as he stood at attention, his feet spread, his arms at his back. Fifteen hundred years ago the seven stones of power were stolen into the human realm and used to seal the gates from the other side. Rumor had always claimed that a single lost gate had been left unsealed, but it had never been found.

Until now.

The king grabbed the slave by the tunic and dragged him forward. "And what of my seven stones?"

The slave's arms waved in agitation. "Only the draggon stone was found, sire. 'Twas the smell of the stone's power that led my master to the gate. But the stone was lost, sire. Lost to the humans who killed him."

King Rith released the creature with a shove. "How is this possible? Humans cannot kill an immortal without the death chant. Surely no humans exist after all this time who remember that bit of magic."

The slave prostrated himself, his voice muffled by the floor. "I beg your pardon, sire, but there are a few. They are the descendants of the mixed bloods, the mortal children of both human and Esri. The humans we once called Sitheen."

Mortals with a drop of Esri blood, Kaderil thought. Just as he was an immortal tainted with human. But the only things they had in common were a lack of true power and the look of the humans. The Sitheen would blend into their world as he never had into his own.

"The Sitheen must die. All of them. They will not thwart us again." King Rith slapped the carved arm of his throne. "*I will have my stones.* Zander, come forth."

As Zander stepped out of the arc of silver tunics and came to stand beside him, Kaderil clenched his jaw. Zander made no secret of his hatred for the human-looking Punisher, yet he had never told Kaderil's secret. Why? Kaderil had spent centuries waiting, tense and wondering, for the day Zander would bring his world crashing down around him.

The king nodded to the captain of his guard, ambition glittering in his eyes. "You will fetch me the seven stones, Zander."

"Aye, sire."

"You will take a team of stone scenters into the human realm at the gate's next opening to find my power stones. I leave it to you to find and kill the Sitheen."

"Yes, sire. But if it please your highness, I should like to take one more." Zander glanced at Kaderil with a gleam that sent a chill of foreboding down his spine. "I would take the Punisher, my lord."

Kaderil jerked. What was Zander up to? Zander knew, as no one else did, he was unsuited for this task. He had no gifts of power, nothing save his great size and strength.

"'Tis well known Sitheen cannot be fooled by glamour," Zander continued. "With Kaderil's barbaric human looks, he has no need for that fine magic."

Zander's voice fairly brimmed with unnatural enthusiasm, igniting Kaderil's wariness, as well as his annoyance.

"Kaderil is the perfect man to infiltrate the Sitheen

and retrieve your draggon stone, my king. They will think him one of them, allowing him to infiltrate their band and slaughter them with ease."

Kaderil opened his mouth to object. There was little to be gained by the time-consuming and dangerous ploy of infiltrating the barbarian's band when the others could fulfill the mission through the power of their gifts. There was little to be gained and much to be lost. If the Sitheen discovered his ruse, they would sing the death chant for him.

Before the words could escape his lips, he felt Zander's palm clap him on the shoulder, silencing him with a river of fire that stole his breath and streaked his vision with jagged flares of light.

Fighting the blinding pain with every scrap of strength he possessed, Kaderil snatched the hand off his shoulder. As he sucked air into his burning lungs, he snapped the man's white forearm with a satisfying crack.

Zander gave a shout and sidestepped Kaderil's reach with a look of venom. "Kaderil will fetch your draggon stone quickly, sire. Between one full moon and the next."

One month. Kaderil struggled against the nearly overwhelming urge to snap Zander's neck and every bone in his body. One month to do a nearly impossible task. He knew now what Zander was about. His enemy was setting him up to fail.

The king nodded greedily. "Aye. Aye, indeed, I will have my stones by the next feast."

Cold tension wove through Kaderil's muscles at the full measure of Zander's treachery. The Esrian king was notoriously unforgiving. Failure resulted in banishment.

And banishment, for Kaderil the Dark, would mean complete and total isolation for the rest of his immortal existence, for who would welcome the Punisher?

Fury burned through him, binding his hands into fists. He would not let Zander win.

Slowly, his fists eased, his heart pumping with cold determination. His mission would be difficult in the extreme. But not impossible. Never impossible. And the ultimate revenge against his conniving foe would be utter and brilliant success.

Chapter 1

Washington, D.C.

Autumn McGinn grimaced with embarrassment as she crawled through the rain-soaked grass, frantically searching for the lighter she'd accidentally sent flying for the third time.

"You okay, Autumn?" Larsen Hallihan's voice darted across the rainy Dupont Circle Park, cutting through the gloom. Light poles bordered the concrete circle at the center of the grassy park, illuminating the huge marble chalice that stood in the middle—the beautifully carved fountain that shared real estate with the invisible gate into Esria.

"I'm fine!" Autumn called back.

Why couldn't she have left her inner klutz home just

this once? For four months, she'd angled for an invitation to help guard the gate, ever since the first Esri, Baleris, had found his way through. For four weeks, Baleris had terrorized the nation's capital, raping young women and enchanting armed cops while he tried to destroy the handful of humans immune to his magic. The humans the Esri called Sitheen. In the end, the humans had won. Baleris was dead.

But the gate remained unsealed. Apparently, it had always been unsealed, but the Esri hadn't known about it until Baleris had stumbled upon it by accident. Unfortunately, after Baleris died, one of his slaves had escaped back through the gate before they could stop him. Chances were good he'd told others and the Esri would invade again.

Fortunately, the gate only opened during the midnight hour of a full moon. One hour a month, four humans who could resist the spell of enchantment guarded the Dupont Circle Fountain. That is, they had until this month, when two of the four Sitheen had been called out of town.

Autumn had been invited to help, finally, though not quite the way she'd wanted. Ordered to stay far back from the fountain, she'd been enlisted as an extra pair of eyes. If one of the creatures came through, her only job was to watch where he went. Not the greatest responsibility in the world, but she wasn't Sitheen. Even though she wore a bracelet of holly which supposedly gave her immunity, they still feared she could be enchanted.

She sighed as she crawled through the soaked grass. If only she could do something truly important for once. But considering she was spending most of her time on her hands and knees, watching was probably the safest job for her...for everyone's sake.

Her numb fingers finally brushed against something hard as the rain beat a tattoo against the raised hood of her jacket. With relief, she grabbed the renegade lighter and scrambled to her feet, her soaked jeans clinging to her legs.

Fire, combined with the Esri death chant, was the only known weapon against the Esri. Logically, she knew her little lighter wasn't going to do an ounce of good in the rain, especially since she didn't know the death chant, but she felt safer with it in her hand. If she could just keep hold of the darned thing.

"What time is it?" Larsen called from the other side of the park. Larsen Vale, now Hallihan, had been her roommate in college and one of her best friends for years.

"One-thirty," Larsen's husband, Jack, replied. The two of them stood on opposite sides of the fountain, each a distance from Autumn. "We'll give it another ten minutes, then call it quits for the night."

Autumn sighed. She hadn't really expected to see an Esri tonight—none had come through the gate the past three full moons. Still, she'd hoped. As a curator for the Smithsonian, she was too much of a history and folklore buff not to be excited by the prospect of other-worldly creatures, even if they were armed with powerful magic and malicious intent.

"I'm heading straight for a hot bath when we get home," Larsen said.

Autumn couldn't hear Jack's reply, but knew it was something suggestive. Jack and Larsen had only been married a couple of months and couldn't seem to keep their eyes—or hands—off one another. Autumn was happy for her old friend, but sometimes life was so unfair. Larsen was blond, beautiful, married to one of D.C.'s hottest cops, and Sitheen. Autumn was six foot four with flaming orange hair, two million freckles and a gene for klutziness. Where was the fairness in *that?*

The rumble of thunder shook the ground as the rain turned to a downpour. Cold and miserable, Autumn huddled beneath the hood of her raincoat while heavy drops beat at her shoulders and back. Okay, *now* she was ready to call it a night. Clearly, the Esri weren't coming.

Jack's shout made her jump. She jerked her gaze to the lit fountain just in time to see a large, dark-cloaked figure leap from the marble base as if he'd been encased in stone all these years.

An Esri!

The creature, taller than Jack, jumped over the low wall of the fountain's pool and took off running at warp speed. Jack sprinted after him, his flamethrower arcing at his side.

A real live Esri.

Excitement pounded through her as she watched the chase until Larsen's yell snapped her attention back to the fountain where three more cloaked figures jumped from the marble base and scattered. Larsen pointed her flamethrower at the nearest one, but the pouring rain doused the fire before it could reach the fleeing target.

Autumn stared in stunned wonder until she realized the smallest of the three was headed straight for her! Her mind screamed at her to run. But as the creature passed within feet of her, some inner need to prove herself had her racing forward on frozen feet to tackle the slender creature to the ground.

As she struggled to catch her breath, she stared down into the face of a skinny, white-as-a-sheet teenaged boy peeking out of a coal-black cloak. Eyes that glowed as orange as her hair stared back at her in furious terror.

What had she done? The hair rose on her arms as she met the gaze of this inhuman monster.

The creature struggled against her hold, his face contorted with his futile effort. Either she was in serious need of a diet, or the kid had no muscle mass. His white face twisted in terror and bravado even as he blinked against the onslaught of rain.

"We'll find the power stones," he sneered. "All of them, as my king demands. You'll not stop us even if you kill me!" His eyes flooded with moisture that had nothing to do with the weather.

Autumn stared at the creature beneath her. He was crying! She'd made a monster cry. This had to be a new low in her life.

"Stop it! I'm not going to kill you."

Beneath her, the Esri youth stilled. "I don't believe you." He continued to thrash until she was sure he was going to give her a headache. "You'll set me aflame as you did Baleris. You...*dark blood.* You *human!*"

She stared at the angry hopelessness that twisted the kid's mouth and felt a sharp stab of pity. She'd told him she wasn't going to kill him, but he was right not to believe her. *She* might not kill him, but Jack and Larsen would. This was war and there was no taking an Esri prisoner. Jack had tried that once. He'd locked up Baleris in the police station overnight. By morning, the Esri had managed to enchant the entire D.C. police force, turning them into his own personal hit squad.

They had to kill him. And yet...*he was just a kid.*

Her mind aimed a swift kick at her heart. She couldn't be soft on this. If she screwed up now, Jack and Larsen would never let her help again.

"Autumn, hold him!" Larsen's voice carried through the rain.

The Esri struggled beneath her. "Release me!" But the anger in his voice was crumbling beneath his fear. "I beg of you, release me. I do not wish to die." The tears ran freely from his eyes, now. "Please, my lady. *Please.* I mean you no harm."

Dear God, what was she supposed to do? He was Esri. Evil.

He was just a kid.

With a groan of despair, she knew she couldn't be the reason he died.

"If I let you go, you have to go back through that gate. *Right now.*"

The boy stilled, his orange eyes widening with hope. "Aye. I shall go back. You'll not regret it. I'll make it up to you. I give you my vow."

"Right. Just make sure you go back through that gate. If you don't, my friends will catch you. And then you *will* die."

She rolled off him into the muddy grass, knowing she was going to regret this. Jack and Larsen were going to be furious. The kid leaped to his feet and made a dash for the fountain as Larsen tried to intercept him with her flamethrower. But the kid was fast. Before Larsen could catch him, he dove into the fountain, his cloak billowing out behind him for one brief moment before he disappeared.

Autumn rose from the soaked grass, her shoulders heavy with guilt.

"Damn, damn, *damn!*" Larsen's epithets rose in volume as she ran toward Autumn. "Did he hurt you?"

"No."

"Do you *know* what just happened?"

Autumn cringed. "If you're asking if he enchanted me, I don't think so. I'm still wearing my holly." She held up her arm, displaying the rough band of wood she wore around her wrist. Holly was the only thing they'd found that protected true humans from the Esris' mind control. "I know I had him. I know I let him go."

"Why?"

All her life Autumn had longed to be smaller. Now she felt about two inches tall. And it hurt. "Larsen, I'm sorry. He looked like a fifteen-year-old kid. And he was crying." Even to her own ears, her reasons sounded lame.

Larsen looked around with a deep sigh, her expression one of frustration, her movements agitated. "All right. Well, it's done." Larsen dug in her pocket and handed Autumn a set of keys. "Go get in the car and lock the doors. The others may come back and I don't want you to get hurt."

Autumn pressed her lips together, wanting to argue that she could help. But she'd just proved she couldn't be trusted.

"Larsen, he said something that might be important. He said they came for the power stones."

Larsen's gaze jerked to hers. "Stones? Are you sure the word was plural?"

"Positive." Autumn shoved the keys and her cold fists deep into her pockets. "He said they'd find them all."

"We thought there was only one. We *have* only one."

"Yeah. That's why I thought it might be important."

"I really wish you hadn't let him go, Autumn."

Autumn met her friend's rueful gaze. "Me, too."

"There's Jack! Did you catch him?" she called to her husband, but he just shook his head.

As Larsen ran to join her husband, Autumn turned to make her way to the car, her heart heavy with the knowledge she'd finally gotten the chance she'd been longing for. A chance to make a difference. To be a hero.

And she'd blown it. Not only had she failed to be of help, she'd become something far, far worse.

She'd become a liability the Sitheen could not afford.

Two weeks later, as the sun set amidst painted clouds, Kaderil strode across the busy street near the D.C. waterfront to the squeal of brakes and the honks of impatient human drivers. He'd learned enough during his short time in the human realm to know he was expected to give way to the vehicles, but he'd spent fifteen centuries making others—powerful immortals—cower before him.

He refused now to submit to humans, regardless of the armor they wore, though he had to admit to a certain fascination with this armor. *Cars,* they called them. And trucks, minivans, SUVs, convertibles. The humans had a different name for nearly every one and he knew them all.

A cold breeze ruffled his hair as he stepped onto the curb and started across the parking lot to the low-slung building of the marina's offices. The human world was not what he'd expected. The humans were not the unintelligent, animal-like beings of Esrian legend. When they were free from enchantment, they were, in fact, surprisingly quick of mind. Much to his relief, he'd discovered that he possessed some small talents against them, talents he hadn't expected. Although he could not fully enchant them as other Esri could, he was able to push thoughts into their heads and borrow knowledge from their brains with a single touch.

Knowledge that had told him he needed documents and a fictitious background that would withstand thorough investigation if he wanted any hope of fooling the Sitheen. A single misstep and he could well find himself burning beneath a death curse.

He'd bullied Ustanis, the third in their party, into setting up his documents and history since he was fully capable of enchanting the humans, forcing them to do his will, and Kaderil was not. It had taken Ustanis nearly a fortnight to accomplish the task, though Kaderil suspected Zander had played a large part in the delay.

He'd worried that a month would be too little time to infiltrate the Sitheen and earn their trust. Now he had only two short weeks.

His stomach burned with tension. The only thing the slave had been able to tell him about the Sitheen was a name, Larsen Vale, and this place, the Top Sail Marina in downtown D.C. They were his only clues. If he failed to find her here, his mission might be lost before he ever started.

Hoping that wasn't the case, he strode up the path toward the door that said Office. He took a deep breath and let it out slowly, caging the Punisher. It was a struggle to fight the deeply ingrained need to fling bodies and demand fear, but he was learning. Humans were fragile creatures, far too easily alarmed by violence. And he had to pretend to be human.

Kaderil opened the door and walked into the marina office.

A solitary, bearded man glanced up from behind the long counter. "Can I help you?"

Kaderil forced his mouth into a semblance of a smile and thrust out his hand. "It's great to see you again!" Human males, it seemed, were incapable of ignoring the invitation of an extended hand.

The bearded one's mouth smiled in a poor attempt to hide his lack of recognition. The moment their hands clasped, Kaderil pushed thoughts into the human's head. *His name is Kade and I know him. I trust him.*

"Kade!" the bearded man exclaimed, the cloud of confusion lifting from his eyes. "What brings you here?"

"Which boat is Larsen Vale's?"

The man motioned Kaderil to the window and pointed to the boat in the last slip. "That's hers down there. That's not Larsen on the boat, though. Looks as if she has company." A lone person walked across the deck, a tall woman with hair like flame. A woman who was not, apparently, his quarry. But she was on a Sitheen's boat. As good a place to start as any.

His pulse leaped with possibility. Even if she wasn't Larsen Vale, she might know her, or be a Sitheen herself. Already, the day was looking up.

Kaderil turned and left the marina office. Behind him he heard a distant, "Good to see you again, Kade. Always a pleasure." Belatedly, he remembered he should have said thank-you or goodbye.

But his patience for the trivial was thin. He had a draggon stone to track down and Sitheen to destroy. And two short weeks to accomplish both.

Long enough, perhaps, for he had an advantage they would never suspect. He looked like them. They wouldn't know he was Esri.

Until too late.

A siren sounded in the distance, rising over the clank and splash of the tie lines, making Autumn's stomach hurt. Every time she turned on the news, another bizarre death was being reported in D.C. Every time she heard a siren, she wondered how many more people had died because of the Esri. How many more murders she might have prevented if she hadn't let that kid go.

A chilly breeze blew a loose wisp of hair in her face as she made her way across the swaying deck of the houseboat to the makeshift desk she'd set up near the back rail. The setting sun over the water blinded her with its brilliance. She grabbed her chair, as much to secure her balance as to move it to the other side of the small table that held her laptop.

Larsen had offered up her unoccupied boat when Autumn had needed a place to stay for a few weeks while her apartment was being repaired after a pipe burst in the unit above hers. In hindsight, she wished she'd taken her less-than-stellar coordination into consideration when she'd decided to live in a moving house. The boat was one of dozens moored at the Top Sail Marina on the Potomac River. Across the river rose the office towers of the very urban Virginia suburbs.

Autumn plopped down in front of her laptop as a pair of gulls cried overhead. For two weeks she'd been trying to find a clue to the other Esri stones. She might not be much of a soldier, but she was a crack researcher, and finding the stones was her only chance to make up for letting that Esri kid go.

Her current research path followed the acquisition records for the Stone of Ezrie: the stone whose scent Baleris had apparently followed to find the gate between the worlds, the stone the Esri called the draggon stone, according to Tarrys. Tarrys was the second of Baleris's slaves, a pretty little thing, barely five feet tall, who had actually helped them defeat Baleris, then stayed after his death.

Before Baleris's arrival, the draggon stone had been doing time as a Smithsonian artifact. A thumb-size pale blue teardrop on a silver chain, the thing had appeared innocuous enough. What made it unique was the seven-pointed star etched on its surface and the legend that it was the key to the gates of Ezrie—a legend, it turned out, that was all too true. If the Esri got their hands on that stone and took it back through the gate, the seals on all twelve gates around the world would instantly dissolve. The Esri could still only get through during the midnight hour of a full moon, but the thought of Baleris's reign of terror times twelve…every month…was enough to give ulcers to the bravest of souls.

She shivered and reached for the zipper on her jacket. If the draggon stone was a key, what was the purpose of the other Esri stones the kid had mentioned? Were they all keys? Or did they serve a different, more ominous purpose? All she knew was they'd better find them before the Esri did.

Her finger smoothed down the copy of the acquisition record she'd copied from the Smithsonian's archives. The page sat beside her laptop, her coffee mug anchoring it against the breeze. She was hoping the previous owner of the draggon stone had been Sitheen with some ability to sense the power in the stones. If he'd owned the one, maybe he'd owned more. She knew she was grasping at straws, but at the moment it was all she had to go on.

She glanced up at her computer, but a movement in the distance caught her attention. Her gaze snagged on a man striding purposefully down the path to the docks—a tall man with dark hair hanging in wind-tossed waves to his shoulders, framing a face that was all strong bones and hard angles. A face darkened by several days' growth of beard. Dressed in jeans and a leather jacket, he looked like some kind of roughrider—sexy and wonderfully dangerous.

As if hearing her thoughts, his head snapped up. He seemed to spear her with his gaze, though he was too far away for her to know if he even saw her. He was probably admiring the sunset. But it still made her pulse race, the fanciful notion that they were destined to meet flitting foolishly through her head.

Which was silly, of course. Even if they were *destined to meet,* it wouldn't be in a romantic way. At least not for him. Though she was definitely a woman who attracted attention, it was never the kind any woman wanted. "Damn, you're tall," was not a comment designed to quicken the pulse. She'd learned a long time ago that men who looked like this one could have their pick of the female population. And no man with choices chose Ronald McDonald's Amazonian cousin.

Toying with her coffee mug, she watched him reach the docks and turn her way. Her pulse leaped. Surely he wasn't coming to see *her?* With suddenly unsteady hands, she lifted the coffee mug, forgetting its role as paperweight. A gust of wind tore the copied acquisition record out from under the lifted cup and sent it soaring over the rail and into the water like a dying moth.

Autumn's jaw dropped at the unfairness of her life, then clamped shut with a snap. "Hell's bells." She lunged to her feet, looking for something to help her fish the paper from the water before it disintegrated. She spied the long, metal boat hook hanging from the side of the cabin and grabbed it, but the brackets were stiff with rust and refused to let go. With a growl, she curled her fingers around the metal, took a deep breath and yanked as hard as she could.

"Hello."

The boat lurched behind her at the exact moment the

long hook came free. Turning toward the deep, masculine voice, Autumn stumbled, the boat hook swinging wildly in her hands. Before she could catch her balance, the metal struck her visitor in the head with a sickening thud. The very man she'd been drooling over!

With a groan, she squeezed her eyes closed. If only she could be someone...*anyone*...other than Autumn McGinn.

Chapter 2

Kaderil snatched the cold metal weapon from the woman's hand, his muscles tensing in preparation for counterattack even as his brain screamed for caution. *Human. Fragile.* She could do him no damage unless she was Sitheen and knew the death curse.

Was she Sitheen? Is that how she'd so quickly seen through his facade?

The boat rolled lightly beneath his feet, forcing him to adjust his stance for balance. But as he prepared for battle, watching for her next move, his opponent inexplicably closed her eyes. An oddly pained expression crossed her face, confounding him. Was this how she drew her power? Even Sitheen were known to sometimes possess the power of the Esri.

The loud hum of a motorboat on the water sounded

in the distance as he waited, muscles bunched, but his gaze never left her face. A detached part of his brain couldn't help but admire the rare beauty of this human with hair the color of fire, and freckles that dotted the pale perfection of her skin like tiny golden jewels. All his life he'd been surrounded by the white-skinned, pale-haired Esri, the standard of true beauty in his land. But he was finding his eye preferred the more varied, more vibrant coloring of humans. And this woman's was the most vibrant of them all.

Her eyes opened. He tensed until he realized their clear gray depths shone not with the light of battle, but with regret.

Kaderil stared at her with wary confusion, freezing when she reached for him not with fists or claws, but with the softest of fingers closing around his wrist.

"I'm so sorry."

Sorry? He watched her, bemused, and allowed her to tug him from the rail.

"Let me look at your head. I can't believe I hit you."

She stood half a head shorter than him, yet she pushed him into the flimsy woven chair with ease, so stunned was he by her reaction to him. Women feared him. He demanded their fear! Yet this one dared treat him like an injured child.

Anger, and some dark emotion he didn't want to acknowledge, had his muscles bunching to right this wrong, but his lucid mind stopped him cold. He *must* pretend to be human. A *nice* human, worthy of trust.

He forced himself to remain motionless. To submit. But when her fingers eased into his hair, his hands curled around the chair's arms until he heard the crack of plastic and felt the sharp bits flake beneath his fingertips. He never let others get this close. *Never.*

"I'm sorry if I'm hurting you, but I've got to find the cut."

She would find no bleeding gash, of course, but a human would let her look. And he must, as well, no matter how difficult.

He sat as still as the statues that dotted the human's city, his senses finely tuned to the intriguing creature hovering over him. Her warm, spicy scent filled his nostrils, sliding through his body, sparking an awareness that surprised him. Her fiery braid drew his attention, the color as hypnotic and exciting as the deadly fire it resembled. His gaze followed the sensuous curve of braid across her shoulder and down to where it teased the tip of one well-mounded breast.

His senses swirled in sudden chaos. She stood too close, confusing him with her gentle touch and lack of fear, ambushing him with the unbidden and unwelcome stirring of desire. *She was human.* He tried to rise, to escape the assault to his senses, but she pressed him down with a perilously soft hand.

"Wait. I haven't found anything. You've got to tell me where it hurts."

He was about to assure her he felt no pain, to escape this tender assault, when his warrior's mind reasserted itself, chastising him for allowing the woman to distract him from his mission, even for a moment. He must find out if she knew the Sitheen Larsen Vale. Or whether she was a Sitheen herself. A probe of her mind would tell him much.

He reached for her hand, slid his fingers over hers and nearly forgot what he was about. The sensual chaos focused, his every sense suddenly attuned to that meeting of flesh. Warmth flowed from her hand into his, a warmth that had nothing to do with the heat of skin against the chilly air, and everything to do with the woman herself. A warmth that traveled up his arm and spread through his body in a flush of awareness that shifted the very foundations beneath his feet.

"Can you show me where it hurts?" the woman prodded.

Kaderil groaned. The woman muddled his mind.

"Here," he said, moving her palm a mere hand's breadth upward. "It hurts here." He used the opportunity, the skin-to-skin contact, to probe her mind, but what flowed into his head was scarce and strangely garbled. Of no use whatsoever.

Kaderil frowned. The woman wasn't Sitheen, for if she were, he wouldn't be able to breach her mind at all. What, then, was blocking him from her thoughts?

The woman tugged her hand loose, her fingers burrowing tenderly through his hair in search of damage. "I don't see anything." She leaned to the side, her thick braid swinging free as she met his gaze. "Does it hurt a lot? Maybe you should see a doctor."

The intensity of the worry in those pleasing features made something pull oddly in his chest. "The pain has receded," he said.

"Are you sure?"

She looked so unhappy, he was almost sorry he had no wounds to offer her.

"Yes." More than sure. He was immortal. Even if she'd split his head open, the flesh would have quickly mended and she'd have found nothing.

"Good." Relief flooded her eyes as she released him and stepped back. She shoved her hands into her jeans pockets, retreating into a charming shyness. "So…what can I do for you…*other* than clobber you in the head?"

His lips twitched. The desire to smile startled him. How long had it been since he'd felt such a need? He grunted with annoyance. He had no time for such foolishness.

Kaderil rose to his full height. "I'm looking for Larsen Vale."

"Larsen's not here." The woman took a step back, but still no fear entered her eyes. A good thing, he had to remind himself. He needed humans *not* to fear him. Especially this human who apparently knew his prey.

"Are you a friend of hers?" she asked.

"No. I need to find her. She's in danger."

She cocked her head, exposing a long expanse of soft, delicate neck. "What do you mean?"

He swallowed the desire she drew so easily in him, needing to play this role with extreme care. "I've been having dreams about her. And a man with pure white skin who means to harm her." He grimaced for effect. "I know that sounds crazy."

"Not as crazy as you'd think." Her brows lifted above sharp intelligent eyes, eyes that clearly understood the significance of his words. Either she'd seen Baleris herself, or knew of him and the Esri. A rarity, it seemed.

Of the dozens of humans he'd touched, not one had heard the word *Esri*. Not one knew of the gates between the worlds.

"I need to talk to Larsen," he said.

The fire-haired beauty hesitated. "Give me your phone number. I'll have her get in touch with you."

No, that was unacceptable. Not only was he awkward with the cell phone Ustanis acquired for him, but he had no time to await a phone call. In barely two weeks, the gate would open and his mission must be complete. This woman would help him whether she wished to or not.

He thrust out his hand. "I'm Kade Smith."

The woman blinked, her gaze softening as she took his hand. "Autumn McGinn."

As before, he felt an enticing warmth flow between them. His instincts warred between backing away and moving closer until he was in danger of falling into those soft gray eyes. With effort, he did neither.

Instead, holding her hand in his, he thrust thoughts into her head. Thoughts that would make her trust him. He watched her eyes cloud with a confusion that should not be there.

Instead of doing as the foreign thoughts bade her, she merely blinked. Other humans had taken his thoughts as if they were their own. Something was clearly interfering with his small power over her. But even as he debated his next move, she cocked her head.

"Why don't you come…inside?"

It had worked. "I will." Belatedly, he added, "Thank you."

She turned and led him to the door, but as she reached for the handle, she stilled and looked down at her hand as if wondering what she was doing. Already his control over her was slipping. She turned to look up at him, confusion shadowing her eyes.

"I don't think..." she began.

Kaderil slid his hand beneath her braid, his fingers gliding across the silken skin of her neck. He'd meant merely to touch her, but the unintended intimacy of that touch parted her lips and lit surprised sparks in her eyes, beckoning him as female eyes never did. His pulse quickened. His gaze fell to those ripe, parted lips and he nearly forgot what he was about.

Control. He was attempting to assert some control. He pushed the thought into her head. *Invite him inside.* But the sparks in her eyes flared into desire.

"Come inside." Her words were low and husky, sending a rush of need barreling through him.

Had he somehow forced her interest with his touch? No. He couldn't have. His power over humans ended with the reading of their memories and the pushing of thoughts into their heads. He had no ability to affect their emotions.

Which meant the attraction he saw in her eyes was real. *Sweet Esria.*

Autumn slid the door open behind her without breaking his gaze, but as she backed into the open doorway, she stumbled over the door's track, the sensual light in her eyes disappearing in a gasp of dismay.

Kaderil grabbed her arm to steady her, careful not to break her fragile bones.

"Thanks." She eased out of the doorway to allow him entrance even as she bared her teeth in a grimace. "I'm not always this clumsy." Color washed her cheeks. "Who am I kidding? Sure I am."

Her admission surprised him, prompting another urge to smile. He liked her, he realized. An odd and inconvenient reaction to have to a human.

"Call Larsen Vale," he commanded. "Please."

The woman peeled off her jacket and tossed it on a stool as she went into the kitchen, revealing a green sweater clinging to soft curves. Jeans covered her slender hips and long, long legs. His body stirred as he watched her charmingly unbalanced walk until she disappeared around the counter. But when she returned, she carried not a phone, but a flashlight.

He stared at her in consternation. Had his thoughts not taken at all?

"Autumn, make the phone call."

She met his gaze without flinching. "I will. As soon as I'm sure I didn't give you a concussion. Now, sit down so I can reach you." Laughter sparkled in her eyes. "I don't think I've ever said that to anyone before. Except my dad. He's not as tall as you, but he's close."

"Does he also have hair the color of yours?"

"Oh, yes." The words came out on a sigh. "I got all my quirky traits from my dad. You'd never believe I was related to the rest of my family. My mom's a five-foot-four blond ballet teacher. Both my sisters look just like her."

"Their loss." He wasn't sure where he'd picked up the term, but the quick grin that lit her face made the breath catch in his throat. She had a smile fit for royalty.

"Thanks." Her expression turned unaccountably shy. "Now, umm, come sit down so I can check your eyes."

"My eyes?"

"The dilation. I want to make sure I didn't give you a concussion." She slid the soft pads of her fingers around the much larger bones of his wrist and tugged him toward the sofa.

Would Esri eyes react like human eyes? He couldn't be sure and couldn't take the chance, not when he'd finally made contact with one who could lead him to his prey.

He was about to try to push the thought into her head that his eyes were fine when she glanced back at him with an impish sparkle. "I've seen this done on TV a million times."

The glitter of self-directed humor told him she laughed at herself, but it was the wry quirk of her lips that drew his gaze and aroused his hunger. And when her soft palm pressed against his chest, urging him to sit, he unleashed the desire that had plagued him from the moment her fingers had first eased into his hair. He kissed her, dipping his head and pressing his mouth against the extraordinary softness of her lips.

The woman stiffened at the contact. Her eyes opened wide with surprise, but she showed no fear, and didn't pull away.

His lips moved over hers lightly, sampling the sweetness of that tempting flesh, drinking the spicy fragrance of her skin. She tasted of honey and cinnamon, and alluring, intoxicating female. He'd had females before, though he'd rarely kissed them, for only those who sought the titillation of fear with their mating came near him. This was so very, very different.

He felt the moment her mouth softened beneath his and began to move, joining the kiss. A sound escaped her throat. Half sigh, half moan. All pleasure.

He didn't touch her except where their lips met, yet the force of that touch swept him beyond himself, beyond mattering, tugging at places inside him that had lain cold and dormant for too long.

Stirring a need…a weakness…

He pulled away. "I have no concussion."

The human…Autumn…blinked, her cheeks flushed and rosy, her expression flustered. "I…umm…right. No concussion." The flashlight slipped from her fingers and thudded against the wooden coffee table, making her jump. She backed away from him, knocking into the table and nearly dislodging a cup, sending it into a precarious wobble. "You…should go. I'll tell Larsen you were here."

He shouldn't have kissed her. Touching her…tasting her…did things to him, weakened him in ways he could ill afford. And with this small aggression, he'd apparently frightened her. A serious mistake when his goal was to win her trust.

His hands fisted and unfisted at his sides as his brain searched for a way to bring her back under his control without frightening her again. Since he couldn't seem to control her thoughts, perhaps he had no choice but to back away and try to approach her again at a later time. As if he *had* time.

What a fool he'd been to kiss her, no matter how pleasant he'd found the experience.

"I'll go, then," he said reluctantly. "Tell…ask… Larsen to call me."

"Oh. Right. I need to get your number." Autumn lifted her palm to her forehead as if trying to gather her wits. As she did, her sweater sleeve dropped, revealing the oddly rustic bracelet twisted around her wrist. It almost looked like…*holly.* Of course! The plant was scarce in Esria, for it had the disturbing ability to thwart and confound magic. No wonder he'd failed to control her.

If he could get the holly away from her, he might salvage this day's work after all.

He followed Autumn to the kitchen counter, standing at her elbow where he could easily reach her, watching as she picked up a pen and a small pad of paper.

Not meeting his gaze, she asked, "What's your number?"

"Two-oh-two," he began, then slowly reached out to stroke her bracelet. "I like the look of this." He allowed his fingers to slide across the soft skin of her wrist while he shoved thoughts into her head.

The holly itches. I need to take it off.

"No." Her voice was a whisper, as if she spoke to herself.

The holly itches. I can't stand having it touch my skin.

"No, I can't," she murmured, but even as she said the words, her other hand grabbed the bracelet, wrenched it off her wrist, and dropped it to the counter.

Kaderil snatched her hand before she gathered her wits, and continued his assault on her mind. *I don't want Kade to leave. I want him to touch me.* As long as he could keep hold of her, he could get her to lead him to Larsen Vale.

With her free hand, she rubbed at her wrist where the holly had been, her gaze fixed on her task. Kaderil brushed her fingers aside and stroked the soft skin for her. "Is that better?"

"Yes." The word was full of confusion, a lost sound that resonated uncomfortably in the hollows of his heart, pricking his conscience.

He pushed the feeling aside. He needed to learn what he could from her, anything that might help him find that draggon stone and destroy the Sitheen. Using the link formed by the press of skin on skin, he reached into her mind and absorbed the wealth of knowledge he found there, an amazing array of facts about archaeology and artifacts, folklore and past human civilizations. And, as often happened when he eavesdropped on a human's mind, he got little in the way of concrete memories, mostly impressions and opinions.

Beneath his fingers, her pulse began to quicken. He was frightening her again. A poor way to earn her trust. He released her arm and was about to step back, when her gaze lifted to his, stopping him.

There was no fear in her expression. No uncertainty at all. And he realized, suddenly, that it wasn't fear driving her speeding pulse. *Sweet Esria,* it was desire. Her eyes fairly blazed with it.

Before he could fully grasp this sudden change in her, she reached for him, pulled his face down, and pressed her mouth hard to his.

Need surged through his body. Shock flooded his brain at the sudden closeness. At the feel of a woman pressed against him, not in fear, but in desire.

His body rose even as his mind rebelled. Too close. He was the Punisher. He kept others at bay for a reason. Just as he never wanted his own people to learn of his great lack of power, he couldn't let the humans know he was more than human.

He grabbed her shoulders, his mind insisting he push her away. But her tongue swept into his mouth and all thought fled. His arms went around her, pulling her tight against him. He reveled in the feel of her soft breasts pressed against his chest, her thighs pushing against his.

He fell into the chaos, sliding and twining his tongue with hers, tracing the contours of her teeth and mouth, drinking the passion she'd suddenly, miraculously, given in to. Her hands roamed his back with growing need. He basked in her heat.

Her hands curved around the back of his neck, pulling him closer, telling him in no uncertain terms that she wanted him. The knowledge rocked him. Never had a woman desired him like this, without fear. Without question.

Her hands lowered and she tugged at his arms, pulling them away from her. Confused, he started to retreat from her kiss, but her mouth followed his, drawing him to her as she shoved his hands beneath the hem of her shirt, sliding his palms over her abdomen. The shock of that warm hidden skin sent hot desire rushing through his veins.

She was his. For this moment, for this hour, his mission was forgotten. His reason for being with her was forgotten in the explosion of pure feeling that had become his body. He slid his palms up to cover the silk-draped mounds of her breasts, eliciting a low moan from her throat. The sound of her pleasure, the feel of the soft mounds beneath his palms, nearly sent him over the edge.

His mouth dipped to her neck, tasting her freckles, drawing a delicious shudder from her ripe, ready body. He wanted her. With everything he had, everything he was, he wished he could bury himself deep inside this woman's heat. Most heady of all was the certainty that she lusted after him every bit as much. Beneath his fingers, her body trembled, begging for release. Her spicy fragrance was a song to his senses, her moans of pleasure driving him to madness. She was made for mating, made for him.

"Touch me," she begged, then pulled back and yanked her soft shirt over her head and tossed it to the floor.

He watched with wondrous anticipation as her hands went to her back to release her bra. But then his gaze flicked to her face, to her eyes, and he froze.

Tears slipped down her cheeks, her eyes filled not with lust, but with frantic need…and panic.

"I need you to touch me," she whispered brokenly.

His own words came back to him, the words he'd thrust into her head. Somehow he'd done this to her with his careless command. It didn't make sense. He shouldn't have this much control over her, but clearly she was not acting on her own.

His body screamed for him to continue. To touch her as she demanded.

But as her bra came loose in her hands, he grabbed her shoulders and thrust new thoughts into her head. *I need to put my bra on.* Beneath his touch, she stilled and pulled the undergarment tight once more, allowing him only a glimpse of the tantalizing flesh hidden beneath. The moment her bra was secure, her arms went around him.

"Touch me, Kade. I need you to touch me."

Need quaked through him as he held her, a war raging inside him. He'd forced this on her.

Kaderil's hands tightened on her back and he kissed her hard, punishing her for his confusion. She met the kiss with equal passion, swamping his senses. He wanted her. *He wanted her.*

But the fingers she raked through his hair reminded him too well of the way she'd sought to save him from the injury she'd inflicted. In his mind's eye, he saw again the gentleness of her eyes as she'd sought assurance she hadn't hurt him.

Kaderil wrenched away from her, breaking the kiss.

"Kade." Autumn reached for him, try to pull his face back to hers. "I *need* you."

He grabbed her band of holly and shoved it into her hand before temptation got the better of him. Slowly, confusion clouded her face, wiping the look of desperation from her eyes.

As he turned and stalked to the window, anger and frustration fueled his steps. In returning her sanity, he'd stripped himself of his own.

He didn't need her! He only desired her in the most base of ways. And he refused to care that he'd driven to tears the first person to show him true kindness in centuries. He was the Punisher. He demanded fear. Exulted in tears.

Behind him, he heard the brush of cloth, then the soft

creak of the sofa. He tried to ignore her, but his body had a will of its own all of a sudden, and he found himself turning back.

Autumn sat, her face buried in her hands, her shoulders shaking.

Foreign emotions raked him. Regret. Pity.

But to his amazement, the sound that broke from her throat was laughter. She lifted her flushed face and clasped her hand to her mouth. "I've never been so embarrassed in my life." Her eyes, miraculously, brimmed with as much humor as chagrin. "I've seriously got to date more."

He stared at her, bemused, as something about her tugged at him, drawing his admiration. There was no doubt he'd distressed her. The tears he'd seen in her eyes told him that clearly. Yet she laughed at herself and met his gaze with strength despite her dismay.

He found himself unaccountably intrigued by her. And uncomfortably drawn to her. He longed for the familiar rightness of the Punisher's scowl and an end to this pretense of softness. Kaderil the Dark was not a soft man. He was not a kind man.

Yet there was something about this woman that called to that weakness. That tempted him to be both.

He fought to conceal his scowl. He could not let this pretense of weakness become truth. She was a means to an end, nothing more. Even if her gray eyes sparkled with an intelligence, a warmth he'd been seeking all his life.

Kaderil went to sit across from her, resting his arms on his knees, clasping his hands together.

"We both lost control," he told her, though it was a

blatant falsehood. She hadn't lost control. He'd stolen it from her.

Damp lashes swept up to reveal eyes that held both vulnerability and strength. "I...um...don't suppose we can forget this happened?" She grimaced, her slender nose wrinkling in a way that set her freckles to dancing, pleasing him. A flirtatious twinkle entered her eyes, making his pulse quicken. "At least until we get to know one another a little better?"

His pulse stuttered at her words. Get to know him better? Overlaying the carnal image was another that left him cold. If she ever truly understood him, she'd know he wasn't human. And that could never happen.

He could never reveal his true self to her. Nor did he wish to know any more about her. Autumn McGinn was a pawn, nothing more. Already, he feared he'd long be haunted by the feel of her fingers in his hair and the laughter in her eyes.

What had she done to him? What had he done to himself by toying with her?

He'd known the human world could hold any number of potential perils for a dark blood with little power. Little had he expected the greatest danger would turn out to be this female with a smile capable of taming even the fiercest of monsters.

Him.

Chapter 3

Autumn pressed her hands to her overheated cheeks, thoroughly flustered by her mortifying loss of control. The sun's last golden rays gleamed through the windows, silhouetting Kade Smith's dark head. He watched her with the bluest eyes she'd ever seen, eyes that smoldered with the memory of the way she'd attacked him. She'd practically begged him to make love to her!

The hunger he'd stoked with his lips and hands still vibrated along her skin. Never in her life had she felt such an intense desire to be touched. She'd nearly climbed out of her skin with the need to have his hands on her. Which wouldn't be half as embarrassing if she'd kept the thought to herself.

If only the ground would open up and swallow her

whole. Since it showed no sign of cooperating, she rose, looking for another way to escape until her face cooled.

"I'll…umm…I'll go call Larsen for you." He looked up at her, his expression unreadable, as he nodded. He must think she was a complete idiot. "Why don't you turn on the television or something?"

Without a backward glance, she fled the room to hide in the tiny cabin that was her temporary bedroom, and dialed her friend.

Larsen answered on the first ring. "Hi, Autumn. What's up?"

My blood pressure, my hormone levels, Kade's… uh… Autumn groaned and yanked her mind from *that* thought and back to the conversation she'd intended. "I've got a guest, of sorts. I think he's Sitheen."

A brief silence answered her announcement, doing nothing for her blood pressure. "Did he tell you that?"

Autumn sighed. "No. He came looking for you. He said he's had some dreams about a white-skinned man he needs to warn you about."

"Why didn't he just call me? I'm in the phone book."

"I don't know." She hadn't thought to ask. Not real surprising considering what *had* been on her mind.

"What if he's Esri?"

Autumn tensed, the word jangling through her like a discordant note. "No. He's not Esri. He's…gorgeous. Amazing. And he has dark hair…and a bit of a tan."

"Autumn…"

"He's not Esri, Larsen! I'd know." But as soon as the words were out, she heard how desperate she sounded. Esri were notorious for hiding their true appearance behind glamour. Yes, she was wearing holly, but who was to say holly worked against all Esri? They just didn't know the extent of the magic these creatures were capable of.

Autumn sank to the bed, her pulse beginning to trip with real fear. "Larsen...what if he is Esri? What do I do?" Tackling *this* man to the ground wasn't going to be an option.

Though it might be fun.

She groaned.

"Do you feel threatened at all?" Larsen asked.

"No." Hot, flustered and thoroughly in lust. But, no, not threatened.

"All right. I hate to ask this of you, but it's important, Autumn. It could be critical. If he's Esri, he's either after the draggon stone or he's after us." The Sitheen. "He's using you to get to us, so he's not likely to do anything to give himself away. I honestly don't think you're in any immediate danger, Autumn. They may be murdering bastards, but they're smart. If he's one of them, we need to turn the tables on him. Are you game?"

"Yes. Of course." What choice did she have?

"I want you to stall him until I can get hold of the guys. It could take me a little while, so maybe offer to fix him dinner or something. I'm hoping it won't take more than an hour or so."

Autumn fell back on the bed, her head swimming, her skin crawling with chills. Kade really could be Esri, as much as she hated to admit it. And she had to fix him *dinner?*

"If anyone's going to walk into a trap it's going to be

him, not us," Larsen continued. "Autumn…be careful. I don't like the idea of you alone with a strange man, no matter who he is."

A man she'd practically thrown herself at. Her chills intensified. *I might have been kissing an Esri.* Even now, he stood in the next room, waiting for her.

God. "Larsen?"

"Yes?"

"Hurry."

"I will. Be careful, Autumn."

She closed the phone and lay on the bed, unmoving. It almost made sense that he *was* Esri, that he'd somehow fashioned himself to look like every dark fantasy she'd ever had. Tall, dark, dangerously handsome. She tried to imagine what he might really look like—the pasty-white skin and pale hair. Was it possible? No. She'd know. Somehow she'd know.

He wasn't Esri. He wasn't *evil.* Then again, if he *was* Esri, he had magic and everything she knew about him was a lie and had been from the start.

She pressed her hand to her forehead. Dear God, what was she going to do? How in the world was she supposed to carry on a polite conversation with a man who could be plotting her rape and murder as easily as her seduction? She couldn't let on that she suspected him of being more than he claimed. If he *was* Esri…if he got suspicious, he might take off. And she couldn't afford to lose a second Esri. Even *she* couldn't be that clumsy.

With a groan, she forced herself up. Hiding in the bedroom wasn't an option, however appealing it might sound. She stumbled twice on her way back to the living room and seriously hoped the boat was rocking more than normal. If not, she was losing what little coordination she had. The sun had finally set, leaving the room in shadows.

Kade looked up from his examination of one of the wall prints, but she kept her gaze averted as she turned on a table lamp, not ready to face him after her mortifying lack of control. And not sure she could keep her doubts about who he was out of her eyes.

But as she crossed to the kitchen and flicked on the light, she felt his gaze on her, felt it vibrate along her skin, and felt her body warm all over again. Oh, this was not good. What if she lost control and tried to strip *him* this time? Oh, for heaven's sake, *he could be Esri.*

Taking a deep breath, she rounded the counter into the kitchen, desperate to reclaim some measure of equilibrium. Or at least the pretense of it. With the counter safely between her and the man who literally and figuratively filled the room, she finally gathered the courage to look up.

He met her gaze, his expression guarded. And what did *that* mean? That he was hiding something…or that he was afraid she was going to attack him again?

If only the floor would swallow her.

The boat swayed, forcing her to grab hold of the counter for support. She swallowed, praying her voice would sound close to normal.

"I talked to Larsen. She wants to meet you after work. You can follow me over there in your car if you want to wait. It shouldn't be much more than an hour."

"I took the Metro. But if I can ride with you, I'll

wait." A gleam that might be satisfaction glimmered in his eyes. But it didn't prove he was Esri. He'd come looking for Larsen. Naturally, he'd be satisfied he was going to get to meet her. And if she doubted every single thing he said, every flick of his eyebrow, she was going to make herself insane.

"Are you hungry? I thought I'd fix dinner."

At the mention of food, that guarded expression in his eyes disappeared. His eyes positively lit up. "I'm hungry."

She laughed. "Of course you are." And what a stereotypical reaction of a male to food. This proved it, didn't it? He *couldn't* be Esri. She'd never heard anything about Baleris demanding food. Virgins, yes. But not food.

Kade Smith was definitely human. And if she could just keep convincing herself of that, maybe she could manage to get dinner on the table.

She started the rice, then pulled vegetables out of the fridge with hands that would not quit shaking, despite her insistence he wasn't a threat. But hormones were as bad as nerves and as long as he was in the room, they weren't about to settle down. As if she weren't clumsy enough. She managed to rinse the vegetables without mishap, then grabbed a knife and a green pepper and started chopping.

Out of the corner of her eye, she saw Kade move to the bar on the other side of the counter. He leaned on it, watching her, shredding the few nerves she had left. Her fingers fumbled the knife, sending it clattering to the cutting board.

With a groan, she snatched it up and tried again.

"What are you making?" The rich timbre of Kade's

too-near voice rattled her even as it sank into her pores, sliding over her skin like liquid silk. Was this how he enchanted her? With his sexy voice? *Stop it.*

"I'm…uh…I've got this great recipe for a Mexican stir-fry. Is that okay?"

"I like all food."

Why didn't that surprise her? The guy had to be close to seven feet tall. Again, she made the mistake of looking up and found his gaze on her face. Those blue, blue eyes caught her, making her pulse lift and soar at the look of hunger in their depths. Hunger she could almost imagine was directed at her, not her vegetables, though she knew better. The knife slipped out of her agitated fingers and clattered to the cutting board once again.

With a rueful sigh, she said, "You'd better go watch TV. I'm not doing well with an audience. At this rate, dinner won't be ready until next Tuesday."

His mouth twitched, gentle laughter warming his brilliant eyes, setting a tingling excitement loose in her body like the bubbles from a soft drink. He wasn't Esri. She simply couldn't believe magic could create such perfect sparkles in his eyes, or that even through enchantment she could feel the bubbly excitement of a brand-new crush. Because that was exactly the way she felt. *Excited.*

Kade rose and took off his leather jacket, revealing a T-shirt that accentuated his hard, muscular arms. Instead of moving to the living room as she'd suggested, he came around the counter and picked up the knife she'd dropped, nudging her aside with his hip. "I have a little experience with cooking."

His warm masculine scent washed over her, his overwhelming nearness stole the air from the room. She took a hurried step back, not wanting to be tempted to craziness a second time. She tried to calm her fluttering pulse as she leaned against the counter and watched him wield the knife with expert precision, his muscles flexing and bulging in all the right places.

"You look like a professional."

"I'm not good with sauces and seasonings, but I can handle a knife well enough." He looked up, capturing her with his gaze as the pepper disappeared beneath his blade. "What else do you need me to chop?"

Autumn grabbed the counter as the boat bobbed, then handed him the red pepper, onion and tomato. "I didn't mean to put you to work."

His mouth twisted with a wry hint of humor. "I don't mind."

"Okay. Thanks. I'll...um...get the rest of the ingredients." They worked together surprisingly well, getting everything into the skillet. Despite Kade watching her, she managed to stir and cook the food without a single additional mishap.

Dinner was almost ready when he leaned over the skillet and sniffed, a look of sheer pleasure on his ruggedly handsome face. "It smells good."

"Thanks." She felt suddenly shy at the sincere compliment.

He turned that look on her, pleasure lighting his eyes and playing around his mouth.

Happiness bubbled out of her throat in a laugh, drawing a full smile from him at last, a smile that was en-

dearingly boyish and a little lopsided, crinkling his eyes
at the corners. Her heart flipped over in her chest. She
swallowed a gasp and turned quickly back to the skillet.
What was she doing?

She was falling for him. Flat-out falling for him. And
she didn't know how to stop.

When the rice started sticking to the bottom of the
pan, she moved the skillet to a cool burner and turned
off the stove.

"Finished?" Kade asked hopefully.

"As ready as it's going to be." She looked at him un-
certainly, wondering how big a fool she was making of
herself. He was *so* out of her league. But as she reached
for the plates, something crashed outside, making her
stop. The wild clanking of the dock lines told her it was
just the wind, but in the next instant, a crack of thunder
had her running for the door.

"My laptop!" She'd left it outside.

The wind buffeted her as she dove out the door. Sea
spray stung her face, but she pushed toward the back
deck and the small table she'd used earlier. The chair
had fallen over, but her computer was where she'd left
it, thank goodness. The sky had turned dark fast with the
rising storm. A distant flash lit the clouds, followed by
a low roll of thunder. She grabbed the laptop, and turned
to find Kade right behind her.

"We've got to get this furniture in the hatch," she
said, yelling over the howl of the wind. "It's here." She
took three steps and tapped the hatch door beneath her
foot. "I'll be right back."

She escaped into the relative calm of the houseboat,

deposited her laptop on the kitchen counter and grabbed the hatch keys so she could lock up once everything was stored. When she returned to the deck, Kade was lowering the table into the hatch, but the chair that had fallen over was on the move again. Lifted on a gust of wind, it was bounding across the deck, end over end, toward the rail.

The boat rocked on the swells, making walking nearly impossible, but that chair belonged to Larsen and she wasn't going to lose it. She lunged for it, lurching across the deck. But as she reached for the escaping furniture, she lost her balance and tipped toward the rail. For one dismal instant, she prepared herself for an icy swim. But at the last moment, a strong arm snagged her around the waist and hauled her against a rock-solid chest.

"I've got you."

Autumn collapsed against him, heart pounding in her throat, then noticed the chair tight in his other hand. "Nice catch."

A low sound that might have been laughter vibrated against her back. "I wouldn't let you escape me that easily."

The boat bobbed, but held by his strong arm, she didn't stumble. Couldn't fall. She felt safe. Protected. And for the first time in years…not alone.

She turned to face him. Their gazes met and locked in the flash of distant lightning and she caught a glimpse of his face, of a brooding intensity in his eyes. Her heart, still thudding from her near fall, began to race as her storm-whipped senses became focused only on the man. The pressure in her chest increased and she lifted her hand and pressed it against his cheek. Gone was the crazed out-of-control need that had gripped her before. In its place was a need for connection as deep as her soul.

As the wind tossed his loose hair, he lowered his face to hers. His mouth brushed hers, gently at first then with more insistence, sending warm desire flowing through her, sliding through her limbs. He tasted like heaven and smelled like the forest and the sea joined in a battle as old as the stars. She wanted this, wanted him, and she kissed him back, losing herself in a whirlwind of sensations. The feel of his strong arm around her, the slide of his tongue against hers drove her excitement with the rising storm.

Lightning lit the sky with a crack of close thunder and the first large raindrops landed on their heads. Slowly Kade pulled back, releasing her mouth even as he continued to hold her. His expression was lost to the shadows until another flash of lightning illuminated his face, revealing a longing in his eyes she didn't understand. Almost a loneliness.

The raindrops began a steady bombardment and they pulled apart. As one, they ran for the hatch. Kade dropped the chair inside and Autumn locked the door then ran for sanctuary. She closed the door behind them and sank back against the cool glass, raindrops tickling her cheeks. Kade ran his hands through his hair, flinging the droplets everywhere, showering her anew.

"Kade!" She laughed and looked at him, but the expression in his eyes caught her fast, silencing her. She couldn't look away. Didn't want to look away. They weren't even touching, yet she'd never felt so close to another, so *aware* of another, in her life. She felt as if he could see into her soul and learn all her fears and secrets. And if she looked closely enough, she could learn his.

Her pulse throbbed with an ache of recognition and the illogical certainty that this man was the one she'd been waiting for.

"Autumn…"

The ring of the phone interrupted whatever he was going to say, breaking that gossamer thread of connection. She ran to grab the phone from the counter.

"Autumn, it's Larsen. We're ready. Drive to Charlie's and give me a call when you reach the parking garage. I'll tell you where to meet us."

"Okay. Bye, Larsen."

Autumn slowly pushed her phone into her pocket, chilled suddenly by the thought of dragging Kade into the Sitheens' trap. She didn't have a choice. If she was right, and Kade Smith was the good, decent man she believed, he'd forgive her. Eventually.

And if she was wrong? Then he was Esri and he deserved to die. There was nothing she could…or would…do to stop it. Though she had a feeling she would regret it for the rest of her life.

Chapter 4

She'd enchanted him. That was the only explanation.

Kaderil stared into the dark at the lights glowing from the windows of passing buildings as Autumn drove him to meet Larsen Vale. The wiper screeched on the now dry windshield and Autumn turned it off, the rain already having stopped.

She couldn't have enchanted him, of course. The woman was fully human. But he struggled for a better explanation for the weakness that grew worse with every moment he spent in her company. He'd smiled at her! He'd told himself he wouldn't kiss her again, yet every time he was in reach of her he could think of nothing else.

The time he'd known her was less than the blink of an eye, yet already she filled his mind. It infuriated him. He was the Punisher, not some besotted fool of an Esri lord.

He would not let her control his thoughts this way. But even as the thought went through his mind, he found his head swiveling to the left, his gaze once more seeking her out.

Unable to fight his traitorous fascination, he drank his fill. Even in the shadows he could make out the shape of her pleasing profile, her slender nose and full, sweet-tasting mouth. Her taste still lingered on his tongue, stirring unwanted need all over again.

Enchanted. That was the only possibility.

The last thing he wanted was to be attracted to her, a human, the very human who was leading him to his prey. He resented the kick of guilt that plagued him.

The Punisher was without guilt. Without conscience. He did his duty with little thought and no remorse. But with every moment Kaderil spent in this woman's company, forced to pretend to be the *nice* human, Kade Smith, he felt the Punisher slipping a little more out of his grasp.

Kaderil forced himself to go back to looking out his window, but his hungry gaze wouldn't be denied. Within moments, he found his head swiveling back toward Autumn. The lights of a passing car illuminated her face fully, revealing a tenseness around her eyes and that lush mouth, a tenseness that made him wonder what was going on inside her head. Did the driving require such deep concentration?

Autumn glanced at him, licking her lower lip with an unconscious nervousness that caught his attention and gave him pause.

"I'm sorry you had to eat so quickly."

"I didn't mind. Eating quickly didn't diminish my enjoyment."

She nodded and returned her gaze to the road, but cleared her throat in a way that told him she had something more to say. "Kade, I need to tell you something. You've had some weird dreams, right? About a white-skinned man? Do you know who he is? *What* he is?"

Kaderil relaxed, realizing her nervousness was a result of uncertainty over how to broach the subject of the Esri with a fellow human who knew nothing. She was easing into it gently, as he was coming to understand was her nature.

He searched his borrowed thoughts for an appropriate response, remembering a thought he'd plucked from her own brain. "Is he an albino?"

A smile flickered over her lips, but didn't ease the tension that gripped her eyes. "No." She glanced at him again, cringing as if with apology. "He's not human."

What was the appropriate response to such a statement? His pulse quickened as he struggled for the right words. He'd done well so far. He'd be a fool to blow this now. Humans doubted. A human would not accept such a statement easily, if at all.

"Of course he's human," he said.

The woman at his side looked away, glancing toward her own side window. "I know you're going to think I'm nuts, but just listen. Please? It's important."

Safe in silence, Kaderil relaxed and listened to her melodious voice as she launched into a fairly accurate explanation of his race and his mission, explaining how

Baleris had terrorized the D.C. area several months ago, raping virgins and attempting to kill the Sitheen.

"We know a certain amount about Esria now," she said. "There are many races, but the Esri are the ones with the most power. They ignore most of the other races and have enslaved the Marceils. The Marceils look like small humans, most five feet tall or less. The Esri can't enchant them like they can us, but they can control their actions."

She slowed in front of a large building and put on her blinkers. "I'm talking too much. And I know this is all too hard to believe. But just keep an open mind, okay?"

She didn't seem to require an answer, which was all for the good, since he wasn't certain he could express adequate disbelief of something he knew so well.

Autumn parked, then without looking at him, pulled out her cell phone. "It's me. We're here." A pause. "Okay. I'll see you in a minute."

She flashed him a weak, apologetic smile, but said nothing more, to his great relief, as they got on the elevator. He didn't have time to play the doubter for longer than absolutely necessary. He must make Larsen Vale believe he was Sitheen and sincerely interested in helping them catch the Esri, if he stood any chance of finding that draggon stone in time. Two short weeks. And Larsen Vale was just the first of the Sitheen. The gatekeeper to the rest. Perhaps, between his own supposed dreams and Autumn's explanation in the car, he could pretend to have already reconciled himself with the truth of the Esri by the time he was introduced to the Sitheen female.

The elevator came to a halt at the top floor and the doors opened. Autumn preceded him into the hall and motioned him to follow. Soon she pushed through a door into a small stairwell and climbed. Kaderil followed, his gaze falling to the enticing curve of her hips, stirring again the desire that he feared wouldn't cease as long as he was in her company.

At the top of the stairs, Autumn opened yet another door and stepped outside into the cool, damp darkness of the night. The roof. An odd place to meet a lone woman.

His hackles rose, his instincts leaping to alert. Not a lone woman. He sensed others. At least three others. And suddenly he understood. Autumn wasn't taking him to meet Larsen Vale. She'd brought him to the Sitheen. On the roof. In the dark. A trap.

Fool.

He'd been so taken with her, so enchanted with her beauty, he'd failed to see the treachery within.

The deceiver had become the deceived.

Even as his muscles bunched for attack, his calmer mind yelled a warning for caution. It might be a test. A test he would fail if he started hurling bodies.

But how could he know until it was too late? These were likely the very humans who'd used the death chant on Baleris. These Sitheen could end his existence this very night.

And if he returned to Esria without the draggon stone, his life would be as good as over anyway. If there was the slightest chance this was a test, he must not attack. If there was the slightest chance he could infiltrate this group, he must take it. He had to make them think he was human, no matter what.

And if he failed? If there was no doubt they knew he

was Esri, he would kill as many of them as he could before they started the death chant. Once they started chanting, if they touched him with flame, his long existence would end. Once they started chanting, it was too late.

The cutting breeze raked ominous fingers across his cheeks. Sharp gravel crunched beneath his heels, ratcheting the tension in his spine. Every muscle in his body readied for battle.

The shadowed forms of three men moved into his line of vision, one moving behind him, cutting off escape.

"Jack?" Autumn's voice held a sharp note of apprehension.

"Come here, Autumn," the voice behind him said.

He felt the brief grip of her hand on his arm. "I'm sorry," she whispered, and moved away.

Was it a test?

In a savage instant, the answer became clear. Fire erupted around him in a blinding flash. The grim sound of the Esrian death chant filled the night.

He was going to die.

Fifteen hundred years he'd lived and this was to be his end!

The heat licked at Kaderil's courage. Three men surrounded him, encircling him in a ring of fire, their threatening faces lost behind the blinding flame. The fire scorched his spirit as he faced the inevitable thrust that would bring his death.

The death chant rose on the night air.

He was a fool! He'd let his weakness for this temptress blind him to treachery. And now he would pay with his very existence.

Tension seared his muscles, strangling his spine. *Trapped.* Unable to fight. If not for the death chant, he would fly through the flames and attack those who would end him, but the moment the flames touched his skin, the chant would dissolve his existence in a shower of light.

His heart thundered in his chest as he turned, looking for escape, but he was well and truly trapped. Waiting. *Waiting.* It suddenly dawned on him his attackers weren't striking. He shielded his eyes against the flare of light and studied the face of the dark-haired human who was doing the chanting. In his eyes, he saw not deadly intent, but wariness. Watchfulness.

Waiting.

A test. A test he would fail if he didn't stop acting like an Esri expecting death. His brain scrambled for a suitably human reaction.

"What in the hell are you doing?" he growled. "If you burn me, I swear, I'll sue you for all you're worth."

The death chant ended abruptly. Kaderil's muscles bunched to leap and attack while he had the chance. He fought the need of the Punisher and forced himself to remain motionless. He *must* convince them he was human. The time to kill would come later.

His heart thudded in his chest as he watched the dark-haired human's gaze shoot to another's, a flash of amusement passing over his features. "Sue?" But when the man's gaze returned to Kaderil, his eyes were once more grave. "Take off your coat."

Kaderil did as he was told, peeling off the leather jacket with hands damp with sweat, then dropped it at his feet. To his surprise, the dark-haired man picked up the piece of clothing and ran his hands over it briskly.

"Shake his hand, Jack," one of the others said pointedly. The man's words sent tension twisting through Kaderil's already taut muscles. Like the Esri, Sitheen could have any of an infinite array of gifts. What magic did the man possess that was about to be turned against him?

As the dark-haired man handed him back his jacket, he thrust out his hand. "I'm Jack Hallihan."

Kaderil had no choice. He wiped his damp palm on his jeans and extended his hand. As the distance between them closed, he felt an odd tingling along the surface of his skin. Magic, but of a kind he'd never before encountered. Not magic so much as the promise of it.

As their hands made contact, an odd jolt shot up Kaderil's arm. Not painful, not exactly. But neither was it pleasant. *An electric jolt,* his borrowed thoughts told him, though he knew he'd never experienced such.

"Kade Smith." Kaderil's tone was unfriendly and wary, but he couldn't do a thing about it. Probably any man's would be the same under the circumstances, human or Esri.

Jack grasped his hand longer than was customary, then released him and went silent. His gaze turned distant as if he were listening to something no one else could hear. The others waited with an air of expectation that had Kaderil's heart pounding. Somehow Jack Hallihan could identify an Esri.

"A mix of human and Esri blood like the rest of us," Jack said, finally. "Though he has a lot more magic."

"So he's Sitheen?" the second man prompted.

"Yes. And a damn strong one."

Kaderil stared at him. The human, Jack, was wrong. He was not Sitheen. Either the man had no true gift or he was lying. Kaderil knew he had a small amount of human blood running through his veins, but he was Esri and immortal.

"What did you do?" he demanded. "Why do you think you know the mix of my blood?"

A low chuckle rumbled from Jack's throat, a sound of honest, if wry, humor. "You wouldn't believe me if I told you. Sorry for the theatrics. I'm not sure how much Autumn told you, but we're dealing with an enemy of unknown abilities. We can't be too careful."

Jack's voice had lost its tightness. As he spoke, warmth slowly replaced the chill. Unless the human was a skilled actor, it seemed he believed his assertion that Kaderil was Sitheen. Human.

Kaderil's knees nearly buckled with relief. Whatever the man's gift, it had failed. The tightness began to seep out of his muscles. The first step of his mission appeared to be complete, but he would be a fool to take these humans for granted again.

The remaining torches went out, the harsh light replaced by the soft glow of man-made illumination. *An electric lantern,* his borrowed knowledge told him. He could finally see beyond the ring of fire and his gaze sought Autumn. He found her standing in the shadows, watching him, her expression one of misery.

"I'm sorry," she mouthed.

Oddly, just seeing her calmed him until he could breathe again.

His attention was snatched back to the circle as the two other men joined Jack. The pair possessed a similarity of facial features that spoke of close relation, though they were built dissimilarly. The taller, more muscular of the two stepped forward. His hair was light and short, his expression friendly.

"I'm Charlie Rand. Welcome to the team." He gave an admiring grin as he met Kade's gaze. "How did the NBA miss *you?*"

The third man stepped forward. "I'm Harrison Rand." No expression crossed his serious face, but when he said "Welcome," acceptance warmed his eyes.

They were too close, but he forced himself to stay where he was, to accept their attention. He must pretend to be human. A *nice* human.

The soft thud of Jack's palm landed on his shoulder and he tensed for the burst of pain before his mind reminded him he was with humans now, not Zander. "Autumn says you've had some dreams about my wife."

Autumn entered the circle cast by the lamplight, easing the feeling of constriction in his chest. The woman with her, a tall blonde, approached him without fear.

"Welcome, Kade. I'm Larsen Vale...Larsen Hallihan." She threw Jack an apologetic smile. "We just got married. I'm still not quite used to the name change." She held out her hand to him, a smile of genuine welcome on her face. "You're one of us, now."

Simple words. *You're one of us.* Confirmation that he had indeed infiltrated the enemy camp.

Words he'd never heard in his entire existence.

The irony didn't escape him. His enemies had
welcomed him into their midst as he'd never been
welcomed by his own.

Autumn edged back into the night's shadows as the
Sitheen circled around Kade, firing questions at him,
welcoming him into their tight group. She was so relieved he wasn't Esri. Her stomach had tied itself into
knots on the drive over, then spasmed into a painful little
ball when the men lit those torches. She never wanted
to go through anything like that again. Clearly, she
needed a thicker skin for this kind of work.

Kade towered over the other Sitheen, his stance rigid,
his expression closed as the wind lifted his dark hair. He
probably hadn't believed a word she'd told him in the
car. Now he was hearing it in four-way stereo. The poor
guy had to be feeling as though he'd dropped down a
rabbit hole.

She felt bad for him, remembering her own reaction when Larsen had called four months ago with her
fear that the Dupont Circle rapist wasn't human.
Autumn hadn't believed that until the evidence had
mounted so high there was no denying it. And she'd
wanted to believe.

As a girl, she'd lived for anything having to do with
fantasy or science fiction. As a student, she'd studied
history, folklore and legend, fascinated by the uncanny
number of eyewitness accounts reported of other-
worldly encounters. The creatures in those legends were
called many things: fairies, elves, brownies, wee folk.
They were creatures capable of tremendous magic and

mischief. She was still marveling that those tales had been based in truth, that other-worldly creatures really had existed in this world…and existed again.

She was just very, very glad that the man who'd turned her world upside down in the past couple of hours wasn't one of them.

Feeling left out, Autumn wandered to the waist-high wall that ringed the roof, and looked out over the lights of the city. In the distance, the Washington Monument stood in a brilliant embrace of light, erect and solid against a changing reality. Behind her, Kade's rich voice filled the night air as he told the others about the dream that had left him with little more than impressions and the certainty he had to find Larsen.

He was human, not Esri, which meant he'd had no ulterior motive to pretend attraction to her. A pleasurable excitement filled her as her mind skipped ahead to dates, a boyfriend. Maybe even a lover.

Of course, the others were bound to draw him into their world, into their war. And the way things were going with the Esri, that would probably take up all his time. If only she could help. But she could do little but sit on the sidelines with her computer and watch.

She turned and leaned back against the damp stone, her gaze going back to the man who suddenly and totally consumed her thoughts.

"What can you do, Kade?" Charlie asked. "Other than your dreams? Any other odd gifts that might be of help against the Esri?"

Kade looked at him like a man being interrogated in an unknown language, uncertain how to respond.

Jack lightly backhanded Charlie's shoulder. "You can't ask him like that, Rand." He turned to Kade. "Look, whatever you've been living with is tough. Believe me, I know. For years I had voices in my head I couldn't understand, voices I thought were madness. It turns out they were the voices of my Sitheen ancestors. My own little advisory committee. The oldest on the committee, a half human, half Esri by the name of Malcolm was the one who told me you were Sitheen."

Kade's eyes narrowed. "How could he know?"

"Hell if I know. I ask questions and they give me answers. When they feel like it. They're not much into explanations."

As the damp breeze chilled her skin, Autumn sighed. She was kidding herself to think she could ever be part of this group. Being at their meetings didn't make her one of them. She didn't have any gifts or super powers. Nothing special at all except a knack for research.

Maybe that knack could be enough. If she could find those stones, she could help them. She could matter. A little.

Kade looked up and met her gaze across the heads of the others, his expression in the lantern light still tense and wary. But as their gazes met across the roof's small light, something happened. Her pulse began to leap and race, her heart lifting on the night breeze. She felt a power in his gaze that called to her, reaching for her even as it burrowed deep in her heart. A power that sent warmth cascading through her chilled body.

He watched her, clung to her, as if she were the only solid thing in his suddenly shifting universe.

He needed her. The certainty filled her, wrapping around her like a soft caress.

But for how long? She was his temporary anchor in a new and unsettling world. Once he felt comfortable with the others and found his place, he'd be fine. He wouldn't need her any longer.

Even if she still needed him.

Chapter 5

"Do you forgive me?" Autumn asked, her eyes wide and earnest.

She'd pulled him aside as the group filed through the door leading back into the building, giving them a moment alone. Now she stood before him on the dark roof, beneath the blanket of endless sky, her beauty pulling at him in ways he couldn't fathom.

"They had to make sure you weren't Esri," she said.

"There's nothing to forgive." He reached out and tugged a strand of fiery hair that had escaped her braid. He let his fingers trail down her jaw, drawing an odd feeling of strength from the contact. Not a power in the natural sense, but a balance. A grounding. A firm hold in the chaos.

And he felt as though he was in the very eye of the

chaos. The humans thought him one of them, but that could change in the blink of an eye. He must be on guard every moment, weigh every word, every action, lest he give himself away.

If that happened, if he was found out and battle ensued, he must find a way to protect Autumn. She must not be harmed.

As he stroked her cheek, her gaze searched his, her eyes soft and a little sad. She smiled and leaned forward to place a gentle kiss on his cheek. A kiss without heat or passion, but soft with an affection that had him brushing his thumb over her own cheek in return.

"I won't doubt you again," she said softly.

He felt the stab from the sharp edge of his own betrayal. She believed in him, yet he was the very thing she feared.

"Are you two coming?" Larsen poked her head around the door. "We're holding the elevator."

Autumn threw him a charmingly embarrassed little smile as she turned to follow Larsen.

He followed the women down the stairs. As they piled into the elevator, Kaderil once more felt that odd sensation of electricity, that promise of magic, and realized Jack was right behind him. He'd never felt quite that sensation from another, and it had him baffled. What kind of power did Jack possess? Was he aware of it? More importantly, what might it mean later, when the time came to kill the man? And he would kill him, all of them but Autumn. He must, even though the prospect had seemed easier before he'd met them and felt their welcome.

They clustered around Charlie as he unlocked the door to the apartment. Kaderil glanced at Autumn and found her watching him in return.

Larsen laughed and he realized she'd been watching them. "So, *how* long have you two known one another?"

Autumn grinned at the woman, color filling her cheeks. "Shut up, Larsen."

Charlie opened the door and they all filed in. Kaderil followed Autumn. Two women were already in the apartment, awaiting their arrival. An older woman in a bright red dress sat nestled on a large chair. Beneath her gray puff of hair, silver crescent moons dangled from her earlobes. Beside her chair stood a petite young woman in jeans and a sweatshirt that read Washington Redskins. Beneath her extremely short cap of dark hair, violet eyes stared at him.

"He wasn't Esri, then," the elderly woman said, drawing Kaderil's fractured attention and eyeing him with a friendly smile. "Welcome, dear. I'm Myrtle. Jack's aunt." With a pat on the younger woman's arm, she said, "And this is my new friend and companion. Aren't you, Tarrys dear?"

The tension that had begun to ease from his muscles rushed back with a vengeance.

Tarrys. The name of the second of Baleris's slaves, the one who'd failed to return to Esria. He'd assumed she'd been ended along with her master, but this woman could be her. She was the size of a Marceil and though she had hair, hers was far shorter than most females wore theirs. She was almost certainly the Marceil. It never occurred to him she'd been taken captive by the humans and remained with them still. He should have considered it, although it was unlikely she'd recognize him. His and Baleris's paths had never crossed. Then again, she was clearly staring at him. If she'd ever seen him, she'd remember.

"Myrtle's a gifted healer," Charlie told him. "And Tarrys is…" He turned to meet Jack's gaze before turning back to Kaderil. "She's not Esri, but she's not human, either. She's an escaped slave from their world with the deadliest aim with a bow and arrow I've ever seen. It's a good thing she's on our side."

Braced for her accusation, Kaderil watched the slave. His mind leaped from one alternative to the next, sorting through the same options he had on the roof. If she accused him of being Esri, what would he do? Attack? Or deny her claims and hope neither she nor the Sitheen had any way to prove him wrong? If only he had the power of a true Esri, he might be able to control her and keep her from giving him away.

"This is Kade Smith," Charlie said. "I haven't decided whether to start calling him Kareem or Hulk." Charlie made a sound deep in his throat. "You two are staring at each other as though you know one another. Did I miss something?"

The Marceil gasped, her wide-eyed expression turning stricken. "Forgive me. I've never seen a man so tall."

She didn't recognize him.

Autumn's arm eased through his, making him jerk. "Tarrys isn't dangerous, Kade. She's very humanlike. Much more so than the Esri."

With a start, he realized he was staring with the Punisher's glower. *Sweet Esria,* he was going to give himself away. He tore his gaze from the small slave, struggling for control as his heart thudded beneath his ribs.

"I'm…sorry." He licked his lips, willing his pulse to calm down as he struggled for a likely, *human* explanation. His gaze eased back to the slave. "I've never met someone who wasn't…human," he lied.

"I should have warned you," Jack said. "But Tarrys is such a sweet little thing, we already consider her one of us. Look at it this way, Kade. If you can handle everything we're throwing at you tonight, you can probably handle anything."

Myrtle rose. "Tarrys, dear, will you help me get the refreshments?"

As Jack followed the two women into the kitchen, Harrison and Charlie each grabbed a pair of dining chairs and set them in front of the sofa to form a loose circle.

"Are you doing okay?" Autumn asked beside him.

Her voice pulled him back from the cliff, easing the tension that was eating him alive.

"Yes. Do I seem a little…" What was the word? "…edgy?"

Her musical laughter wrapped around him, pleasing his ears even as it settled his leaping mind.

"*Edgy* doesn't begin to describe it. But you're not going ballistic and you haven't run away in fear, so I'd say you're doing a lot better than most people would under the circumstances."

"Good." Apparently his reaction was within the range

of normal for a human. Never in his long life had he felt so uncertain of himself. The role of Punisher he knew all too well. The role of nice human, not at all. And he could not afford mistakes.

"How many of them are Sitheen?" he asked Autumn. The more he knew about his enemy, the better. He wanted no more surprises.

"All but Tarrys."

"And you."

He heard her sigh, heard the unhappiness in the sound. "Yes. And me."

"How did you get involved in this?" He wished she weren't. It was too dangerous, especially for one without any of the gifts of the Sitheen.

"I went to college with Larsen. When they started realizing Baleris wasn't your run-of-the-mill bad guy, Larsen called me to see what I could dig up in the way of folklore and superstitions that might help them. I'm the one who figured out holly might work against enchantment." She pulled back her sleeve to show him her bracelet. The bracelet she didn't realize she'd already lost to him once today. "Right now I'm trying to help them find the other Esri stones."

On the drive here, Autumn had told him what the humans had learned about the seven stones. They had the draggon stone, and knew its purpose well enough. But they knew little about the others.

"Have you had any success?"

She wrinkled her nose, making her freckles dance in the lamplight. "No. I keep hoping something will turn up, but so far nothing has."

He saw the unhappiness in her eyes and was sorry for it. Sorry for her. He knew what it felt like to be on the outside.

"They're lucky to have your help."

She gave a soft, humorless snort and rolled those gray eyes.

Jack carried in a tray laden with cups, set it on the coffee table then came over to join them.

"Kade, I need to ask you some questions, if you don't mind. Where you live, work, those kinds of things. Don't take it personally. We have to check out anyone we bring into this group."

Kaderil nodded. "I understand." As Jack went through his list of questions, Kaderil recited the detailed background Ustanis had put together for him with the help of an enchanted human.

Apparently satisfied, Jack smiled. "Good enough."

"Have a seat, everyone," Charlie said.

Larsen patted the seat beside her. "Come on, Autumn."

Autumn looked at him with soft eyes before she slipped her arm from his and joined Larsen on the sofa.

Kaderil sat on one of the dining chairs, as did the two brothers, Harrison and Charlie. Jack sat beside Larsen, sliding his arm around her shoulders. A look passed between them, filled with more raw caring than he'd ever seen between two people. It was not unheard of for Esri to mate for life, though such devotion was unusual. He'd not expected to see such strong ties develop between creatures whose existence could be measured in a few short score of years. He had to wonder why they bothered.

But then his gaze slid to Autumn and she smiled at

him in a way that did funny things to his insides, and he thought he understood. They developed ties with one another because they couldn't help it. Perhaps it was just one of the many weaknesses of being human. A weakness, he was all too afraid he shared.

Myrtle and the slave joined them, each carrying a serving plate.

"Oatmeal cookies and spiced cider," Myrtle announced.

"Spiced?" Larsen asked with a knowing look. "Or spiked?"

"Spiced, dear." But the older human pulled a small green bottle out of her apron pocket with a grin and set it on the table. "A shot of whiskey for those who want it."

"Bring me up to speed," Charlie said, grabbing one of the cookies off the plate Tarrys held for him. The small Marceil's gaze softened as she gazed at the man, but Charlie appeared not to notice. "Kade and I both need to know what's been going on."

Myrtle handed Kaderil a cup of the warm drink. "Whiskey?"

"No. Thank you."

She shook her head, a gleam in her eye. "You're as bad as my nephew. Or as good, I suppose."

"They're just leaving more for us," Charlie said, waving her over. "Let's have some of the good stuff, Auntie M."

As Myrtle served the drinks, Jack filled them in. "Four Esri came through the gate two weeks ago during a downpour. Larsen and I were guarding the portal, and Autumn came along to help keep watch since neither of you Rands were in town. I went after the first one who came through, but the bastard ran faster than any human I've ever seen. There was no way to catch him. The other three came through a minute later and scattered."

"Three more?" Charlie looked confused. "I thought there were three in total."

Jack nodded. "Autumn caught one, learned that they're here for the *stones,* emphasis on the plural, and sent him back through the gate."

"He was just a kid," Autumn said, defensively.

Kaderil looked at her thoughtfully, with a new understanding of that night's events. He'd been the first through the gate. With his greater speed, the intent was for him to draw off any Sitheen who might be present. Zander's intent was likely to see him captured, but it hadn't worked out that way. When he'd first entered the human realm, the attack of water had briefly unnerved him until he'd realized it was falling from the sky and not coming from the humans. He'd easily outrun his pursuer, then waited for Zander and the others to catch up with him.

When they did, they'd been one short. Ustanis had turned around in time to see his son going back through the gate and had feared the boy a coward. But it seemed the youth had been captured by a kind-hearted woman and given a chance to live. How much courage it must have taken for her to attempt to capture an Esri, knowing what she did. His admiration for her rose another notch.

"Did he say how many stones?" Charlie asked.

Autumn shook her head, looking chagrined. "No. I've been searching for any hint of them, but so far I haven't found anything."

"So we've got three Esri loose in the city looking for stones that are probably dangerous. And we can't keep them from finding those stones since we don't know the first thing about them, not even how many there are."

Autumn winced, clearly blaming herself for letting the boy go. "Right."

Kaderil shifted the subject away from Autumn and onto a subject that suited his needs more. "But you have one of the stones? The key?"

Jack nodded. "The draggon stone."

"I wish to see it."

Jack looked at him for a moment before answering. "Nothing personal, Kade, but the whereabouts of that stone is on a need-to-know basis only. These bastards are powerful and clever. We can't take any chances."

"I understand." He hadn't expected them to trust him so quickly, but Jack's answer was not what he wanted to hear. What would constitute this "need to know," and how could he get it within the short time he had left?

"We have no way of knowing whether they've found any of the other stones. But we know they've been busy. The murder rate in the Dupont Circle area has skyrocketed since they got here. The reports are all over the news."

Charlie shook his head and reached for the whiskey bottle. "I haven't seen any news. Do you think they're finding that many Sitheen?"

"No." Jack pulled his arm from around Larsen and leaned forward, resting his arms on his knees. "About ten o'clock this morning, we had another incident. Apparently, a man killed everyone aboard a Metro bus except the driver and one small boy whose mother had hidden him beneath the seat. From the kid's description, it appears the man walked down the bus aisle, touching people, making them scream and then die. People were running for the back of the bus, yelling for the driver to stop the bus, but he ignored them. He just kept driving. The driver didn't remember a thing."

"Enchanted," Harrison said. "The son of a bitch."

Zander, Kaderil thought. Zander had the ability to send a shooting pain through his hands strong enough to drive Kaderil to his knees—a fire Kaderil had no doubt could kill an Esri if such destruction were not strictly forbidden. A pain no human could survive.

"Sounds as if they're not just going after Sitheen this time," Charlie said.

Jack sighed. "We don't know what they're doing other than terrorizing the city again."

Kaderil knew. Centuries ago, in the days before the gates were sealed, Zander's mate had been killed by humans. Sitheen. Kaderil had always suspected his own resemblance to the mortals was behind Zander's unreasoning hatred for him. Now he was sure.

"Have we had any sightings of the Esri at all?" Charlie asked.

"A few by the cops," Harrison said. "None by us. Jack, Larsen and I have been patrolling the Dupont Circle area night and day, but we're only three and it's a big area."

As the discussion moved from one man to the other, Kaderil followed with his gaze, watching, listening, and marveled at the fact that they paid him no more attention than anyone else in the room. They thought him one of them, though he wasn't. Never before had he blended in. One of the group.

He enjoyed the novelty rather too well.

"I'm back now." Charlie grabbed another cookie. "I've been granted two-weeks leave."

"What about you, Kade?" Harrison asked. "How much time can you give us?"

Kaderil jerked back from his thoughts and dug through his borrowed memories for an appropriate answer. "I have vacation built up." He wasn't certain that phrase even made sense, but Harrison nodded.

"All right, then." Harrison pulled a folded paper out of his back pocket, opened it and laid it on the table. "I've been tracking the locations of the suspicious murders and the few sightings from the police. They're centered around Embassy Row. I've drawn up a new patrol schedule that includes Kade and Charlie. We'll have to patrol individually to cover as much square footage as possible. Jack's got the cops out there covering the streets we can't. If anyone spots an Esri, keep him in sight and call Jack or me. We'll get word out to the rest. Don't try to take him. He may not be alone."

This wasn't going to work. How could he possibly earn their trust enough to be shown the whereabouts of the draggon stone if he was off walking the streets alone? He'd foolishly thought infiltrating their group would be the difficulty. That part had been surprisingly easy. Getting them to trust him would not.

He'd give it a few days. But if he'd made no progress by the end of the week, he would be forced to take stronger measures, using their very caring for one another against them.

The thought was surprisingly disagreeable. He scoffed at the sentimental thought. He'd been sent to kill them and kill them he would, even if they *had* welcomed him warmly into their midst.

Autumn would be the only one who would survive the slaughter, for she wasn't Sitheen, thank the spirits.

As Jack explained the Metropolitan Police Department, or MPD's, unofficial role in the search for the Esri, Kaderil's eyes slid to Autumn. Her gaze was on her lap where her fingers laced and unlaced, playing with one another as the talk went on around her. She glanced up without lifting her head, her gaze spearing his with perfect accuracy as if she were as aware of him as he was of her. A smile started on her mouth and rose to her eyes, causing a strangely erratic sensation deep in his chest. A sensation not altogether unpleasant.

What would happen to that smile when his work in the human realm was done? Would it be forever destroyed?

It didn't matter. His only concern must be the fulfilling of his mission and the finding of that draggon stone. Nothing else mattered.

But that smile eased into his pores. His longing to taste her again grew with every heartbeat until he once more feared he was the one being enchanted.

"Autumn found some paintings," Larsen told the group, breaking the spell. She nudged Autumn, forcing her gaze from his. "Tell them."

Autumn accepted the attention with a self-conscious shrug. "I've been looking for anything with a seven-pointed star. A couple of days ago, I discovered the star was used by a mid-nineteenth century Danish painter as his artist's mark. He was a man who was known for his wildly fantastical subjects. I managed to get copies of two of them. The subject is a strikingly pale blond woman wearing the draggon stone."

The grunts of surprise and interest told him Autumn had impressed the others, and he felt pride warm him, as if he'd somehow contributed to the accomplishment himself. He watched as she pulled an envelope out of her purse and laid one of the pictures from it on the table. They all scooted forward or pulled their chairs closer to get a better look.

Kaderil glanced at the picture, then started as recognition slammed into him. The place was Esria, the Forest of Light, with its blue thornewood trees and the sparkling rainbow mists. In the middle of the painting stood a young woman in a gown of royal emerald, her pale hair tumbling around her shoulders. She looked toward the distance, her exquisite face haunted with worry.

"Princess Ilaria," Tarrys gasped. "She must be. The royal gown and the green eyes. A Sitheen must have seen her in his dreams and painted her likeness."

"Hot damn." Charlie breathed. "She's gorgeous."

"She's Esri," Harrison snapped.

Kaderil had only seen the princess once, many centuries ago, long before her banishment.

"She's the daughter of the old Esri queen," Tarrys explained. She glanced at Charlie, then away, as if she were too shy to hold his gaze. "When King Rith seized power three hundred years ago, he destroyed the queen and imprisoned the princess in the Forest of Night-mares. She remains there still."

"She's still *alive?*" Charlie asked.

"Yes. All Esri would know the moment she died."

"But she must be…*centuries* old."

Tarrys met his gaze and held it this time. "The Esri are immortal, or virtually so. A normal lifetime spans many thousands of years. Princess Ilaria has likely aged little. Except…the Forest of Nightmares is a difficult place. It's hard to know what she's endured."

"Why doesn't anyone rescue her?"

A dread Kaderil understood all too well darkened the little slave's eyes. "None can make it through the woods to find her." It wasn't called the Forest of Nightmares for nothing.

"There's another picture," Autumn said. "I doubt you'll think she's so pretty, Charlie, once you've seen it." She pulled a second photo from the envelope and set it on the table. In the painting, Ilaria stood in the human world beside a large oak tree, in the throes of power, the draggon stone glowing as brightly as her eyes.

Larsen gasped. "That's just how Baleris looked when he was raping all those young women—his hair flying above his head like a troll doll's, his eyes glowing like Christmas bulbs."

"It's what happens when an Esri gains or uses great power," Tarrys said.

Larsen looked up at him. "From what we managed to piece together—and Tarrys has confirmed this—Baleris was able to spot virgins on sight. Apparently they put off a glow some Esri can see. When a girl grows to womanhood, her body creates an energy that's released the first time she has sex. If an Esri male is her first partner, he absorbs that energy, greatly increasing his own power. It's one of the things that made Baleris so hard to catch. With each rape, his power grew, faster than we could keep up. Fortunately for the women he raped, he enchanted them first and none remember."

Kaderil nodded as if hearing the explanation for the first time even while the magnitude of the challenge before him hit him squarely in the chest. Even with all that added energy, Baleris had not been able to defeat these humans. Had he taken foolish risks? Underestimated their cunning and intelligence? Had they outsmarted him? Or truly overpowered him?

He was going to have to be on guard every minute and take nothing for granted if he wanted to be the victor this time and not end like Baleris.

Tarrys knelt by the table, pointing to the draggon stone around Ilaria's neck in the second painting. "It's glowing. It is said it only glows when it's being used as the key."

"What do you mean?" Harrison asked.

"I think I understand," Larsen said. "The draggon stone is the key to opening the gates between the worlds. Or sealing them." She looked at Tarrys. "Princess Ilaria was the one who sealed the gates and gave us the stones, wasn't she?"

"It would seem so."

Kaderil grunted. So Princess Ilaria's was the hand that had swept the stones out of the Esris' reach. Why? While Esria had not suffered too greatly without their power, the trees no longer bore fruit with the same abundance, the grass no longer grew on most of the slopes and hillsides, and the Esri themselves had found, over the years, a waning of their gifts. Power that was once sharp and strong had dulled and weakened. And would continue to do so. Why would the princess have disposed of the stones? Perhaps she'd become enamored of the humans and wished to keep the Esri away from them?

"Too bad we can't rescue the lady and get her to help us seal this last gate," Charlie mused.

"Don't even joke about going into that hell hole," Harrison said. He rose. "I've got to get going. I've made copies of the schedule." He reached for a small pile of papers on the corner table and began handing them out, bypassing Myrtle, Tarrys and Autumn.

Kaderil saw the way Autumn's head dipped as Harrison passed her by. He felt her rejection as if it were his own. She wasn't one of them, thank the spirits, or he'd have to kill her, too. But, like him, she lacked the blood heritage necessary to be accepted by her peers. He knew the feeling all too well.

"I've put everyone's cell-phone number on the list but Kade's. Kade, why don't you give us your number and we can add it to our lists."

Kaderil recited the number Ustanis had acquired for him, a number he'd yet to use.

They all rose. Autumn crossed to him with a smile, making his hands itch to reach for her and draw her against him. The woman was becoming a weakness he could not afford.

"I'll take you home," she said.

"No." It was best if none of them knew where he

lived. The address he'd given Jack would check out, but it wasn't where he was staying. And it was best if he didn't see Autumn again. He didn't need her any longer. Not for his mission. She'd led him to the Sitheen and any further involvement between them would not only complicate his mission, but would also put her at risk. And that was the last thing he wanted to do.

"Okay."

He saw the hurt in her eyes and hated that he'd put it there. Words came to him. "I'll walk you to your car."

She smiled and he knew he'd chosen right. When they reached Autumn's vehicle, he held the door for her. "Good luck finding your stones," he said as she slipped inside.

She looked up at him, those gray eyes soft and welcoming. "You can give me a call anytime." She gave a small grimace. "Anytime you need to talk. I know this is all a bit much."

"Thanks." He closed the door, shutting out the temptation to pull her into his arms, the temptation to kiss her until he forgot his mission, forgot why he was here. But no sooner did the door close, than the barrier dissolved with the lowering window.

"Kade. You don't have my phone number." She turned away, then back, with a pen in her hand. "Give me the paper Harrison gave you and I'll write it down."

Even here, in the muted glow from the bulbs lighting the parking garage, she shone like a brilliant fiery gem. As he watched her write the number, he felt her beauty like an ache in his chest. How was it possible he would never see her again?

She looked up, meeting his gaze with her soft eyes, and handed the sheet back to him. "I'm glad you're not Esri."

"Did you really think I was?"

"No, not really." A soft smile lifted her lips. "But I wasn't sure. I've never dealt with magic before."

"I hope you never have to…. You shouldn't be involved in this, Autumn. It's too dangerous."

"I know." Her brows pulled together. "But I want to be involved."

"Why?"

She gave him a self-deprecating look even as her eyes began to sparkle. "Because it's exciting and important. And fascinating."

He understood, he realized. This was *her* place, as the royal court was his. And like him, she struggled against the accident of birth that would keep her from being part of it. Perhaps he could help her. There was one small gift he could give her that wouldn't compromise his mission or her own safety, but would give her a purpose. For now.

"You keep talking about stones," he mused. "Every time you do, I see the same picture in my head. I believe it's from one of my dreams."

Autumn's gaze sharpened. "Tell me."

"I can't remember the details, only that there are six rocks."

"*Six?*" Her voice rose with excitement.

"Yes. Pale green, about the size of a nickel, but of varying shapes." He'd never actually seen the six lesser stones, and he certainly hadn't dreamed about them, but he'd heard them described often enough to know what she sought.

"Pale green," she breathed. Her face lit up in a smile of such brightness it took his breath away and made him doubt his decision to not see her again. "Kade, this is wonderful! Now I know what I'm looking for."

"It was just a dream, Autumn. It might be nothing."

But her laughter filled him with pleasure. "The dream of a Sitheen is nothing to take lightly. You saw them, Kade. I'm sure of it. I'll start researching as soon as I get home."

Sharp intelligence gleamed in her eyes as the excitement visibly bubbled within her, pleasing him immensely. What he wouldn't give to pull her into his arms and taste the happiness on her lips.

"You're an amazing woman, Autumn McGinn. If anyone can find those stones, you will." That thought, that certainty, gave him pause. Perhaps he shouldn't have told her the truth about the stones. What if she really did trace them quickly? Surely even Autumn couldn't locate six forgotten stones in this large world in less than two weeks. And by then, Ustanis would have followed their scent and tracked them down himself.

"Thank you." Her gaze turned soft and shy as she smiled at him.

Every intent flew out of his head as the need to taste her became too great to fight. He leaned low into her window to capture her lips one last time and was blindsided by the fire that leaped between them. Need rolled through him as her sweet taste caressed his tongue. He drank of her, reveled in the sweetness for a few stolen moments before forcing himself to pull away.

"Goodbye, Autumn."

"'Bye, Kade."

As he watched her drive away, he knew he should be feeling relief that she was out of danger. And gratitude that she'd led him to the Sitheen. But all he could think about was that he'd just said goodbye to the woman he'd been waiting for all his life.

Chapter 6

Autumn trudged along the graveled path on the National Mall beneath a bright sun and a sky as blue as Kade Smith's eyes. A week ago, she'd gone to bed with stars in her eyes, her heart racing with excitement over a brand-new crush, thinking that maybe her luck with men had finally turned. But Kade had never called.

She knew it was time to forget him, to accept that he'd been every bit as out of her league as she'd feared, despite the way he'd looked at her, the way he'd kissed her. But the ache in her chest refused to go away. And she just couldn't seem to quit coming out here every lunch hour to scan the pathways and sidewalks that Harrison had assigned him to patrol, hoping for a glimpse of the tall, dark and devastatingly handsome man who consumed her thoughts.

Clearly, he'd forgotten about her easily enough. Five days ago, she'd taken a chance and left a short, friendly message on his answering machine, but he'd never called her back. Obviously, the man wasn't interested. If only she could say the same. Somehow she'd fallen prey to a ridiculous case of love-at-almost-first-sight. And it *was* ridiculous. She barely knew the man. But she couldn't deny he'd turned her world upside down. She thought about him every minute, wondering where he was, wondering if he was okay. Wondering why she'd been so wrong in thinking they'd discovered some kind of connection.

She buttoned her coat against the chilly wind, then shoved her hands in her pockets. At least meeting him hadn't been a total loss. His dream about the six green stones was starting to pay off. Once she knew what she was looking for, she'd had little trouble picking up the trail. The stones *had* been part of the same estate as the draggon stone, but not part of the jewelry, as she'd expected. She'd found a picture of them set in the rim of an antique pewter cup, a cup no one seemed to have wanted. She'd tracked the cup to a local antique store where the dealer told her it had sat on his shelves for years until one of his neighbors had expressed an interest in the stones for his craft business, and he'd sold it to the man for next to nothing. She had a call into the neighbor, Jerry Robertson, now. It was too soon to call her search a success, but her hopes were flying high.

It was about time, too. The death rate in D.C. was going through the roof and the vast majority of them were too odd not to be Esri-related. In the past four days alone, there had been more than thirty cases of apparent suicide—people walking in front of moving cars, jumping off bridges or diving out the windows of office buildings. Just yesterday, four tourists from Minnesota had drowned in the Reflecting Pool in front of the Washington Monument. The pool was three feet deep! They had to have been enchanted.

Every time she heard of another murder, her stomach tightened with sharp, fresh guilt. Maybe if she hadn't let that kid go, he could have told them something that might have helped, that might have stopped the murders. Her only chance of helping to stop the Esri was to find those stones. With the help of Kade's dream, she fully intended to succeed.

Even if her relationship with Kade himself seemed destined to go down as just another failure.

Twenty-four hours later, Autumn's mood was soaring as she drove through the busy streets of D.C. Kade still hadn't called, but she could almost forgive him for his lack of interest in her because of what he *had* given her. He'd made her believe in herself. He'd told her that, if anyone could find the Esri stones, she could.

And maybe, just maybe, she had.

Nervous excitement had her tapping the steering wheel as she waited for the stoplight to turn green. Jerry Robertson had returned her call last night and confirmed he'd bought the cup and used the stones from it in his creations. Junk art, he called them.

She was on her way to his house now.

Autumn rolled her gaze to the roof and back even as

the butterflies beat at the insides of her stomach. She'd all but promised the man a showing of his collection at the Smithsonian if he let her come see his work. Her boss was going to kill her.

Despite the hope firing her excitement, she knew finding the Esri stones was a long shot. Jerry Robertson was a crafter who sold his work at shows and fairs around the city. Crafters rarely kept records of their customers. Those stones could be long gone by now with no way to track them.

She'd know soon enough.

The street came into view and she started searching for the row house. Autumn spied the address she was looking for and parked. The house, like many in this neighborhood, was ill kempt. Weeds had long overtaken whatever grass had once blanketed the yard and the door badly needed paint. Overgrown holly bushes lined the front of the house, half-covering the windows.

As Autumn approached, the front door opened to reveal a man who was the antithesis of the yard. He looked like a lawyer in his suit and tie, his thinning hair brushed carefully to one side. No, she realized. He looked like a man on his way to an interview. She groaned. Of course he was dressed for an interview— an interview with a Smithsonian official. *Her.*

"Mr. Robertson? I'm Autumn McGinn with the Smithsonian." At least she was wearing nice slacks and a blazer.

"How do you do, Ms. McGinn? Please, come in, won't you?" He led her into a small, neat living room lined with shelves overflowing with sculptures. There must be more than a hundred of them! Junk art, he called them, and the description couldn't be more accurate. The works all stood about six inches tall and included everything from a spray of bottle-cap daisies to the Empire State Building made from gum wrappers and paperclips. Most of the sculptures were made from a hodge-podge of cast-off components—a lightbulb base, an old toothbrush, the glass from a pair of spectacles. Strange and yet fascinating in an odd sort of way.

Her stomach churned. Even if the Esri stones were here, how was she ever going to find them in this mess? There were too many!

She forced herself to calm down, to take a deep breath. There was only one way to do this, she decided.

"I love them, Mr. Robertson," she enthused, hoping he mistook the edge of panic for excitement. "How many would you allow me to take for the exhibit?"

The man's eyes lit with excitement. "You're going to accept them?"

Autumn smiled, swallowing her guilt. "Yes, of course. I'd like to take twenty, if that's okay, but it may take me a little while to decide which ones."

"Of course, of course. The only one I can't part with is this," he said, and pulled a floppy-eared dog sculpture from the top shelf.

The sculpture was different from the rest. Instead of junk, the dog was made from pieces of silver, or silver plate, and semiprecious stones. *And his stone ear was pale green.*

Her heart skipped a beat. "May I see it, please?"

The man hesitated only a moment before handing it

to her. At once she saw the faint etching of a seven-pointed star on the surface of the stone. Her heart began to pound. She'd found one of the Esri stones! Without screwing up one single thing.

Yet.

Perspiration broke out on the back of her neck beneath her thick braid. She had to get this sculpture without making him suspicious.

"I can see why you wouldn't want to give it up, Mr. Robertson. It's beautiful."

"Well, that's not exactly why I can't let you have it. It's for my latest grandchild. I've made special sculptures for each of the other ten. Number eleven is on the way and it's going to be her baby gift when she's born."

Eleven special sculptures. Six of which she'd bet money, possessed pale green stones. The trick was getting her hands on them. She should probably tell Jack and let the police confiscate them, but the thought made her ill. The man was so excited about this exhibition and so proud of these sculptures, she couldn't do that to him if she could find another way. Besides, she wanted to do this on her own. She had to prove to Larsen and the others that she was good for more than just research. That she could be counted on to come through when it mattered.

Kade's words came back to her, as they had two dozen times this week. *You're an amazing woman, Autumn McGinn. If anyone can find those stones, you can.*

And she had. She could do this, too.

"Mr. Robertson, this is spectacular. Truly a work of art. Couldn't we borrow the sculptures from your grandchildren?"

"Oh, dear. Oh, no, I don't think so."

Autumn's stomach clutched with panic. She had to get that stone.

She tried a different tactic and waved her hand airily. "You don't have to give me an answer today, but why don't you talk to your children about it? Your grandchildren might be thrilled to see their gifts on display in the Smithsonian."

Mr. Robertson's head began to nod and as it did, he started to smile. "You're right. Why, I can take them there myself and show them my art. *My* art, in the Smithsonian."

Oh, she was going to have to make this happen.

"I'll have my daughter bring her kids' sculptures to me tomorrow," he said. "None of my boys live in the area anymore, but they could overnight them directly to the museum."

"Better yet," Autumn said. "Have them mail them to me at home. That way I won't have to hunt them down." The truth was, she didn't want to have to explain these pieces to anyone at the museum. Especially when she still had some removing and replacing of stones to do. She took out one of her business cards, wrote the marina address on the back, and handed it to him. "I'll take this one with me today."

"Yes, indeed." The older man grinned. "This is such a proud day."

Autumn smiled and shook his hand. "You *should* be proud, Mr. Robertson. You have an amazing talent." She said goodbye and started down the walk with a grin that just wouldn't be contained. One of the most powerful stones in the world—in two worlds—was safe in her hands.

A giddy euphoria bubbled up inside her, making her want to laugh. She should call Kade and tell him what he'd helped her accomplish by sharing his dream. He'd want to know. Even if he wasn't interested in her romantically.

And it was the perfect excuse to hear his voice again.

"Here," Ustanis said. "This is the area where I keep smelling the stone."

"Park the car," Zander ordered the enchanted driver. With a scowl he turned to Ustanis. "I'm disappointed in you, Ustanis, as the king will be when we return with only half the stones."

Ustanis met his scowl with one of his own. "This world is too large, Zander. If the king knew the impossibility of his demand…"

"If you are not up to the task, Rith will find one who is."

Dismay pulled at Ustanis's expression. "One of the stones is nearby. I've smelled it for days, but can't find it. I fear something's blocking it. I had hoped you could tell me if there's a Sitheen in the area causing the disturbance."

Zander opened his own senses. "No Sitheen. Holly. The plant dampens the magic that would pass through it." He searched the houses on both sides of the street and found holly bushes in abundance. "You'll have to enter the dwellings."

"The task could take me days."

"Then you had best begin."

Ustanis released a frustrated breath. But as he

reached for the door handle, he froze. "I smell it clearly." He pointed to a dwelling three houses down from which a tall, red-haired woman emerged. In her hand she carried some kind of object.

"There! The stone's power follows her path."

His hand closed around the door's handle, but Zander stopped him.

"That deadness of energy follows her, as well. She's wearing holly and will see through your glamour. Best to approach her where she cannot escape. We'll follow. When the time and place are right, we'll retrieve what is ours."

Autumn climbed into her car, set the sculpture carefully on the seat beside her, then locked the doors. She pulled her phone from her purse and pressed the speed-dial number she'd foolishly thought she'd be calling often. Kade's. As the phone rang, she pressed her head back against the seat, listening to her pulse pound as she waited for him to pick up.

"Hello?"

The sound of his deep, rich voice brought such a rush of longing she nearly couldn't talk around it. Every minute of the past week, she'd longed to hear his voice.

"Kade? It's Autumn." Terrified he'd think she was stalking him and hang up, she rushed forward. "I found one of the Esri stones. I thought…I thought you'd like to know. Because you helped me."

The silence on the other end was deafening.

She was an *idiot* for thinking he'd want to talk to her. "I shouldn't have called. 'Bye—"

"Autumn, wait. What do you mean, you found one of the Esri stones?" His voice was harder than she remembered, but hearing her name on his lips again sharpened the ache in her heart.

"I have one of them with me right now. And I think I know where the others are."

He made a sound of disbelief. "I didn't think you'd manage the impossible quite so quickly." After a moment's silence, he added, "I'd like to see it. Where are you?"

"On my way to the houseboat."

"I'll meet you there."

"Okay." She hung up then stared, unseeing, at the kids playing on the sidewalk. Slowly, she tucked the phone in her purse and started the car. Kade was coming over. But not to see her. To see the stones.

What had she done?

She was going to have to pretend to be completely uninterested in him, or she'd send him running for cover. Yes, she was dying to see him again, but he wasn't interested in her. And by inviting him over, she'd guaranteed her heart was in for another pounding.

"Can't you drive any faster?" Kaderil's feet tapped an urgent rhythm as the taxi crept through the city traffic.

"No. No tickets," the man said in a heavily accented version of the local human tongue.

Kaderil's fists pressed against his knees. If it were night, he might risk a run through the city streets, for his natural speed was far faster than this vehicle was able to move through the creeping traffic. But that might draw attention to what he was.

Still, the thought of the danger Autumn had placed herself in, the danger he'd placed her in by giving her that hint, made him consider the risk. It amazed him that she'd found not one, but all six stones this fast. He continued to underestimate the humans—a mistake that would be the death of him. Or the death of Autumn. He didn't know why Ustanis hadn't found the stone before now, but if it was truly one of the six, whatever had blocked Ustanis's power to find it would likely disappear now that Autumn had removed it from its resting place. Ustanis would follow the stone's scent to Autumn. Kaderil could only hope Zander wasn't with him when he did.

He shouldn't care. A simple human shouldn't matter to him one way or the other. But there was nothing simple about Autumn McGinn. She'd enchanted him. Somehow, with her feminine ways, she'd cast a spell that had made him unable to forget her. That had caused her to matter to him in ways no woman ever had. For a week, now, he'd thought of her night and day, wondering what she was doing, if she was safe.

A dozen times he'd nearly broken and gone back to her. For a single smile. A single kiss. But he'd recognized the weakness and refused to give in.

Now, he hoped he wasn't too late.

Finally, the taxi pulled up in front of the marina. Kaderil handed the driver bills that more than covered the fare, then unfolded himself from the vehicle and strode with barely restrained speed down the path to the dock. But as Autumn's houseboat came into view, he knew he was too late.

Zander and Ustanis were on the deck of her boat, their silver tunics shining in the sun's afternoon glare. As he broke into a run, they opened the sliding glass door and slipped inside. Zander would know Autumn wasn't Sitheen, but the holly would protect her from their enchantment.

Unable to control her, Zander would kill her.

With a surge of pure fear, Kaderil sprinted down the dock, leaped onto the deck of the houseboat and wrenched open the door. Autumn was holding some sort of rock pile, backing away as Zander advanced on her.

"Leave her alone!" he shouted.

Autumn speared him with fearful eyes. "Kade!"

Zander glanced at him with surprise. "Kade, is it?" A gleam entered his eyes that sent fear spearing through him. If Zander poured his pain energy into her, he'd kill her.

"She's not Sitheen," Kaderil said.

Zander scowled. "She's *human*."

Using the speed and strength that had earned him the position of the Punisher, Kaderil leaped, knocking Zander away from her. He grabbed Zander's wrists, immobilizing those deadly hands, then with a satisfying snap, broke them.

Zander yelled with pain, nearly drowning Autumn's cry of outrage. Kaderil looked over his shoulder to find Ustanis now had the odd pile of stones. Autumn was trying to block the shorter man's escape. "Kade, he has the stone!" Beneath his hands, he felt Zander's bones reknit, so he broke them again.

"Autumn, let him go!"

"*No.*"

"Autumn…" His words strangled in his throat as fiery pain seared his skin and poured through his body. While he'd been distracted by Autumn, Zander had twisted his hands until he was able to touch Kaderil's skin, attacking him with mind-numbing, strength-stealing pain.

"Autumn," he gasped. "Run!"

"I'm not leaving you!"

Loyalty. So precious. So ill-timed.

"Ustanis, take her bracelet. *Holly.*" Enchanted, she'd remember nothing more that she saw or heard. If Ustanis touched her quickly, she might never realize Kaderil was in league with her attackers. He fell to his knees. Out of the corner of his wavering vision, he saw Ustanis drop the stone pile back on the counter and face Autumn. The stricken look on her face tore his heart from his chest. She'd heard him. She understood he was one of them.

Autumn fought Ustanis valiantly and managed to get past him, but as she ran for the door, the Esri grabbed her from behind and wrenched the band from her wrist. Instantly, she stilled.

Enchanted.

Kaderil pushed Zander away from him, freeing himself from the source of pain. But even with the source removed, the pain itself continued to scorch his body. He stumbled to his feet, gasping for breath. His gaze leaped between Zander's scowl and Ustanis, who was watching him with wide-eyed disbelief. The Punisher driven to his knees was not something most Esri expected to see.

Kaderil tried to glare at him, but Zander started for Autumn and all he could manage was a grimace as he lurched forward to cut him off. He stood in front of Autumn and turned to face Zander.

His enemy chuckled, an ugly sound. "So the Punisher has fallen for a human."

"I haven't…fallen for anyone." He must talk fast to convince Zander she was important to their mission or her life was over. Zander, who had killed so many humans already, would destroy her just for the pleasure of hurting Kaderil. "We need her, Zander. She's located the other stones."

Ustanis's eyes widened. *"Where?"*

"I'm not sure," Kaderil admitted. "How many have you found?"

"Only two other than this one. The others are too far away, their scent too faint to follow. I had despaired of finding them, but if she can get them for us…"

"Enough!" Zander looked from one to the other of them in disgust, then speared Kaderil with that yellow gaze. "Get them and bring them to us. Ustanis, take the one here."

"No," Kaderil said. "Leave it. It must be here when she wakes from the enchantment."

Zander scoffed. "She already knows you're Esri, Punisher. I saw the knowledge on her face as clearly as you did."

He glowered at the pair, pulling himself back into the role of Punisher. Between clenched teeth, he growled, "I will find a way to convince her otherwise. But that stone must be here!"

He took a threatening step toward Ustanis. The smaller man thrust the stone into Kaderil's hand.

Zander scowled. "If you fail, *dark blood,* we all fail. Beware your loyalties. I fear you identify a little too closely with the Sitheen. You are, after all, both mixed bloods."

Kaderil glared at the captain of the royal guard. "Sitheen are mortals, human but for a small trace of Esri blood. I am the oppostie. Immortal. Esri but for an unfortunate trace of human. You needn't question my loyalties, Zander. She's critical to my mission, nothing else." If only that were true. If only he'd been able to stop thinking about her for a single moment over the past eight days. "When the gate opens at the full moon, I'll have the remaining stones, including the draggon."

"We go," Zander said. But as Zander turned toward the door, Ustanis reached for Autumn.

Kaderil growled and Ustanis leaped back, both hands raised. "I—I only seek to release her mind."

Kaderil sucked in a hard breath around the slowly easing pain. "Do it."

Ustanis touched Autumn's hand and she collapsed. Kaderil swept her into his arms.

Zander made a sound of cruel laughter. "They're such gratifyingly fragile creatures, aren't they?"

Kaderil held Autumn tight against his chest as the two Esri went out the door and closed it behind them. What was he going to do? She'd seen too much. Heard too much.

He regretted the need for magic against her, but he had to convince her she was mistaken. And if he couldn't?

He must, that was all there was to it. The alternative was unthinkable.

Chapter 7

Dreams. Just dreams.

Kaderil held Autumn's cold hand and pushed the thoughts into her head as she slept the unnatural sleep of enchantment. Over and over again, he pushed the thoughts into her brain, desperate to make her believe.

I fell and caught my bracelet. I hit my head.

She lay stretched out on the sofa, her head cradled in his lap. With the hand that didn't grip her own, he stroked the loose tendrils of hair from her face. His heart still raced from the fear of seeing Zander stalking her. If he'd killed her...

It wouldn't have mattered, his Punisher's brain avowed. She was just a human and had already served her purpose.

But deep inside he knew that wasn't true. She did matter. More than he wanted to admit.

He pushed more thoughts into her head. *I dreamed Esri came after the stone. I dreamed Kade rescued me.*

He had to make her believe she hadn't truly seen the Esri. That he wasn't one of them.

A growl rumbled out of his throat. She was a weakness he could not afford. He'd thought staying away from her would end his infatuation, but every night she entered his dreams, laughing, the sun shining in her hair.

She'd become his obsession. A weakness, yes. But also a gift. Light shining for the first time into a life of darkness.

He *must* make her believe.

Autumn stirred, causing tension to scream through his body.

It was all a dream.

Her lashes fluttered open, blinking with soft confusion.

"How are you feeling?" He'd spent much of the past week working to make his speech more varied, more human, and working on what the humans called "people skills."

Her gaze snapped up. "Kade?"

A sweet smile curved her lips, then froze half formed and he knew she'd remembered. Fear flooded her eyes as she jerked. "The sculpture." She struggled to sit up, but he kept firm hold of her hand. "The Esri stole the stone!"

Dreams. Just dreams. They weren't really here.

She escaped his grasp and stumbled to the kitchen. At the counter, she pulled up short and stared at the silver dog.

Kaderil rose and followed her, afraid to let her out of his reach and the reach of his thoughts. He slid his hand beneath her braid, cupping the soft skin at the back of her neck. To his surprise, she leaned into his touch instead of pulling away with fear, easing some of the constriction in his chest. But it was too soon to relax. She'd not yet remembered everything. And when she did, if his thoughts weren't enough, she'd be backing away in fear.

For the first time in centuries, the thought of seeing fear in another's eyes brought no satisfaction.

I had the weirdest dream. He pushed the thought into her head, then pointed to the pile of rocks. "Is one of these the stone you were looking for?"

She nodded, the sunny room glistening in her fiery braid. "This one." She pointed to the stone in the green ear with the star etched on its surface. Her gaze found his, her brows pulled tightly together. "I am *so* confused. I swear, the Esri followed me, Kade. They want that stone."

His fingers slid up and down the back of her neck. *No, the Esri weren't here. It was a dream. Just a dream.*

"If they followed you, why didn't they take it?" He gave her a moment, then supplied the answer to her head. *They didn't follow me. It was just a dream.*

She turned to him, her lashes sweeping up to reveal twin gray pools of confusion. "It was just a dream." Her gaze broke from his, sweeping down with a shake of her head. "But it seemed so real."

Kaderil massaged the tense cords forming beneath his hand, his fingers on either side of her neck. He had to remember to ask the questions the human Kade Smith would have asked had he truly stumbled upon her as he claimed.

"Tell me what happened, Autumn. Did you fall?"

I fell and hit my head. I dreamed the Esri came and Kade saved me. But it was all a dream.

Her hand shot out and she clung to the counter, though the boat barely rocked. "I...fell. I had a dream." When her gaze swept back up, her eyes were filled with a pain that went straight to his heart. "I dreamed you were helping them, Kade. You were helping the Esri."

But it was all a dream.

He turned her to face him fully, sliding his hands over her speckled cheeks, wanting to ease the confusion in her soft gray eyes. "Are you okay?" He didn't think enchantment could harm a human. Not by itself. But he couldn't be sure.

"Yes. I think so." She looked at him with that grave confusion. "How did I wind up on the sofa?"

"When you didn't answer my knock, I looked in the window and saw you lying on the floor. You were unconscious."

Dismay tightened her features and she turned away with a groan. "I'm such a klutz! Someone needs to put me in a padded room where I can't hurt anybody, especially myself."

"You're not a klutz." He wrapped his hand around her braid and gave a small tug, hating that he was forced to make her doubt herself.

But the boat gave a gentle rock and she grabbed the counter with both hands. Looking down, she gasped. "My bracelet. The Esri took it off me." She whirled to face him, her eyes large and accusatory. "It wasn't a dream! You came in. You stopped the one who was going to hurt me. Then you told the other one to take my holly."

Sweet Esria. Kaderil pressed his free hand to her cheek. "I wouldn't have helped them." *It was just a dream.*

But she didn't seem to be listening, her gaze darting around the small room, then back to him. Her brows pulled together, dipping to his shirt. "You were wearing these same clothes."

"Autumn..." He was losing control. He framed her face with his hands. "This is the same thing I was wearing last week when I met you, so of course you would see me in it in your dream. I would never do anything to hurt you."

That much was true, but her eyes were too sharp, too full of doubt. So he did the only thing he could think of to distract her from the thoughts spiraling out of his control. He pulled her against him and kissed her.

The moment his lips touched hers, the moment he tasted her again, he forgot everything but his need for her. For eight long days he'd craved the taste of her, thought of little but having her in his arms again.

She melted into the kiss with a moan of pleasure. Her mouth opened over his hungrily and he met her aggression with a sweep of his tongue, devouring her with a hunger that had only built with every day he'd been away from her. She was everything he remembered, everything he wanted. Sweetness and strength.

Her fingers slid over his cheeks and into his hair, stripping him of all control. All thought flew from his head as he fell headlong into a well of passion. Her tongue twined with his, stroking and sliding against his, sending heat flowing hotly through his veins.

She smelled of cinnamon and spice, of rain and beauty, and he couldn't get enough. His hands slid over her back, pulling her hard against him. He wanted to be inside her, deep in her warmth, embraced by her sweetness.

The violent longing tore through him, jarring him out of the passionate storm and he pulled back, stunned by his loss of control. She was just a pawn. The kiss was just a ploy. A ploy that had made mush of his brain.

But he couldn't let her go.

Autumn looked up at him, her eyes glazed with desire, her lips damp and swollen from his kisses and it was all he could do not to kiss her again. Instead, he pulled her against him, cradling her head to his shoulder where he wouldn't be as tempted to give in to his needs. But as he held her against his heart, it wasn't need that surged through his head, but a keen protectiveness.

She lifted her head, looking at him with wide, luminous eyes as if searching for the truth of him. Desire smoldered in those gray depths that held both strength and vulnerability.

He could never harm her. Yet he knew that was precisely what he would do if he stayed with her any longer. But he had no choice. He was all that stood between her and Zander…and certain death.

The confusion and questions in her eyes slowly dispersed the passion and she pulled out of his embrace.

"Where's my bracelet?"

He sucked in a breath and thought fast as he searched for where Ustanis might have dropped it. His gaze caught on the circular wood lying on the carpet.

He didn't want to return it to her. Not yet. Not when he wasn't sure she believed the thoughts he'd pushed into her head.

But if his thoughts hadn't taken by now, they probably never would. Besides, having the holly again might calm her.

"There," he said, motioning to the bracelet on the floor. "Right where I found you unconscious," he lied. "It must have come off when you fell."

Autumn retrieved the bracelet and slipped it on. She sighed as her fingers caressed the rough wood. "Maybe it *was* all a dream." Her gaze rose back to his. "I've got to tell Jack about the stones. I thought I could protect them, but I was fooling myself. The Esri might not have come yet, but they will."

His heart gave a lurch. If that stone went into Jack's keeping, he'd never get his hands on it again. He took a step toward her, then stopped himself. Autumn McGinn was an exceedingly clever woman to have found the stones in the first place. Perhaps he should discover her plans before he thrust his own thoughts into her head.

"Why didn't you tell Jack you'd found the stone in the first place?"

"I don't know." She sighed and made a rueful twist with her mouth. "Yes, I do. I had this foolish dream of handing all the stones to them at once in some grand flourish, making them think I was brilliant and special."

"You are brilliant and special."

She looked up at him and rolled her eyes. "Yeah. So brilliant I can't even walk straight without falling and knocking myself out."

He smiled, the act almost natural. "That has nothing to do with brilliance. It's a small matter of coordination."

"A small matter...? Easy for you to say."

The self-doubt was rife in her eyes again, and he was immensely sorry for it. "Tell me what you'd planned to do with the stones as you found them. Had you planned how you'd hide them?"

"Sure." She shrugged. "Though it probably wouldn't have worked anyway."

"Tell me."

"I'll show you." She rose and went to retrieve a small cube from the dining table. She came to where he stood by the counter and handed the box to him. "It's lined with lead. My plan was to put the stones and some holly into the box, tie it to the boat, then drop the whole thing in the water. I've done a lot of research on old superstitions and I think the combination might work. The Esri shouldn't be able to smell them."

Kaderil grinned at her. "Clever girl. Let's do it."

She frowned. "I don't know, Kade. That dream spooked me. I just want to give the stone to Jack. I don't want the responsibility for it."

He could offer to take it to Jack for her, but then she might tell Jack and he'd start asking for it. No, he needed her to keep the stones here. Hidden and—possibly— safe. "Let's hide it in the water for now, at least. I really think it might be safest there." Kaderil took her hand and tugged, not wanting to give her too much time to think. "Let's hide the stone."

She frowned, then gave a resigned nod. "All right." She gathered the sprig of holly and the rope, then carefully pried the stone loose from the sculpture. As she worked, the confusion and concern slowly cleared from her expression.

"Do you want to do the honors?" she asked.

Kaderil hesitated, unable to make sense of the words. "What do you mean?"

Autumn smiled, lifting his spirits. "Here." She handed him the stone and when he opened his palm, she dropped the rock in his hand. "You can be the one to put everything in the box."

Kaderil smiled, feeling oddly pleased that she was giving him a special role in this simple task. He placed the stone, one of the most powerful in all his world, into the small black box, then dropped the sprig of holly in on top of it. Autumn snapped the lid closed and tied the rope to the box's handle.

As they stepped outside, Kaderil searched for sign of Zander or Ustanis, but saw no sign of either. He accompanied Autumn to the back of the boat and watched while she tied the rope to the railing and dropped the box carefully into the water.

If this worked, Ustanis was going to wonder where the stone had gone, but that didn't concern Kaderil at all. *He* knew where it was and that was all that mattered. And when Autumn found the others, he'd know where those were, too. When the time was right, he'd take them all, as long as they stayed here, within his grasp.

When she straightened, Kaderil took her hand.

"All done?" he asked.

She smiled at him, but the smile didn't ease the creases in her forehead. She was worried the Esri would return. As was he. The only way he could hope to protect her was to keep her close by his side. And the only way to do that...

His pulse began to quicken. He must profess soft feelings for her. Pretend to be besotted. A role he had never played.

A role too close to the truth.

With a deep breath, he dove in. "We need to talk."

"About what?" She shivered and tugged on his hand. "It's cold out here. Let's go in."

He followed her inside and closed the door. When she turned around, he pulled her into his arms, attempting to mirror the look he'd seen on Jack's face as he gazed at his wife. But as he looked into her soft gray eyes, he lost himself in her beauty.

"I tried to stay away from you," he murmured. That wasn't what he'd meant to say.

The aching softness that entered her eyes forgave him his honesty.

"Why didn't you call me?"

"Because..." He couldn't think when she looked at him like that. "Because I was...I don't know. I couldn't stop thinking about you. You were...everywhere. In my mind every time I closed my eyes."

A charming little smile tilted her lips. "And that scared you?"

"No. Yes. I don't...let people get that close." He didn't know what he was saying, but the words wouldn't stop. "I thought I could forget you if I stayed away. I was wrong."

His pulse was thudding now. He'd meant to give her

platitudes memorized from the numerous human thoughts he'd borrowed. Instead, he'd spoken...he'd spoken the truth.

He released her and tried to pull away, but she wouldn't let him go. "Don't, Kade. I feel the same. I haven't been able to stop thinking about you since I met you. But it doesn't scare me. I think it's a rare miracle. We should embrace it, don't you think? Maybe it won't last. Maybe it's nothing to be afraid of."

She lifted onto her toes and kissed his mouth. "And maybe it was meant to be."

Meant to be. That was the one thing he could be sure it was not. She was human. He was the Esri sent to kill her friends. This was a relationship that could never be. But the knowledge did nothing to tame the need for her that raged through him. His arms tightened, pulling her closer. If only...

His cell phone rang, the tune annoying in its jauntiness. With regret, he released her to answer it.

"Kade? It's Jack. We've got a sighting of an Esri downtown, near the Warner Theater. How soon can you meet us there?"

"I'm on the waterfront. I'll leave now."

He closed the phone and turned to Autumn. "It was Jack. I've got to go."

Her gray eyes watched him with tight concern. "I'll drive you."

He wanted to say no. He didn't want her anywhere near Zander again. But the only way he could ensure her safety was to keep her at his side no matter what.

"All right. Let's go."

And as he ran for the car, he wondered how, when the time came, he was ever going to let her go.

Kaderil's mind raced as Autumn zipped through the streets. This was the opportunity he'd been waiting for, a chance to actually work with the Sitheen after a week of patrolling alone, but the situation carried serious risks.

The Sitheen might expect him to help them kill one of his own and that was something he couldn't do. It was strictly forbidden. With the magic that tied all Esri together, all knew both murdered and murderer the moment one of them died. They'd all felt Baleris's death and known he'd been killed by humans. If Kaderil were to be involved in the ending of either Zander or Ustanis, his own existence would end when he returned home. Somehow he had to find a way to pretend to help the Sitheen without actually helping them. And at the same time, keep Autumn safe.

"The intersection is at the next light." Autumn glanced at him, her eyes clear of enchantment and sparkling now with excitement. Something he didn't want to see. He wanted her far from danger. But there was no such place now.

A car pulled out of a parking space ahead of them, and Autumn slid into it with little difficulty, then jumped out of the car and joined him on the sidewalk, the thrill of the chase lighting her eyes. He held his hand out to her and she took it, sliding her fingers between his in a move that felt natural and right. As he scanned the area for sign of Esri or Sitheen, he caught sight of Harrison Rand, the quietly intense Sitheen, rounding the corner behind them.

Harrison raised a hand in greeting and caught up to them with quick strides. "Jack got a bead on one of the bastards. We thought he was heading for the Warner, but he kept moving."

He probably sensed the Sitheen and took off, Kaderil thought.

"Jack and Larsen are on the next street following him," Harrison continued. "We'll go this way. I hope we can cut him off."

When they reached the corner, he held up his hand and peered carefully around the corner. "There's Jack. We must have lost the Esri, dammit."

Kaderil squeezed Autumn's hand, relieved but not surprised. Zander couldn't be taken unaware and Ustanis was unlikely to be. Zander's gift of sensing power in others allowed him to track the Sitheen. They would never get near him unless he wished them to.

Harrison straightened but didn't relax his guard as the three rounded the corner to meet with Jack and Larsen. The street was narrow and cast into shadow by the office buildings rising on either side. Half a dozen business types strolled the sidewalk across the street, but this side was all but deserted, thanks to the small band of street punks lounging against the building midblock.

All at once, the punks straightened as if pulled upright by unseen strings.

Kaderil's instincts screamed. In a synchronized, fluid motion, the punks whipped out guns and began shooting, half in each direction. But Kaderil was quicker. He pushed Autumn against the building, shielding her with his body as he took two slugs to the gut. The bullets pierced his flesh, burning with surprising pain, but they wouldn't kill him as they would her.

Harrison dove into a nearby doorway. Kaderil pushed Autumn in after him.

Autumn grasped his arm, trying to turn him. "Are you okay?"

"I'm fine." He brushed her seeking hands aside and fumbled with the zipper of his leather jacket, hiding the bullet holes in his shirt.

"Harrison's shot."

Kaderil swung around, meeting the other man's pained gaze.

"Just the leg," Harrison said, his voice tight.

As suddenly as it began, the shooting stopped with a series of empty clicks. Kaderil looked out. One of the shooters was on the ground, likely shot by Jack. As Kaderil watched, the five remaining shooters collapsed in a single fall.

"Enchanted," he murmured. When Zander had sensed the Sitheen, he hadn't run, but had set up an ambush for them.

Autumn's hand gripped his shoulder. "Is it over?"

"I think so."

"Are Jack and Larsen okay?" A quaver of fear laced her words even as his gaze traveled to the other end of the block.

His stomach clenched as he saw Jack fall to his knees beside the prone body of his wife. Blood ran down the side of the man's face. Blood spread in a pool around the woman. Kaderil's skin turned cold as he stared at the destruction.

Such gratifyingly fragile creatures, Zander had said.

"No." The word that came from his lips sounded strangled. "No, they're not okay."

Autumn slid past him and with a cry of heartbreak, took off running toward her friends.

"Autumn!"

"Go," Harrison said behind him, his voice tight with pain. "I'll call 9-1-1."

Kaderil took off after Autumn. He searched for Zander as he swept up the guns from the unconscious shooters, but saw no sign of him. The Esri captain could be anywhere, enchanting another armed human, readying another attack.

He had to get Autumn out of danger. His hands filled with guns, he hurried to the scene of the carnage. Autumn looked up from where she knelt in the blood beside her friend, tears sliding down her freckled cheeks. "She's bad, Kade." The grief in her eyes tore at his heart.

Jack cradled his wife's head in his lap, tears mixing with the blood on his cheeks as he pulled the phone from his ear and snapped it closed. His desperate gaze rose to Kaderil. "Did you drive?"

"Autumn drove."

"Get your car, Autumn. Quick, before the ambulances arrive. I have to get her to Myrtle."

Autumn gaped at him. "Jack, she's going to need surgery."

"The doctors may not be able to save her. Myrtle can." His head snapped up, his anguished eyes blazing with determination. "Go!"

Autumn scrambled to her feet. Her gaze met

Kaderil's for an instant before she turned and ran for the car. He was about to go with her when Jack's words stopped him.

"Kade. Where's Harrison?"

"Shot in the leg."

"Help him." Jack eased Larsen's head out of his lap and struggled to his feet. Blood ran in rivulets down his face and bloomed from his shoulder. "We've got to get out of here. The bastards could be planning another attack." His eyes were filled with such pain, such grief that Kaderil felt his own emotions twist in sympathy.

Yet even in the face of such destruction, such disaster, these humans rose with courage and determination. Their bodies might be weak but their spirits were as strong as any he'd ever encountered. For the first time in his life, he felt a stirring of pride for the human blood that ran through his own veins.

Autumn's car screeched to a halt by the curb. The door slammed and she flew toward him, her gray eyes wounded. "Is she still alive?"

"Yes."

As Jack bent down, his arms sliding beneath his wife as if he meant to lift her, something fell from his shirt to dangle on a chain around his neck. A light-blue, teardrop-shaped stone.

The draggon stone.

The hair rose on Kaderil's arms. Victory flushed his skin as he stared at the prize he'd been sent for. The strange magic he felt around Jack suddenly made sense. It wasn't Jack's own power he'd been feeling, but the stone's.

His muscles clenched as he watched Jack struggle to

lift Larsen, the human's skin turning nearly as white as an Esri's. Sweat broke out on Kaderil's brow. The time was at hand. He could end his mission right this moment with nearly flawless ease. The Sitheen, badly injured, were in no position to stop him.

Jack swayed. Kaderil dropped the empty guns at his feet and lunged forward to pluck the injured woman from his arms. "I've got her. Sit down before you fall."

"Myrtle," Jack choked out as he sank to his knees. "I've got to get her to Myrtle." The eyes he turned to Kaderil were desperate. "Help her. *Please*." He fell forward, collapsing onto his side as his injured arm failed to hold him, the draggon stone lying against his heart.

Autumn grabbed his arm. "Quick. Get Larsen in the car, then help Jack."

"No," Jack said. "Leave me. Myrtle can only heal one. I'm going to need that ambulance." His pleading gaze bore into Kaderil. "Save her."

"Come on, Kade," Autumn cried, and his gaze swung to her. Tears and Larsen's blood streaked her face. Misery and strength filled her eyes. "We don't have any time. We've got to get her to Myrtle before she dies."

He was helpless to deny her.

Later, he would complete his mission. Later, when there were no witnesses. Later, when Autumn wasn't staring at him with a soft plea in her eyes.

Kaderil rode in the back, needing the extra room for his long legs and the dying woman in his arms. Autumn's emotions swirled around him, thickening the air, as she drove. How did the humans bear it? The fragility of their existence? Yet even as he wondered, he was beginning to understand. It was that very fragility that leant such a sharpness to the living and to the relationships they formed with one another. Bonds that ripped the heart to shreds when broken.

What must it be like to matter that much to another?

"Is she still breathing?" Forced to stop for a red light, Autumn turned in her seat to look at him. His chest ached with her sorrow.

"She's alive." But only just. The woman had little breath left within her.

Autumn met his gaze in the rearview mirror, her eyes heavy with the understanding that she was about to lose her friend.

"I'm sorry, Autumn." The words came from his heart. He was sorry for this loss she was about to suffer. And the others to come. The ones from his own hands.

She pulled up in front of a nondescript brick apartment building, then jumped out and ran around to open his door. While she'd driven, he'd felt the bullets that had penetrated his own flesh ease their way to the surface of his skin. As he slid out of the car, Larsen's limp body in his arms, he felt them slide down his legs to ping on the pavement, one after the other.

He tensed for Autumn's questions, but her attention was focused elsewhere.

"Is she still alive?" Her hand, where it touched his arm, shook.

"Yes." Barely. They hurried up the steps to find Tarrys waiting for them at the entrance, her feet bare beneath a pair of too-long jeans, a Redskins sweatshirt hanging to her hips, tears in her eyes.

"Jack called. Myrtle is preparing the ritual." She held the door for Kade, then followed him to the elevator.

"Hey!" A man shouted. "You can't bring her in here. She's bleeding!"

Kaderil sent the man a glower that had him scurrying backward.

"Kade!" Autumn held the elevator door for him as he strode inside.

"I'll call the cops!" the man shouted, but his threats were quickly drowned by the closing of the doors.

Tarrys's eyes widened. "Is it illegal to harbor the injured?"

Autumn scoffed. "He doesn't want the blood on his floors." She hit the wall of the elevator with the palm of her hand. "Come on, come on. *Faster.*"

When the doors finally opened, Kaderil followed the women down the hall to where Jack's aunt Myrtle stood in the same red dress he'd seen her in before, her expression grave.

Kaderil eased his dying burden through the door of an apartment that looked as though someone had plucked it from a flower garden. He followed the silent Myrtle to a bedroom as blue as the sky.

"Put her down, Kade."

He laid Larsen onto the striped bedspread, watching her head roll to one side, her face without color. He eased his arms out from under her and stepped back, his gaze seeking Autumn. She took his hand and held it tightly, her eyes bright with tears, her lips tight with misery.

"Oh, dear," Myrtle said, her words choked with tears.

The blood still flowed freely from Larsen's abdomen. She covered her mouth, tears springing to her eyes. "This is far more than I can do. We must call an ambulance."

"Myrtle..." Autumn said. "There isn't time. Jack believed you could save her. He believed you were the only one who could. You have to try."

Tarrys joined the older woman beside the bed. "I'll help you," she said softly. Myrtle lowered her hand and enfolded the smaller woman in a tight hug. Against her shoulder, Tarrys said, "I haven't much magic, but what little I have is yours."

Myrtle pulled away. "All right, then. Let's try." She pulled a stoppered bottle from the lace-trimmed basket sitting on the bedside table. "Open her shirt, Autumn. All the way. You can leave her bra."

Autumn released Kaderil's hand and moved to Larsen's side. But as her fingers moved from one button to the next, a sob caught in her throat. "I can't do this."

"You must, dear. I must see the wounds."

Kaderil stepped forward. He gave Autumn's shoulder a squeeze, then wrapped his arms around her and helped her pull the bloody fabric from the ruined flesh. Pressure throbbed between his eyes at the damage wrought by such small bullets.

The wounds bared, Myrtle unstoppered a small vial of oil, filling the room with a smell that burned the insides of his nostrils.

Tarrys slapped her hand over her nose. Autumn pulled out of his embrace and turned to face Myrtle with a grimace. "It smells like dead animals."

Myrtle said nothing, merely poured a small puddle

of oil between Larsen's breasts and laid two rocks on top of the glistening pool. She replaced the oil in the basket, then pulled out a stack of candles and handed them to Autumn with a pack of matches.

"Replace the other candles with these, then light them. Quickly. And pull the drapes."

Autumn gave the matches to Kaderil while she and Tarrys changed the candles. Kaderil stared at the small package. He'd never struck a match, for Esria was lit by magic, but he searched his borrowed memories and found the trick. On the third try, the match sparked and burst into flame, a small triumph as long as no one started murmuring the death chant. As he lit the candles, Autumn and Tarrys lifted them to light others until the room flickered with candlelight.

"Silence please, children." Myrtle sat on the bed, placed one hand on the rocks, the other on Larsen's forehead, and began to hum, then to sing under her breath, her words only sporadically audible.

With a shock, Kaderil recognized the words as Esrian. He shouldn't be surprised. Sitheen magic came from the Esri.

"Heart beat with life…illness flee…vanquish death. Tarrys, your hand, please, dear."

As Tarrys sat across from Myrtle on the bed and placed her hand atop the older woman's, Autumn came back to stand beside him, tears in her eyes. Kaderil pulled her against him in a movement that felt as natural as breathing. He enfolded her tightly in his arms as her grief buried sharp claws in his heart, his chest filling with the echoes of her misery and heartache.

As he stroked her back, she trembled and clung to him and he felt needed, truly needed, for the first time in his life.

The seconds turned to minutes as they stood, breath shallow, hearts racing, waiting for a miracle.

Myrtle's voice rose, the chanting turning more urgent, more frantic with each repetition.

Autumn's grip on him tightened as Myrtle lifted the stones, poured more oil and set them down again.

"It's not working." Autumn's words were light as the wind, for his ears only. But Myrtle's gaze snapped up and speared them with anguished eyes.

"No. It's not working." Myrtle's words rang with a devastating hollowness. "Oh, my dears. I can't save her."

Chapter 8

Grief thickened the air, weighing on Kaderil's heart as Autumn clung to him, her arms like a vice around his waist. Kaderil's arms tightened around her quaking body, offering what comfort he could against Myrtle's devastating words, words that still echoed in the small blue bedroom.

The elderly healer sat on the edge of the bed, her dress as red as the blood still flowing from Larsen's prone body. Tears and hopelessness shimmered in her eyes.

Tarrys sank to the mattress on the other side, weeping softly. Though Myrtle was purportedly a gifted Sitheen healer, the devastation to Larsen Vale's...Larsen Hallihan's...mortal body was too great for even her skills.

Autumn's tears started to come in great sobs as she

buried her face against his neck. Her misery sliced through him, making his chest ache with her sorrow. So much grief. So much suffering over a single mortal life.

How did the humans stand it?

None of this should bother him. He should, in fact, be rejoicing over this death. But he felt no joy. No relief. Only the echoes of Autumn's distress and fury that Zander, by enchanting those shooters, had caused Autumn such pain.

If there were any way to spare her this, he would.

He stilled. Maybe he could. His power wasn't great. But combined with Myrtle's and Tarrys's, it might be enough.

Refusing to think too hard about the foolishness of saving one he was only going to have to destroy later, he squeezed Autumn's shoulders lightly, then released her and crossed to the bed and Myrtle. The smell of the oil was even more pungent up close, and his eyes burned from the assault.

"Try again," he said to the woman.

Myrtle looked up at him, her faded eyes swimming in tears. "I've done all I can," she said softly.

"Jack said my power is strong. We must try again." He looked across the bed at Tarrys. "All of us."

The violet-eyed slave nodded, wiping away her tears. She pushed up the overlong sleeves of her sweatshirt and placed her small hand on Myrtle's. Kaderil covered both of them with his own.

Myrtle tried to resume chanting, but her throat was clogged with tears and she had to clear it twice before she could get any sound. Finally, she began to sing.

Even as his logical mind ridiculed this soft-hearted,

foolish action, the overpowering need to end Autumn's suffering had him clearing his mind and pushing his energy, his power, into the broken body of her friend.

He felt Autumn move to his side.

She knelt at his feet and slid her free hand over Larsen's where it lay motionless on the bed. "Can I talk to her?" she asked quietly, her gray eyes glistening with unshed tears.

Myrtle nodded, but never ceased her singing.

Autumn leaned over, close to her friend's ear, her braid slipping over one shoulder. "Larsen...you have to get better. Jack's okay. He's hurt but waiting for you. He's worrying about you." Her voice broke.

Kaderil squeezed her shoulder and felt a strange surge of energy, as if the power arced as it traveled between the unintended circle. The energy rose, like a humming through his body, an odd blend of Sitheen, Marceil and Esri power and Autumn's love for her friend.

"You have to get better," Autumn murmured. "Fight, Larsen. *Fight*. Jack needs you. We all need you."

As the vibration inside him grew, heat began to build in both his hands, the one that covered Myrtle's and the hand that clung to Autumn's shoulder. A faint glow began deep within Larsen's body as if she were suddenly lit from within.

Autumn gasped and pulled away. At once, the glow died, the magic failed.

Kaderil squeezed her shoulder. "Don't let go! Hold her."

Her startled gaze snapped to his before she nodded and grabbed Larsen's hand. "What's happening?"

"I don't know, but somehow you're part of it. I can feel it. The circle must not be broken."

She reached up and pulled his hand off her shoulder, lacing her fingers between his. Her hand was cold and trembling, and he clasped it tightly, offering comfort and assurance even as he drew them from her.

Myrtle's song grew slowly louder, filling the room, as if the power that flowed between them strengthened her as much as it did Larsen. The glow within Larsen's body grew and changed, shimmering now with sparkling, iridescent color.

"That's it, Larsen." Autumn's grip on his hand tightened. "Fight for your life. Fight for Jack."

The room was getting hot, the air charged with power. Sweat began to roll down his spine. Before Kaderil's eyes, the torn flesh began to heal visibly, slower than any Esri's, yet a thousand times faster than human flesh. The bullet appeared in the wound, then slowly rose to the surface.

Autumn's hand convulsed around his. Kneeling at his feet, she pulled their clasped hands to her face, pressing his knuckles against her soft, damp cheek. Tenderness and a keen protectiveness clutched at his chest.

Myrtle's song rose in volume, the Esri words as clear as her voice. "Death I banish you. Death be gone." Tarrys began to take up the chant and Kaderil joined her until their voices filled the room. Little by little, the bloodied flesh reknit itself until all that remained of the deadly injury was a single bullet lying atop Larsen's unblemished skin. The rainbow of light that had filled her body gathered at the surface and began to rise until it hovered inches above her.

Myrtle's voice rose higher, then abruptly ceased even as Tarrys and he continued to sing. Kaderil could feel her drawing their power, feel it building inside her until finally she took a deep breath and with a last surge of magic, shouted in Esri, *"Be gone!"*

The hovering light exploded, blowing out the candles, sending the magic scattering to the corners of oblivion. Myrtle collapsed across Larsen in a dead faint.

Autumn scrambled to her feet. "What's happened?"

"Are they all right?" Tarrys asked.

Kaderil scooped up the healer and laid her carefully at Larsen's side, feeling the magic still swirling inside her. "This one's pulse is strong."

Autumn's fingers pressed beneath Larsen's ear. She looked up at him with eyes shining with joy. "So is Larsen's. She did it. Myrtle saved her."

Laughter bubbled out of Autumn's throat. The smile that lit her face filled all the empty places deep inside him. She threw her arms around him and he lifted her off her feet and swung her around, laughing. The sound felt foreign, yet even the strangeness delighted him.

Slowly he lowered her to her feet. The laughter died from his throat as he fell into her eyes and fed his parched soul on the tender joy he found there. Their heads bent together and he kissed her, tasting the salty sweetness of her tears. This was wonder. Perfection. And if he could stay here like this for the rest of his life, he'd be the happiest of men.

"What happened?" Larsen's soft, weary voice had them jerking apart.

Autumn's laugh held a touch of embarrassment, but she

grinned at him without shyness, then turned toward the bed. She leaned over Larsen and pressed her cheek to her friend's. "You scared us to death, that's what happened. Myrtle just performed one of her famous miracles."

Kaderil stepped back, giving the women room. The smile continued to play at his mouth as his spirit soared. But as he watched them, the happiness slowly drained out of him as the truth of who he was, and what he must do, rushed in.

He turned from the room, suddenly unable to face Autumn. Knowing the suffering she was doomed to endure.

Kaderil went to the living-room window, his hands fisting on the sill as he watched the late-afternoon traffic clogging the streets below. The phone rang. From the bedroom, he heard Larsen say Jack was on his way. Then the women's talk turned to clean clothes and baths. And still Kaderil stood, rooted, a war raging inside him. Jack was on his way, the draggon stone likely still around his neck.

The opportunity he'd waited for was finally about to fall into his hands.

His heart tried to rebel, but his mind was strong. Taking that stone, killing these people was his job. His life. If he failed this mission, Zander would win. Rith would banish the Punisher from court, leaving him to wander his world alone, feared and hated.

If he failed this mission, his life was over, his place in his world lost. And for what?

For Autumn.

A foolish sentiment. Any heartache he saved her

would be temporary. If he failed to complete his mission as directed, others would step in. Zander, who would not only kill the Sitheen, but any humans he could catch, as well. His blood went cold as he imagined the way Autumn would suffer at Zander's hands.

Autumn's laughter carried from the bathroom, twisting his heart, but his mind stood firm. He was the Punisher. This was his mission and he could not fail.

The thoughts circled, over and over, as he stood before the window, his heart as cold as chiseled stone. He heard Jack arrive. Heard the tearful reunion between the man and the wife he'd thought he'd lost. And Kaderil continued to stare out the window, unseeing, as his Punisher's brain took over.

Completing his mission—retrieving the draggon stone and killing the Sitheen—would be a simple matter now. Jack trusted him and would allow him to walk up behind him. Kaderil had broken dozens of necks as the Punisher, though this would be the first that would kill his victim.

Once Jack was dead, Larsen would die next. Then Myrtle. Both women were weak from the healing and would put up little resistance.

The problem was Tarrys. The Marceil should be returned to Esria where she belonged. And this one had knowledge of humans and their world that would be greatly sought. Zander and Ustanis would be able to bring her quickly under control, for true Esri had the power to control a Marceil's every action with the touch of a hand.

So, the Sitheen had to die. Tarrys had to go with him.

And that left Autumn.

His stomach clenched at the thought of her in the midst of such destruction. At the thought of her watching him destroy the people she loved. The pain in her eyes. The horror.

The betrayal.

Sweat rolled down his scalp. His pulse pounded behind his eyes.

What would he do with her? He couldn't leave her here to warn Charlie and Harrison that he'd turned traitor. But neither could he escape the building with two struggling females without attracting far too much attention. If only he had the power of a true Esri! He could enchant Autumn and control Tarrys. But he didn't. So what would he do with Autumn?

The obvious answer hovered at the edges of his mind like dark, ominous smoke threatening to suffocate him. He needed to kill her with the others. That was the obvious answer.

And one he couldn't accept.

He would not hurt her.

His arms began to shake as he gripped the window sill. He wiped his mouth, feeling the beads of sweat on his upper lip.

All his life he'd been feared. And he'd demanded that fear. But he hated the thought of it in Autumn's eyes. He'd seen a glimmer when she woke from the enchantment, but that was nothing compared to the terror that would fill her eyes if he acted now.

And he must act.

His life depended on it.

Yet his muscles quivered and shook at the thought.

He was turning weak. The Punisher threw bodies without compunction, dealt destruction without a second thought.

Yes, but to beings who *could not be hurt*. The Punisher had never ended a life. It wasn't the same.

It was his mission. His duty. He must act. He must deal this death.

He jerked at the feel of a hand on his back, nearly attacking until he realized it was Autumn's.

"Are you okay?"

"Yes." The word came out harshly. The Punisher's voice.

He made the mistake of looking at her. What he saw in her gray eyes nearly broke him. Concern and softness. Deep, strong caring. For him. She pulled at him with her eyes, coaxing him into her warmth, into that place of smiles and belonging. That place the Punisher could never go.

Her hand slid up and down his back in a slow, steady rhythm meant to comfort and soothe. But he was beyond calming. His body was strung tighter than a bow with the knowledge of what he must do.

"It's been an eventful day." Her smile was small, but sweet, filling him with the nearly unbearable urge to pull her against him and bury his face against her hair. "Why don't we go back to the houseboat? I'll make you dinner."

The devastating need to hold her again was almost too great to breathe around.

Weakness. It is weakness.

She cared because she thought him human. The moment she knew who he was...*what* he was...she'd run from him in fear.

He was the monster. He would always be the monster.

He'd never minded being the Punisher, his brain railed.

Because he'd never known anything else.

But it didn't matter. None of it mattered. He was what he was.

And he knew what he had to do.

Autumn stroked Kade's muscular back, her hand sliding up and down the cotton, feeling the tense vibrations beneath her palm. For more than an hour, he'd stood here, staring out Myrtle's window, even though the sun had set and he could probably see little through the glass but his own reflection. He'd clearly taken all he could take of blood and miracles, and she didn't blame him for being unnerved by it all. She was suffering from a bad case of emotional whiplash herself.

Larsen had almost died!

Then they'd saved her...*all* of them. Autumn still didn't understand how her own involvement could have possibly mattered, but it seemed to have made a difference. Every time she thought of watching that bullet rise out of that gash, she got chills and tears in her eyes. She'd witnessed a miracle. She'd helped *create* a miracle. And if she never did anything worthwhile for the rest of her life, this day would be enough.

She looked back at the sofa where Jack sat hugging his wife. He looked much worse than she did now, with the bandage on his head and his arm in the sling. Her happiness for them was so great, her eyes welled up all over again and her heart soared with the pure joy of knowing Larsen was fine.

She glanced back at Kade. If only he could share in the happiness instead of being unnerved by it all.

"Myrtle's taking a nap," Tarrys said, closing the bedroom door behind her and joining them in the living room. "The healing exhausts her." She stopped behind the lone empty chair, resting her arms on the back as she addressed Larsen. "How about you?"

Larsen smiled at the small woman. "I feel a little tired, but otherwise pretty amazing, all things considered."

"What happened?" Tarrys blanched and straightened as if embarrassed to have asked the question. "Forgive me…but I would like to know."

"Tarrys, stop that," Larsen scolded. "You're not a slave anymore. If you want to know something, ask. If it's not a question we want to answer, we'll tell you so."

A slow smile lit the former slave's delicate features. "My thanks. I know that my will is my own now. But the knowing is easier than the doing." Her smile disappeared. "Was Charlie injured?"

Jack smiled and squeezed Larsen's shoulder. "Charlie's fine. He didn't get there until the ambulances were arriving. He's still at the hospital with his brother. Harrison's going to be there for a couple of days while they repair his leg, but he should be fine. All in all, we were incredibly lucky."

He turned to look at Larsen, so much deep, rich love in his eyes that a lump formed in Autumn's throat just watching the two of them. She'd always wondered what it would be like to feel that strongly for someone. Now she thought she was beginning to understand.

She turned back to Kade and was lifting her hand to resume stroking his back when she caught his reflection in the window. Alarmed, she stepped forward where she could see his profile. At the sight, apprehension shivered through her. He looked angry. *Furious.* His dark brows low and straight over hard eyes, a muscle leaping in his jaw with the rhythmic clenching of his teeth.

"Kade? What's the matter?"

If he were another man, she might have been frightened by the look of fury on his face. But he was Kade and he wouldn't hurt her. She knew that.

But when she reached for him, he reared back, turning that mask of rage on her. *"Get back. Get away from me."*

Her heart lurched. Autumn stumbled back, staring at the man who'd suddenly become a stranger. "Kade?"

Jack came up beside her, pushing her behind him. "You doing okay, big guy? You've been through a lot today. We all have. Why don't you have a seat?"

But Jack's words weren't working. If anything, Kade was getting angrier.

She watched Jack's stance shift ever so slightly, as if he were bracing himself for Kade's attack. Which was ridiculous. Of course Kade wouldn't attack him. But second after second, the tension built, the air growing so thick she could hardly breathe.

Then suddenly, without a word, Kade whirled and stalked to the door. He left, slamming the door behind him.

Autumn stared at the place he'd been, her heart pounding in her chest. Then ran for the door.

"Autumn!" Jack called. "Give him some time."

But she couldn't do that. In the instant before he turned, Kade had met her gaze. In his eyes she'd seen an ache, a misery so profound she'd felt her heart tear. She ran out into the hallway, turned toward the elevator and stopped. Halfway down the corridor, Kade stood, back against the wall, his head tilted as he stared at the ceiling. His body shook so badly she could see it vibrating from there.

She started toward him with wary steps, unsure of her reception. But as she neared, he turned toward her with eyes so bleak, they tore at her soul.

"Do you want some company?" she asked.

"I want you." His words were low and raw.

She didn't move, but kept her gaze firmly on his and nodded. "I'm here for you."

In some corner of her mind, she wondered if she'd just agreed to go to bed with him. And realized that whether that's what he'd asked, that's how she'd answered. She wanted him. All of him. For now and always, or at least for as long as he wanted her.

Chapter 9

Autumn didn't reach for him, nor did he reach for her. But he turned and they walked together to the elevator, not speaking again until they were in her car.

Autumn turned on the ignition. "Do you want to come back to the houseboat with me?"

"No. My apartment. I'll tell you how to get there."

They drove in silence except for Kade's brief directions. Autumn found a parking space on the street and together they took the elevator to the fifth floor. Kade let them into his apartment and turned on a light to reveal an attractive room with simple, clean lines, the earth tones relieved by the colorful splashes of modern art that dotted the walls.

Kade went to the kitchen and flicked on a light, his back straight and tense.

Autumn shoved her hands into her back pockets, suddenly unsure of herself. He'd said he needed her, then hadn't said a word to her other than "Turn left" or "Turn right" since. Had he only been looking for company? Was she supposed to just hang out and watch TV?

He pulled a bag of carrots and a bag of celery out of the refrigerator, grabbed a knife and started chopping.

Autumn eased closer until she stood in the kitchen doorway. "What are you making?"

He chopped two more carrots, cutting them into tiny chunks, before answering. His gaze flicked to hers, then back to the carrots. "I don't know."

Oh, Kade. In his eyes, she'd seen an isolation so profound he didn't know how to breach it, even with her standing here. He was chopping carrots, she suspected, because he had to do *something*.

He did need her. More than she'd realized. Probably more than he knew. He needed the touch of another, but was too strong, too alone, to know how to ask.

So she made the move he didn't know how to make. She pulled her hands from her pockets and went to him.

"Don't stab me, okay?" she said softly as she walked up behind him, slid her arms around his waist and pressed her cheek to his back. He didn't answer, didn't quit chopping, but he accepted her comfort with a tremor that rippled down his body.

He felt so good against her, solid and warm. More than anything, she wanted to reach that deep loneliness she sensed inside him and banish it. He wasn't alone anymore. He wouldn't be again, unless he wanted to be.

But first she had to break down the thick walls he'd erected around himself.

She slid her hands beneath his zipped jacket to tug at the shirt tucked into his pants. For a moment, he stilled while she pulled it free, then resumed chopping. The warm skin of his abdomen caressed her palms, making her breath catch at her own bold move. His abs were rock hard, delighting her fingertips and heating her blood. She wanted to feel more of him, see more of him. Taste him.

But despite the increasingly urgent pressure of her hands beneath his shirt, Kade didn't respond. Though he allowed her this pleasure, he gave her no indication he shared it.

Autumn's confidence faded. She'd acted purely on instinct, but she was the first to admit she had way too little experience with men to think she knew how to please one. She pulled her hands from his shirt and stepped back, embarrassed.

The knife went silent. "Don't stop." His words, though low, ached with a need beyond the flesh.

She stared at his stiff, proud back, as a tenderness almost beyond bearing engulfed her. He needed her. The thought trembled through her with the sweetness of a warm wind on a cold day.

Gathering her battered confidence, she closed the distance between them and slid her hands over the soft leather that covered his back, making large circles designed to calm and comfort.

But the play of muscles beneath her fingers was anything but calming. Her pulse accelerated as she drank in the scent of leather and warm male. She wanted more. Needed more.

Her hands slid down to his waist and with unsteady fingers, she lifted the back of his shirt, pushing up the leather, exposing the strong, fine lines of his back inch by delicious inch. Emboldened by his need for her touch, Autumn leaned forward and planted kisses on one side of his spine and then the other, feeling the muscles quiver beneath her lips, though Kade himself remained rigidly still, his vegetables forgotten.

She shifted her kisses to his spine. But when her tongue darted out to taste the ridge of bone, he jerked, arching away from her.

"Autumn." The word came out on a strangled laugh.

Autumn grinned, delighted. "You're ticklish. Put down the knife before you stab one of us." But when she tried to kiss him again, he pulled out of the grip of her hands, turned and hauled her into his arms.

The look on his face was part humor, part surrender and all desire. With a groan, he covered her mouth in a kiss that exploded through her, sending chills of need tearing through her body.

The kiss was hard and urgent, his lips moving over hers with hot demand and something more. A desperation. In his kiss, she tasted the darkness of his self-imposed prison and the confusion that still swirled within him. He needed her, she realized, to lead him out of that darkness.

Love for him swelled until she could hardly breathe around it.

When his tongue slid into her mouth, she welcomed

it, twining her arms around his neck and pressing herself against him, feeling the hard ridge of his arousal.

Excitement and need heated her blood, pooling dampness between her legs. This was what love was all about, she realized. This fierce tenderness combined with a desire so intense she thought it might tear her limb from limb. This need to give herself up to it…to *him*…in every way.

Kade's big hands roamed her back, then slid down to her bottom where they gripped and kneaded. Desire spiraled out of control, spiking in a gasp as he rubbed her against his erection, telling her in no uncertain terms what he wanted.

Was she ready for this, ready *finally* to know a man in that way? To know Kade in that way?

Oh, yeah. More than ready.

Autumn gripped his face with her hands and drank of him as he devoured her, telling him silently of her love, her need. Comforting him even as she stole comfort in the knowledge he needed her. He wanted her.

She felt his hands on her braid, his fingers tugging it loose.

"I want your hair against my skin." His tongue slid across her lower lip, then dove back into her mouth with a sound of pleasure. As the kiss grew more frantic, she felt his fingers slide against her scalp and shoulders as he unbraided her hair.

He pulled away and she groaned in protest until her passion-dazed eyes focused and she saw the look on his face. He watched her with an expression of such softness, such caring, she wondered if he, too, were falling in love. Tears stung her eyes at the sweet perfection of the thought.

With gentle hands, he lifted her unbound hair over her shoulders. "You're so beautiful," he whispered, the truth shining in his eyes.

For the first time in her life, she *felt* beautiful.

With excruciating deliberateness, he leaned forward, grazing his lips across her cheek, sending shivers of pure delight tingling through her body. Tenderly, he trailed kisses along her jaw, then down the sensitive skin of her neck. The shivers intensified a hundredfold, tightening her nipples, sending more damp heat to pool between her legs. She clung to his shoulders, tilting her head to the side, encouraging his gentle, exquisite attack. Need built inside her, pulsing and growing until it was alive in every vein, every muscle, demanding release. Here. Now.

With this man.

As his lips pressed against her neck, he pushed the blazer off her shoulders and let it slide to the floor. Then his fingers moved to the top button of her shirt.

Autumn kept her eyes closed, drowning in sensation, reveling in the feel of his lips pressed against her upper chest, moving downward with the release of each button of her shirt.

When he pushed the shirt off her shoulders, she opened her eyes to find him watching her with sharp desire. His hands cupped the pink lace of her bra, his thumbs sliding over her sensitive nipples, nearly buckling her knees.

He leaned forward until his lips brushed her mouth.

"I want you, Autumn McGinn. I want to be inside you. I *need* to be inside you." His mouth slid across her cheek to tug at the lobe of her ear. "If you don't want that, tell me now. Before I go any further."

She forced her arms, heavy with wanting, to grasp his face. Her fingers slid through his hair. "I want you, Kade. All of you. Inside me."

He pulled back, searching her eyes with his brilliant blue gaze, as if not quite believing the truth of her words. Deep in his eyes, behind the hard alpha pride, she saw uncertainty. And wonder. As if he weren't God's gift to women, but a man all too used to rejection and denial.

"If you want me, let me see you," he murmured. "All of you."

Autumn felt heat rise up her body, flaming in her cheeks. She breathed in quick, shallow breaths, her pulse racing, but she felt powerful.

A slow smile pulled at her mouth as she reached behind her and unfastened her bra. She pulled it off and tossed it to the ground, standing before this amazing man, bared and proud, offering him...everything.

As her fingers groped for the button on her pants, Kade lifted his big hands to her breasts, sliding his palms across her ultra-sensitive nipples until she was gasping for air.

His hands clenched gently around the soft mounds as he stroked one nipple with his tongue, then the other. Need shot through her, doubling when he took the second breast wholly into his mouth. She arched against him, holding his dark head against her as she drank in the exquisite feel of him. When his damp tongue slid across the hard, sensitive tip, heat spiraled so deep, so low inside her, she wasn't sure how anything could feel any better.

His mouth moved to her other breast, lavishing upon it the same exquisite attention until her hips were rocking against his chest, her fingers digging into his scalp. When he pulled back, the expression on his face was sheer triumph, his eyes burning with a fire hot enough to melt her where she stood.

With his gaze locked on hers, he slid her pants down over her hips and thighs, stopping only when he reached her knees where Larsen's blood had soaked her jeans and dried, causing the fabric to stick.

Autumn sighed with pained disappointment. "I need a shower."

Kade pried the fabric loose and pushed the pants down to her ankles where she stepped free of them.

Kade rose to his feet, his blue eyes smoky with desire, the violence she'd sensed in him when they'd first arrived channeled now into an entirely different passion. She felt his gaze like a tender caress as his fingertips grazed her face. "You are so beautiful," he whispered again, his words aching with emotion.

Her hands splayed against his leather-covered chest. "So are you."

With a daring she'd never before possessed, she reached between his legs and stroked the hard, thick ridge inside his pants. He closed his eyes and threw his head back, a groan of pure pleasure rising from deep in his throat. "Autumn…" He opened his eyes and pulled her hard against him, his kiss barely controlled.

The metal zipper of his jacket pressed against her abdomen, reminding her she was the only one un-clothed. She needed to feel the warmth of his skin beneath her fingertips. And she needed to feel not quite so exposed.

"You have too many clothes on," she murmured against his mouth, then reached for the zipper of his jacket, but his hands snatched hers and gently pushed them away.

"I'll do it." He turned away from her and retreated to his bedroom.

Autumn followed and watched as, back turned to her, he shed his jacket, then pulled his polo shirt over his head and tossed it on the floor. Her breath caught in her throat as her gaze took in the sight of his muscular back, perfectly proportioned, with wide shoulders nar-rowing to a trim waist.

He glanced down at himself, then turned toward her, a rueful look on his face. "We're both going to need showers." Blood stained the skin of his abdomen, but did nothing to hide the hard muscles. Standing there, shirtless, covered with blood, he looked like a warrior of old returning from battle. Deadly, dangerous and very, very sexy.

The flash of devilish amusement in his eyes set the butterflies to flight in her stomach. "We'll share one."

The very thought made her legs tremble, but when he held out his hand to her, she hesitated less than a heartbeat before placing hers in his palm, giving him her heart, her body and her unquestioning trust.

He led her to the bathroom, turned on the shower, then pulled her into his arms, his eyes shining with desire and tenderness. She'd always felt too big, too clumsy and ungainly. But in Kade's arms, pressed against his far larger frame, she felt feminine and perfect. Beneath his gentle touch she felt delicate and cherished.

Loved.

He leaned in and kissed her again, capturing her mouth, her emotions. Her very spirit. Desire exploded between them, sweeping her away. She wanted him.

Kade's hands encircled her waist, then slid over her hips and behind, to cup her buttocks. His fingers dug gently into her soft cheeks, through the silk of her panties, making her gasp with the sheer excitement of his touch. Her breath quickened until she wondered if he would steal it altogether.

Everything about him excited her. The smell of his skin. The taste of his mouth. The tenderness and fire in his eyes. *This* was what lovemaking was supposed to be. Not just a joining of bodies, but of minds, of spirits.

Of hearts.

The fingers of one of his hands slid down to the bottom edge of her panties, then beneath the edge to stroke the flesh of her bottom. She felt his finger slide slowly, shockingly, between her legs until it brushed her most private and sensitive flesh. Wondrous sensation shot through her body, weakening her knees. She grabbed for his shoulders, holding on as he pushed her panties over her hips and down her legs until she stood naked and ready before him.

Then he stripped himself of his remaining clothes, freeing his engorged flesh to her curious eyes. He was *huge*. Of course he was. Everything about him was giant-sized. She knew, from a clinical aspect, he'd fit. If she was ready for him, he'd fit. But *how?*

She had no more time to worry the question. With a strength nothing short of miraculous, he swept her into his arms and ducked into the shower.

The warm spray pelted her body as he lowered her to her feet, letting her slide down his long length. The thickness of his arousal brushed her hip and abdomen, stoking her excitement. When her feet reached the floor, Kade turned her in his arms and kissed her beneath the spray, stealing all thoughts, all doubts, everything but her spiraling need for this man.

The water ran down their faces, blending with the heat of the kiss until she couldn't breathe. With a laugh, Autumn pulled away, gasping for air. Kade's answering grin was nothing short of evil as he turned her away from the water, pressed her back against him and covered her breasts with his hands.

"Let me wash you," he said in her ear as his large hands stroked her breasts from beneath, then captured her tight nipples between strong fingers.

"Yes," she said, though anticipation and nervousness warred within her. She'd never had a man's hands on her body like this.

He released her to pick up the bar of soap, then slid his soapy hands over her shoulders with studied care. His hands traveled across her body, sliding over her breasts, her abdomen, then turning her in his arms to soap her back. His broad, muscular chest was too much temptation and she slid her fingers through the dark, springy hair. His low sound of approval drew her gaze to his and the heat in his eyes burned through her flesh, all the way to her soul.

The moment was so right, so perfect, tears sprang to her eyes. Kade saw, his expression softening as he cupped her face, his soapy thumbs stroking her cheek. When his head bent to capture her lips, the kiss was the most tender, most precious she'd ever imagined. A kiss filled with love and caring and need.

Finally he pulled back, reslathered his hands and knelt in front of her to wash Larsen's blood off her legs. Autumn braced herself with his shoulders while his palms slid over her calves and knees, but when his hands slid higher, her fingers dug into his flesh.

His thumbs led the assault, sliding with perfect friction up her inner thighs, pressing and teasing, rising until they touched the very heart of her fire. As his thumbs played between her legs, his mouth covered her breast, sucking, making her arch against him as fire erupted in both places. She gasped as his fingers stroked her pulsing heat and dipped inside. Hot tremors wracked her body.

"Kade, I need...I need..."

As he released her, a sound of dismay escaped her throat. But he rose to stand before her, his eyes glittering with passion and tenderness.

"I want you." His words set rhythmic spasms clutching inside her.

"Yes," was all she said, was all she could get out, but it was enough.

Kade pulled her into his arms, pressing his hips to hers, his thick erection between them. He covered her mouth and the kiss was hard and wild, his tongue thrusting against hers, driving her beyond reason. She had no thoughts, no fears, only feeling. *Need.*

His hands grasped her waist. "Wrap your legs around me," he murmured against her mouth, then lifted her until her eyes were at a level with his.

She complied without thought, desperate for release from the terrible pressure building inside her body.

Not until she felt the brush of that hard thickness at the juncture of her thighs, did she start to tense. But he was already sliding into her, already stretching her in a way that felt heavenly and right. She closed her eyes, lost to the exploding sensations until the pinch of pain made her gasp.

She felt Kade tense and prayed he hadn't noticed she was a virgin. It would be too embarrassing and it no longer mattered. All that mattered was that they were joined.

If he'd noticed, he didn't stop, but pulled partway out of her and thrust himself inside her again, this time without hurting her. Again and again, he moved inside her, harder, faster as her own need, her own desire built in a way she'd never imagined, in a way she'd never expected. It was like energy filling her, sweeping her up in a frenzy of lust and power.

Hands locked at the back of his neck, her head thrown back, she rode the incredible storm, each thrust of Kade's hips driving her higher.

A sharp tingling began at her wrists where her arms pinned Kade's hair to his shoulders. The discomfort barely registered through the haze of passion until her wrists started to burn. She snatched them away, grabbing his biceps.

Her eyes flew open and she froze.

Kade's dark hair was standing straight up, whirling around his head, heedless of the shower spray that should be beating it down.

She stared at him, uncomprehending, her mind struggling free of the delicious sensations of the flesh. His hair looked just as Princess Ilaria's had in that painting. Tarrys's words ripped through her head.

It's what happens when an Esri uses or acquires great power.

Terror ripped through her, freezing her lungs on a gasp.

This wasn't happening. This couldn't be happening.

But at her sound, Kade's eyes snapped open. His eyes, so blue before, now glowed like blue light bulbs.

"No." Fear speared through her. Her head spun as the truth assailed her.

Kade Smith wasn't Sitheen. He wasn't human.

The man who even now thrust inside her, stealing her virginity…the man who'd stolen her heart…was Esri.

Chapter 10

She was a virgin!

Kaderil thrust into Autumn's tight sheath over and over, trapped in the power, as the enormity of his error crashed over him. He'd released her virgin's power, revealing himself as Esri.

"Stop!" The terror in Autumn's eyes speared through his heart, shredding the ecstasy that had enveloped him just moments before, destroying something deep inside him.

"I can't." He held her in his arms beneath the hot spray of the shower, her legs locked around his waist, his hips rocking against hers in a hard, carnal rhythm. His muscles bulged as he struggled to stop, strove to at least slow down, but all control had been wrenched from his grasp the moment he'd spilled her virgin's blood.

Water ran in rivulets down Autumn's face, her vibrant

hair a dark cloak around her shoulders, her expression desperate as she beat at his arms with her fists. He knew the look of fear, had forced it from others a million times, but seeing it on Autumn's face was more than he could bear.

"Kade, *stop!*"

"I…can't. The magic…won't let me." His words came out low and hoarse, a strangled gasp in the throes of what had been the most wonderful event of his life and was quickly becoming the most horrible. The unnatural energy heated his blood, flowing through his body like stinging sparks of fire, making him feel stronger. Filling him with power as the tight heat of her body drove him toward ecstasy.

"Kade." Tears slid down her face, slaying him with her misery.

The uncontrolled passion that drove their mating was too much for her untried body. Her fear only made it worse.

"Autumn, close your eyes."

But she continued to stare at him, terror whirling in those gray depths.

"Close your eyes!"

She turned her head, dipping her face until he couldn't tell if her eyes were closed or not.

It was all he could do to talk, all he could do to *think,* so great was his hunger for her body and the completion to come. "I don't want to hurt you, but I can't stop. The magic won't release us until the act is complete. Until I've climaxed."

"Then do it," she said between clenched teeth.

Her desperation twisted inside him. "Come with me."

"No." Her face jerked up, her eyes flashing with hatred beneath her fear.

"Close your eyes!"

She did, her mouth tight and quivering and he gentled his voice.

"Listen to me. I'm not what you think. I don't…want to hurt you."

"You're hurting me now!"

"I know." Her anguish tore at his heart. "When this is over, you can hate me. You can claw my eyes out. But for right this moment, *feel me*. Your body wanted me before. Give yourself back to that need."

Her fingernails dug into his shoulders, her head shaking in denial.

"Feel me inside you, sweet one. Open yourself…to the pleasure. You were so close."

"I can't."

But his words were working. Deep inside she was softening, melting, easing his way. The exquisite feel of her body's welcome nearly sent him over the edge.

"You can."

He couldn't talk anymore. Couldn't think. His own climax was too close, too powerful. But he didn't want to go there alone.

"Come with me." He kissed her cheek. "Fly with mc, Autumn."

"No." The word was more moan than denial as pleasure tightened her features. He felt her climax building almost as clearly as he felt his own. Her breaths began to come in small gasps.

"I hate you for this."

"I know. Steal the pleasure my body has to give. *Feel me.*"

With each thrust, her tight sheath became more slick. Her gasps grew, turning to small screams of delight. Her rising passion stoked his own, driving him higher and higher until the promise of completion was only a breath away.

He dipped his head, seeking her mouth, half expecting her to bite him, or at least turn away. But she met his kiss, eyes closed, with an open mouth and seeking tongue. Her arms wrapped around his neck and for one glorious moment, she was his again.

He drank of her pleasure, swallowing both their moans, as their joint passion roared toward climax. She tore her mouth from his and threw her head back, cresting that final mount with a guttural scream of pleasure that sent him tumbling after her.

As her inner muscles contracted over and over, milking him of every last drop of pleasure, power roared through him with the suddenness of a storm. The lights in the bathroom flickered and flashed, the rows of light bulbs breaking, one after another, in a cascade of tinkling explosions that cast them into the dark.

Autumn jerked and tensed in his arms. "What's happening?"

"The power we raised blew some lights."

She pulled back, her body going stiff. He gripped her slick waist and pulled himself out of her, then set her on her feet in the tub, his body already railing against the loss. She tried to step back, out of his reach, but he held on to her, hating that she was beginning to tremble beneath his touch.

"Stay here so you don't cut your feet. I'll open the door and let in some light." He reached for the towel he'd left hanging on the rod and pushed it toward her in the dark.

The glass crunched beneath his soles, stinging his flesh with little quickly healed cuts as he crossed the bathroom and opened the door. Light washed in from the living room. He glanced at himself in the mirror, relieved to see his eyes and hair were back to normal.

Misery crushed his chest as he turned back to Autumn.

"I'll carry you out of here." He reached for her, avoiding her gaze, unable to bear seeing that terror in her eyes again, but she backed away.

"You're Esri." Her words were tortured.

"Yes." He tried to look anywhere but her face, but the white-knuckled grip on the towel she'd wrapped around herself did nothing to ease his guilt, and he finally met her gaze.

The fear was there, as he'd known it would be. But shimmering beneath the fear lurked a deep hurt that was nearly more than he could bear.

"You knew I was a virgin."

"No. I don't possess that ability. If I'd known, I never would have touched you." He gave a harsh, humorless laugh. "Revealing myself was not my intent."

"But the power…you gained power. I felt it."

"Yes." He raked the wet hair back from his face. "I gained something. Virgin's power merely enhances a man's gifts, it doesn't add to them. And my gifts are scant. I may be physically stronger, now. Physically faster." He snorted. "Of little use in my world."

He looked into the pools of torment that were her eyes and needed her to believe him. "I mated with you because I wanted to. Because I've been attracted to you since I first saw you standing on the deck of your boat with the sun's fire in your hair. Not because I wanted anything from you except the sharing of pleasure."

And her warmth.

He'd craved her sweetness, her gentle kisses. The laughter in her eyes and the joy of her smile. Her acceptance of him, the Punisher. The monster.

And her lack of fear. Above all, her lack of fear.

But he'd lost it all.

She gripped the towel tighter against her breasts, the dark red tendrils of her hair raining droplets on her arms. "You came through the gate in one of those dark cloaks."

"Yes."

Her brows lowered as her face contorted with confusion. "But...Jack said you're Sitheen. Why can't they see through your glamour?"

"I have no glamour." He held up his hands. "What you see before you is all I am. I'm what the Esri call a dark blood. An Esri tainted with human blood. I don't know my heritage, so I can't tell you which of my forebears was human. All I know is that I am not one of you. I have lived many, many of your lifetimes."

He held out his hand to her. "I didn't mean to hurt you."

She snorted in disbelief, but her eyes still ached from his betrayal. "What do you want from me?"

Kaderil sighed. "In the words of you humans...hell

if I know. Let me carry you out of here, then I'll find a vacuum and clean up this mess."

Her mouth tensed. Her eyes glittered with fear and wariness, but she stepped forward and he swept her into his arms, gathering her rigid, towel-covered body against his. Her arm hooked around his neck to hold on as her other hand grasped the towel tucked at her breast. She smelled of soap and that sweet spicy scent unique to Autumn. Just holding her made the need begin to stir in him all over again.

A need that would never be fulfilled.

Kaderil walked through the glass again to deposit her on the carpet in the hall. Without a backward glance, she fled to the nearest bedroom and slammed the door, shutting him out, casting him adrift.

He stared at that closed door, feeling the world shift back to a painful and familiar axis. He was well and truly the monster, now. Kaderil the Dark, of both worlds and yet of neither. Feared and reviled by the Esri for being part human. Feared and hated by the humans for being Esri.

Of course he was. He'd never expected it to be any different. That he'd let himself get caught up in the lie was his own fault. That he'd allowed a woman's gentle smile to touch his heart, her warm hand to lead him into a dreamscape of heroics and friendship and caring, was the mistake of a fool.

There were only roles to play. Duties and missions and responsibilities.

He was the Punisher. That was his role, the only role available to him. A role that allowed him no conscience, no emotion, no remorse. A role that required him to be a man who would fulfill his duty no matter what that duty asked of him.

Autumn locked the bedroom door with shaking fingers, then turned and sank against the flimsy wood, gasping for breath.

He's Esri.

How could she have been so stupid? So gullible?

Her heart raced, her scalp tingled with horror as she sank to the carpeted floor. Everything she'd thought… everything she'd believed…was a lie. She'd thought she was falling in love! And he wasn't even human.

She pressed her hands to her knotted stomach, struggling to suck air into her lungs. How could she have given her heart…*her body*…to one of those creatures? He'd betrayed her in every way possible. Worse, he'd made her betray herself. Even after she knew what he was, she'd found pleasure in his arms beyond anything she'd ever imagined.

Dear God, she was such a fool.

Her head fell with a soft thud against the door. She'd thought he was Sitheen. They'd *all* thought he was Sitheen.

Her stomach clenched.

The others still did.

She had to warn them. He was after the draggon stone. He had to be. And once he got it? Like Baleris, he would try to kill the ones who couldn't be enchanted.

Heart pounding in her ears, she pushed herself to her feet and searched the room for a phone. Nothing. Her cell phone was in the purse she'd left in the living room.

Mind leaping, she considered her options. The apartment was on the fifth floor, so there was no going out the window. Which meant she was going to have to go out the front door. Without Kade noticing.

Right.

At least it was a plan. Maybe not a good one, but a plan. And she needed something to wear. She reached for the nearest drawer and dug through the clothes until she found a pair of sweatpants and a flannel shirt. Underwear, she'd have to forgo. She wasn't likely to find ladies' underwear in Kade's house. But as she pulled on sweatpants that were barely big enough for her, and several inches too short, the truth hit her.

Kade was Esri.

These weren't his clothes. This wasn't his apartment. Which raised the obvious and tragic question: What had happened to the true owner?

A chill slid down her spine. She didn't want to know. While she knew full well how Esri worked, raping and murdering at will, her heart refused to accept Kade capable of such slaughter.

Her logical mind scoffed. Of course he was capable. He was Esri. Magic. Everything she thought she knew about him was a lie. Who knew how many times he'd enchanted her?

She stilled as memories washed over her—the confusion she felt around him sometimes, the way she'd jumped him, peeling her clothes off the first time she met him. Had he made her do that?

And what about a few hours ago?

The hair rose on her arms as she thought of the

dream. The two Esri forcing their way into the house-boat, Kade's running in to save the day, only to tell the one called Ustanis to take the holly off her wrist.

She'd been so confused, so certain it was real. And, she'd bet money now it *hadn't* been a dream at all. They *had* tried to attack her. Kade had stopped them. Not because he was being chivalrous. But because he needed the stones she was tracking down. If only she'd never told him about those.

As she buttoned the shirt, the dull roar of a vacuum cleaner erupted outside the bedroom door. Her eyes darted around the room as her brain leaped. *Now.* She had to escape now, while the noise covered her movement.

Autumn reached for the bedroom door, heart pounding. She couldn't blow this. She might never get another chance. The doorknob clicked as the lock sprung, sending her heart to her throat, but the vacuuming continued. With shaking hands, she eased open the door and slipped into the hallway.

Kade, dressed in jeans and nothing else, stood half in and half out the bathroom door, his muscular arm shoving the vacuum back and forth into the now-dark room. Broken glass clinked as it disappeared into the machine. Beyond the bathroom, the living room, lit by two table lamps, was light and welcoming.

Her gaze traveled that infinite expanse to zero in on the front door and escape. The phrase *so close and yet so far* had never resonated quite so clearly.

Autumn stood rooted in the bedroom doorway, her palms sweating, her pulse racing. She couldn't do this.

She *had* to. She alone knew Kade Smith was an Esri

imposter. If she failed to get word to the others, he could kill them all.

Slowly, she forced herself to take a step, and then another, her bare feet barely sinking into the carpet's worn pile. All she had to do was sneak past the bathroom.

The blood thundered in her ears, vibrating through her entire body. Now or never. Now or never.

She took a deep breath, gathered every bit of courage she possessed, then eased past the bathroom door. But just as she thought she was going to make it, the roar of the vacuum died. Kade stepped into the hallway, nearly backing into her. Autumn panicked.

With an explosion of fear and adrenaline, she ran for the apartment door, moving with a speed she could hardly credit. Within a handful of seconds, she was wrenching open the front door.

And just as suddenly, it slammed closed again, held there by a large, bare arm.

Panic thudded in her chest as she yanked at the door, but she couldn't budge it. A silent scream vibrated in her throat, fueled by desperation. She had to get away.

But the door wasn't budging.

Autumn released the knob and whirled, fists swinging. With a miraculous bit of luck, she caught Kade under the chin with her right fist, hard enough to snap his head back. Her eyes went wide. *No way*.

But the monster of a man didn't go down. He didn't even stumble, just stared at her, the surprise in his too-blue eyes hardening into determination.

She tried to hit him again, but he caught her right wrist so fast, she didn't even see him move. With her left hand, she aimed for his eyes, but he deflected her hand at the last moment and her nails bit into his cheek instead, ripping through the skin in two places, drawing blood. Jaw clenching grimly, he snagged her left wrist and slammed both hands to the door above her head, pinning her.

But her gaze was caught on his cheek as she watched, scalp crawling, as the bloody gashes disappeared, leaving only the small smear of blood.

Dear God. The truth of what he was punched her in the stomach all over again. Terror whipped through her like an icy wind, prickling her scalp and making her mouth as dry as sandpaper.

"Let me go!" In desperation, Autumn struggled against his steel hold, trying to kick him or knee him. *Anything.*

She had to get away!

But his hold on her appeared almost effortless, though his face was set in grim lines.

As she fought him, an odd buzzing ignited deep in her body. Within seconds, the living-room lights exploded, one after the other, shattering like the bulbs in the bathroom, casting them into shadow. Only the light from the kitchen and the bedroom lit the apartment, now.

"What's happening?" Autumn flinched and tensed for another explosion. Her voice quaked with the fear that was spreading like poison inside her. *"What's happening?"*

Kade shook his head, his gaze tight and wary. "I don't know. It's the magic—the power we raised. But I don't know why it's doing this."

Terror twisted inside her. Panic clawed at her throat and she tried to jerk her hands out of his hold. "Let me go!"

Kade's blue gaze focused on her, pulling on her.

I don't want to leave Kade. I trust Kade.

Autumn jerked and stared at him, breathing hard. "You just talked in my head."

His eyes narrowed. "You heard *my* voice?"

"Yes!" She struggled against his superior hold and the insanity that was quickly becoming her life. "Let me go!"

He pressed his body hard against hers, pinning her to the door as he grabbed both her wrists in one hand and wrenched off her holly.

"No!" Without the holly, she'd be completely at his mercy. Enchanted. *Controlled.* "No, Kade, no!"

The lights in the kitchen blew, the fluorescent hissing as it died. Only the dim light from the bedroom cast a small glow into the room. But still she fought. She managed to free one leg enough to kick at his shin with her bare toes and stomp on his foot with her heel.

"Be still!"

She froze. *Literally.* Staring at his chest. As if he'd waved a magic wand and turned her to living stone.

She couldn't move. Dear God, she couldn't breathe. *Kade, no! Don't do this.*

"That's better," he muttered. His voice sounded clearly in her head. *I trust Kade. I don't want to leave.*

He didn't know what he'd done to her! And she couldn't tell him. Couldn't move.

Her lungs cried for air.

Kade!

But he couldn't hear her.

And if he didn't release her soon…she was going to die.

Chapter 11

Slowly, Kaderil loosened his grip on Autumn's wrists, testing. His thoughts should have taken, now that he'd removed her holly. She no longer struggled against his hold, but neither had she relaxed. She remained pressed against the front door as if she sought to get as far from him as the small space between them would allow. She stared at his chest, refusing to meet his gaze.

He terrified her, and as much as he told himself he didn't care, he did. "I'm not going to hurt you."

Little by little, he released her wrists, preparing himself for her renewed attack. But she didn't move. He released her wrists entirely, and still she didn't move. Her arms remained above her head as if he'd frozen her. As if…

In a flash he understood. He'd seen Marceils enchanted in just this way—told to hold still and unable to move until they were freed. They weren't even able to...

"*Breathe,* Autumn. Move!" He grabbed her as she collapsed against the door, gasping for breath. *Sweet Esria,* he could have killed her. "Autumn, I didn't know. I *vow* I didn't know what I'd done to you. I've never been able to control another like that."

She coughed against his chest. "What...what did you do to me?"

He pressed her against him, holding her up, stroking her back. "I must have acquired more power than I thought. When I told you to be still, I meant only for you to stop fighting me, but the magic forced you to obey my command. In every way."

His mind leaped between horror at what he'd nearly done to her and wonder that he'd been able to do it at all. He raked his damp hair off his face as thoughts swirled in his head. "I still can't enchant you, which would mean controlling your mind. But apparently, I can control your body."

Autumn pulled away from him, her eyes wide with dismay and fear.

He reached for her, then dropped his hand when she jerked away. "I won't hurt you. I've seen..." Memories rose to sicken him. The Esri controlled their Marceil slaves in just this way—body, but not mind. He'd seen the horrors visited upon slaves in the name of discipline and amusement. Never had he had that kind of power over another. Other than the recurrent wish he wasn't so different from his brethren, he'd never wanted it.

But now that he had it, he'd be a fool not to use it.

Autumn stood just out of his reach, hugging herself, her breaths labored, as if she'd run a long race. Regret hammered him hard. He hated the fear in her eyes, longed for the closeness they'd shared for such a short time.

She watched him with fear and wariness, tendrils of fiery hair drying around her face in a soft cloud. The clothes she'd found in the bedroom did nothing to hide the curves of her body, curves he'd only started to know and would never know again.

He wanted to beg her to forget what he was, but knew it was far too late.

Kaderil reached for her and grabbed her wrist before she could back away. "You will not fight me."

Instantly, her struggles ended. Her eyes filled with dread, deepening his regret.

He loosened his grip on her wrist, trailing his fingers down her soft skin until he cradled her hand in his. "You will not make any phone calls or leave this apartment unless I tell you to. You will not raise your voice above normal level. I don't want you calling for help."

Against his palm, her hand began to quake. "Is that all?" she asked bitterly. She watched him with hard, frightened eyes. He'd been out-magicked all his life, but never so utterly controlled by another, and he ached for her plight. Yet he could do little to change it without endangering himself and his mission.

There was one thing he could do. He squeezed her hand gently and stared into those frightened eyes. "If ever again you're in pain or discomfort or danger, you will shout my name even though I've told you to keep your voice normal. This command supersedes all the others."

Her mouth tensed and trembled with misery. "I don't even know your name."

"Kaderil. But call me Kade." The thought of his real name, the Punisher's name, coming from her soft lips turned him cold. His arms ached with the need to pull her against him and erase the desolation he saw in her eyes. But for her, too, he'd become the monster.

And the monster needed to know his strength. Never would he have chosen this path, destroying the precious connection he'd developed with Autumn. But now that he had, now that it was done, he needed to understand the power he'd acquired. It could be critical to his mission...even to his survival.

"I know all you want is to be free of me," he told her. "But we have some work to do first."

"What kind of work?" she asked warily.

"Stay here." He released her and went into the kitchen to retrieve the pack of spare lightbulbs he'd found several days ago. "Are you okay?"

"Yes. Can I turn around?"

"You can try." He paused as he reached for the light-bulbs on the top shelf of the cabinet to watch her. She didn't move. "Are you trying to turn?"

"Yes." Her voice was tight with effort. Then suddenly she let out a sound that was half gasp, half scream.

Kaderil rushed back to her. "What happened?"

Her eyes were wide, but a little sheepish. "It hurt. I think I did it wrong."

"Does it still hurt?"

"No."

He looked at her thoughtfully, his gaze straying to the

amazing fall of hair that was starting to curl as it dried. As he watched her, she watched him back with a stubborn thrust of her chin, cutting him with her gaze. Myriad emotions swam in those gray eyes—fear, betrayal, anger, hatred and probably a dozen more. But the tears were gone, replaced by a gleam of steel that drew his admiration. And his profound, if fragile, relief.

She was afraid of what he was. Of what he could do.

But, despite all that had happened, deep down she wasn't afraid of *him.*

Yet.

He desperately wanted to keep it that way. More than anything in his life, he would miss the softness he'd seen in her eyes. He wouldn't hurt her. Not physically. When he left her world, he would leave her safe and whole. As whole as he could leave her after he did what must be done. That much he could vow even though he knew she'd truly fear him then, and hate him with a fury that would grind the last spark of light from his soul.

"I'm going to try to turn you without touching you."

"Can you do that?"

"Doubtful. Most Esri can only control through touch, though there are a few who can use their minds or voices." He concentrated on turning her around, but nothing happened so he took her hand. "Face whichever direction you wish, but don't leave this spot."

She jerked her hand from his, watching him warily, then turned as he went to get the lightbulbs and exchange them for the broken ones. The living room once more glowed with light.

"What are you going to do?" she asked.

"I want to see if we can break more bulbs. First, I want to know if I can do it alone." Kaderil focused, drawing the invisible energy up through his body until he could feel it radiate along his skin. But it was only a shadow of the power he'd felt with Autumn. Mentally, he flung the energy toward the nearest light.

Nothing happened.

He peered at Autumn. "Did you feel anything?"

"No. Was I supposed to?"

Kaderil sighed. "I was hoping to raise the energy alone this time. Maybe we can only do it together. Or maybe it's already gone. Virgin's power doesn't last."

"Good."

He raised a brow. "You don't like the extra speed and strength?"

Her eyes narrowed with confusion. "Were they real?"

"Real enough." He rubbed his chin where she'd clipped him.

"I thought only the Esri got the virgin's power."

"Only the male benefits. I've never heard of a virgin growing stronger, not even an Esri virgin. I don't know why this happened."

"But it's not going to last?"

"I don't know." He'd never been with a virgin before, so he wasn't entirely sure what was normal, especially for a dark blood. A dark blood and a human.

He went to stand in front of her. "Hold my hands."

She lifted that stubborn chin, drawing his attention back to that full, ripe mouth and for a moment, all he could think of was kissing her again, tasting the sweetness of her lips. Desire slammed into him anew.

He forced his gaze to her eyes, startling a flicker of answering need in her eyes, before she closed it down.

She glanced at his waiting hands. "If I say no, will you make me?"

He shrugged. "Yes. Come, Autumn. Give me your hands."

With a frustrated roll of the eyes, she laid her hands in his. He forced himself to ignore the feel of her skin against his sensitive palms.

"Do you feel the power rising?" he asked.

"No."

"Me, neither. Fight me." The moment the command left his lips, she began to struggle against his hold. He held her fast as she kicked his shins and tried to wrench free of his grasp, but still no energy stirred inside him.

"You're fighting me with your body. Because I told you to. I want you to fight me with your mind, Autumn. *Hate me.*"

Almost at once, her eyes flashed and a faint stirring of power charged the air.

"That's it, Autumn." But in her eyes he saw anger. An anger she'd been directed to feel. If they were going to raise the kind of energy they'd raised before, he was going to have to stir in her real, honest rage. "I release you from your spot."

At once, she tried to pull away from him.

He pushed her back against the door and pulled her arms above her head as he had before, pressing his body against hers. The moment his bare chest came in contact with the soft, flannel-covered mounds of her breasts, blood rushed to his groin.

She struggled against him, her breaths coming faster.

"Fight me." He leaned closer, filling his senses with her intoxicating scent until his lips brushed her temple. "Hate me for my lies, for the way I used you to find your friends. For the way I pretended to be one of them in order to win their trust."

With each word, her hands tightened in his until her nails dug into his flesh, until her eyes sparked with her fury. The power buzzed around them, swirling in and around their bodies like a swarm of bees. But the lights remained whole and bright.

"I'm going to kill the Sitheen, Autumn."

"No."

He ignored the way that single pain-filled word squeezed his chest. "Yes, Autumn. It's what I was sent to do, I'm going to kill them all. Jack, Larsen, Charlie, Harrison. Even Myrtle."

She struggled against him with an inhuman strength, forcing his muscles to bulge and strain to control her. Her hips thrust against his throbbing erection as she tried to kick him, driving his lust to a fevered pitch.

The nearest light burst. Heat began to build in their hands.

He ground his hips against hers. "They'll die because they were foolish enough to think I was one of them."

"No." Her face contorted with fury, with the effort she poured into the silent battle—a battle without punches. Without weapons. Nothing but the straining of their bodies as he fought to hold her considerable strength under control.

The second light burst and he growled with triumph,

but didn't stop. The energy was riding him now, driving him higher. He wanted more. He *needed* more.

"They'll die because I'll never release you to warn them. You're my prisoner. I can make you do whatever I want, Autumn. Whatever I want! Hate me. *Hate me!*"

A reddish glow erupted over their skin in a flash of light, as if they were lit from within. The heat of power rushed through him in a charge of pure energy, power that strengthened but didn't burn. Power that...

"Kade!" His name burst from her lips, throbbing with agony, tearing him from the power's greed.

Autumn's face was contorted with pain and he wrenched his hands away from hers. "What happened?"

But she didn't answer, just sank to the ground as the glow died, casting them back into shadows.

What had he done? Kaderil swept Autumn into his arms before she hit the floor, then strode back to the lit bedroom, fear lending unnatural speed to his steps.

He laid her on the bed, but instead of curling in on herself, she flung her arms and legs wide, arching her back.

"Autumn, what happened? Where does it hurt?"

Squeezing her eyes closed, she gasped with pain. "Fire. My body's on fire."

He'd felt the flames, but no burn. But neither was he mortal. His stomach clenched with self-directed anger. Would he *never* cease hurting her?

"I'm sorry." He reached for her, then stilled, wondering if his touch would help or only cause her more pain. Could his control over her body control the fire within her? He had to know, had to try.

Kaderil laid his hand lightly over the back of hers, barely touching her heated skin, but even with that barest of touches, her tension leaped into him, stringing him as tight as a bow.

"Feel no pain, Autumn," he murmured softly. Power, he was beginning to realize was a double-edged blade. And in the hands of the inexperienced, he thought ruefully, a dangerous and unpredictable weapon.

He lifted his hand, fearing he was doing more harm than good. "Did I help at all?"

Her lashes fluttered open, freeing tears that slid silently into her hair. "A little," she said, her voice tight, her gaze filled with pain.

He lifted his hand and slid it over his mouth as he struggled with the sharp ache of guilt.

"Forgive me. I never meant to hurt you, Autumn. If you believe nothing else of me, believe that. I only said those things to drive your fury and raise the power, but your human body is too fragile for the energy we raised. I won't do it again."

She said nothing, just watched him with eyes filled with a misery that called to the dark ache in his own soul. He took her hand, watching that he didn't cause her more pain as he tried to ease the fire tormenting her.

Slowly, the arch eased out of her back. Her gray eyes lost their focus, filling with an empty hopelessness that tore out his heart.

"You said those things to drive my fury," she said softly, her words flat and hollow. "But they were true."

Kaderil turned his head, unable to watch those empty eyes. "Yes."

"Leave me." Her words rang as hollow as her eyes as she pulled her hand from his and rolled onto her side, turning her back on him.

He stared at her rigid back and knew a pain unlike any he'd felt in centuries.

All his life he'd been feared. He'd thought himself immune to emotional pain, immune to hurt. He'd thought his heart's armor strong enough to withstand anything.

But he'd been wrong.

Nothing in his life had prepared him for the cutting pain of watching eyes that had once looked at him with warmth and affection suddenly slice him to shreds with loathing and fear.

He forced his feet to move, to leave the side of the woman who, for a few short days, had brought such light into his life. In the hallway, he closed the door behind him, then squeezed his eyes closed against the stunning sharpness of his own unhappiness. If only he could let her go.

For her. For him, so that he wouldn't have to continually face her hatred and misery. But he couldn't afford to be so weak. She knew he was Esri. If she warned the others, he might never get his hands on that draggon stone. His mission would be forfeit.

And his mission was all he had now.

Chapter 12

"You'll drive us to the marina." Kade's touch on her hand was light, but his voice was not as he handed her the car keys the next morning before they left his apartment. He was dressed in jeans and a black silk shirt that, on his muscular frame, made him look dark, dangerous and way too sexy. Even knowing he was Esri wasn't enough to stop her body's response to his potent masculinity.

Autumn's gaze roamed over the features of the man she'd thought she was falling for. The strong bones and straight nose, the brilliant blue eyes. How could she have been so blind? He still looked like the man who'd kissed her so tenderly, but there was a hard light in his eyes this morning that chilled her to her core.

Overnight, something had changed in him. Or maybe she was just seeing him clearly for the first time.

"You will keep your eyes downcast and you will speak to no one on the way to the car." He stood in front of her, compelling her to meet his gaze. "You will drive carefully and legally and park the same way once we're there."

"Yes, master," she said sarcastically.

Though he hadn't said why they were returning to the houseboat, she knew. He wanted that Esri stone. And with the control he had over her now, there was nothing she could do to stop him from getting it. If only she hadn't told him about Mr. Robertson and the sculptures. If only she *had* told Jack and the others. Her foolish, foolish wish to impress the Sitheen might kill them all now.

Kade tugged on her hand, but unlike before, the feel of his strong fingers engulfing her own made fear lance her heart. He led her out the apartment door and she followed because she had to. If only she could find a way to thwart him. But the man seemed to think of everything.

The elevator door opened and they walked hand in hand to the car, looking to all the world like lovers. She was still in sweatpants and the flannel shirt she'd found last night, but in the second bedroom she'd at least found women's underwear and a pair of flip-flops that were a little short, but not too bad. She kept wondering about the woman they'd belonged to.

She unlocked the car doors as they approached the vehicle. "What happened to the owners of your apartment, Kade?"

He glanced at her over the roof of the car. "I don't know. Ustanis procured me the apartment."

"So they could be dead."

"They could also be on vacation. Don't automatically think the worst, Autumn."

"Thinking the best certainly hasn't worked." Bitterly, she remembered thinking he was a kind and gentle man. She'd imagined she'd seen a loneliness inside him, and a need for connection that had called to her.

Foolish, foolish Autumn.

"Get in the car," he said, and she did, unable to do otherwise. When he told her to start the car, she fought against the command with everything she had.

She wasn't going to drive this car!

But though her mind refused, her body obeyed him, starting the ignition, easing out of the parking space, shifting to drive.

Her hands gripped the steering wheel until her knuckles turned white as she tried to turn the wheel toward the parked cars. Sweat broke out on her brow. A groan of sheer effort escaped her throat.

"You can't fight it," Kade said beside her, his tone flat.

With a low cry of frustration, she quit struggling as her unwilling self joined the heavy morning traffic. "Why is this necessary? What are you going to do with those stones? The least you can do is tell me what I've done."

"You already know what they do. The draggon stone opens the gates. The others will revitalize the magic in my world."

"Is the magic in your world low?"

"Not desperately so, but yes. Lower than it should be."

He didn't say any more and didn't look at her again as she drove to the marina and parked. As she pulled the key out of the ignition, his hand covered hers. The brush of his warm flesh on hers sparked a quick rush of excitement before her mind recoiled and doused the pending fire.

"When I release you, you'll get out of the car and wait for me silently."

"Do you really think I could escape you?"

"No. I'm still faster than you. But we'd attract too much attention."

Her gaze flicked to his. "Two giants chasing one another at superhuman speeds? Go figure."

For an instant, his expression softened to something slightly shy of granite, then hardened again. "Let's go."

Autumn got out of the car and couldn't move until Kade slid his warm fingers around her wrist. Angry frustration flared inside her. "I *hate* this. You might as well put a choke collar around my neck and attach a leash." Her gaze rose to his. "I used to love it when you touched me. Now I hate it."

His eyes flinched and she thought her barb had hit its mark, but the look was gone a second later and he pulled her with him to the marina office.

"We're going to check your mail in case one of those stones has already arrived. Act natural."

"Yes, sir, master, sir," she muttered.

He opened the door for her and ushered her inside.

"Good morning, Kade!"

Autumn's head jerked up in surprise, a chill raising her skin to gooseflesh. How in the *heck* did the desk guy know the Esri? Had Kade enchanted him, too?

Kade lifted a hand in greeting, but said nothing to the

man, whose name even Autumn didn't know. "Retrieve your mail and bring it to me, including packages."

She silently wished that none of the sculptures had arrived yet. But when she opened Larsen's mail slot— hers for now—she found a telltale slip of paper announcing that a package was being held for her at the front desk.

Led as if by unseen puppet strings, she marched to the counter and retrieved a small box that was about the size of a tissue box. A quick glance at the label said the sender's name was Robertson.

Hells bells.

This son had spent a considerable amount of money to overnight the sculpture for morning delivery. Poor Mr. Robertson was so anxious for this exhibit. If she managed to get out of this alive, that exhibit was going to happen if she had to tie up her boss and do it herself.

Against her will, she took the box to Kade, afraid she was turning over another power stone to the enemy.

"See you later!" the man behind the counter called as they left the office.

They walked down the path to the docks, the river-scented wind whipping loose tendrils of hair into her face. The day was as gray as her mood. Was it only a week ago that she'd dreamed of walking hand in hand with this man she'd fancied herself in love with? Now here she was, she thought bitterly. Hand in hand. But their closeness had nothing to do with affection and everything to do with control. And her dream had turned into a nightmare.

When they reached the houseboat, Kade helped her

on board, then handed her the box. "Hold this and wait here." Then he turned and went to the rail where she'd tied the lead-lined box. Out on the river, a lone sailboat bobbed as it cut through the rough water. Free.

Beneath her, she could feel the gentle sway of the houseboat, but for once the movement didn't unbalance her. What if she fell and the box landed in the water? Could Esri swim? She tried to fall, tried to *move,* but his words, no matter how casually stated, bound her. It wouldn't matter anyway, she thought with a soft snort of resignation. He'd simply tell her to go in after it. And if she drowned trying to retrieve the thing? At least he wouldn't be able to control her anymore.

She watched Kade lean over the rail, the leather jacket stretched taut across his broad back. Her fingers remembered all too well the planes of that back, and the hard muscles of his arms and chest. Heat rushed through her as her body warmed and readied itself to welcome his. She tore her gaze away and forced herself to look elsewhere.

How could she still want him, knowing what he was? She didn't, not consciously. But her body was not so particular and her gaze wouldn't be denied, following him as he lifted the dripping box over the rail and opened it, pulling out the stone she'd worked so hard to find.

His expression closed, he came to her, taking the box out of her hands, then ushered her inside.

The houseboat was as she'd left it yesterday, the blinds open, muted daylight filling the living room with a gray gloom.

Kade set the box on the kitchen counter. "Would you like to open it?" There was no softness in his voice. No

kindness. Yet his words offered a measure of consideration completely at odds with his role of evil Esri.

He was letting her be the first to find the stones if
there were any.

"Why do you do that?" she asked, frustrated.

"Do what?"

"Pretend to care how I feel."

He turned away. "Do you want to open it or not?"

"Of course."

"Then do it." His voice remained without heat, without warmth. Without any inflection at all.

She crossed to the kitchen, able to move freely for
the first time all day. Her pulse leaped as the breath of
opportunity pricked her scalp. What if he *couldn't*
swim? What if she could grab the stone and dive into
the water before he grabbed her? Before he gave her any
orders? If he couldn't follow, she'd be free.

But she'd never outrun him. Not unless she could
figure out a way to slow him down.

The blood began to pound in her ears as she opened
the drawer to grab scissors to cut through the tape. She
stared at their sharp, pointy ends. *A weapon.* They
wouldn't kill him. From what she knew of Esri healing
powers—and the little bit she'd seen for herself—the
stab would barely hurt him at all. But it might slow him
down enough to give her a chance to escape.

Her mind leaped in an excited panic from one thought
to the next. She needed time to think this through.

There was no time.

Kade stood by the counter, watching her. She moved
around behind him, gripping the scissor handles in her

fist. But as she lifted the weapon, intending to aim for his heart, the boat rocked, knocking her into him. The scissors slipped from her fingers, landing with a glancing blow that sliced a painful cut along the top of her bare foot.

"Ow, ow, ow!" Her fingers curled into the silk of Kade's shirt as she tried to get her balance. Blood oozed from the shallow, burning cut.

Kade's shirt slid out of her grasp as he turned to face her. "What happened?"

"I dropped the scissors." And lost her one chance to stop this travesty and get away. Tears of pain and frustration swam in her eyes. She was *such* an idiot.

She gasped as Kade swung her into his arms. "What are you doing?"

"We have to stop the blood." His voice sounded so dire, she might have laughed if she'd had any laughter left in her.

"It's just a cut. Not a big deal."

He looked at her with solemn, worried eyes. "A human cannot withstand too much blood loss."

She knew he was remembering Larsen. The memory jarred her. Why had he helped *save* Larsen? To keep from blowing his cover? Probably.

"The human body is designed to stop the blood loss on its own if the cut isn't too deep or the damage too extensive," she told him. She thought of the way her fingernails had torn his cheek, and shivered. "My cut won't heal as fast as yours, but it will heal."

His eyes narrowed in concentration as if he were thinking about something carefully. "You need a bandage."

"There's a box of them in the bathroom medicine cabinet." She grimaced. "I don't go anywhere without them."

He set her down on the sofa and patted her hand. "Wait here."

Damn. She wondered if he even knew he'd given her another order. She tried to rise and couldn't budge. With a defeated sigh, she let her head fall against the sofa back as she waited for him.

Kade returned with the bandages and a sterile gauze pad and knelt at her feet. With big, gentle hands, he lifted her foot onto his lap and gently dabbed at the blood.

She stared at the top of his dark head in bewilderment. "I don't understand you."

His gaze lifted. "What don't you understand?"

"Why you're being so gentle."

Emotions flickered through his eyes, but she couldn't read them. "I've hurt you enough." He bandaged the cut then rose and looked down at her, his eyes shuttered. "Does it hurt?"

"A little." It was hard to remember he was Esri when he was being kind like this, when he was acting like the man she'd fallen for. "Thank you."

He nodded, then he went to retrieve the box and the scissors. He sat beside her and cut through the tape himself, then handed the box to her for her to open.

As she lifted the flaps, she felt a tingling of excitement she couldn't manage to quell. The sculpture was wrapped in Bubble Wrap. She lifted it carefully from the box and unwrapped it. In her hands she held what appeared to be a silver and green frog. Her heart leaped and then plummeted as her gaze fastened on the pair of etched stones that acted as his feet.

"How many?" Kade asked.

"Two." She couldn't see any advantage to lying.

He thrust out his hand to her. "Let me see them."

She handed him the frog and watched as he turned the small rock-encrusted animal over in his hands, cradling it with surprising care. Tension pulsed from his big body, palpable and unsettling. But not frightening.

The man was an enigma. Inhuman, certainly. Intense. But not cruel.

"Do you see more than two?" she asked.

"No." Using the scissors, he carefully pried the two stones loose.

As he set the footless sculpture on the coffee table, she reached out and touched his arm. "Kade." She raked her teeth over her bottom lip, suddenly nervous. "Couldn't you pretend you didn't find these?"

He covered her hand with his, his grip tight and unpleasant. Any kindness she'd seen in his eyes evaporated.

"Don't *ever* doubt my loyalty to my king." His jaw clenched, throwing his cheekbones into hard relief. Making her pulse race with real fear.

"Kade, I'm sorry, I didn't mean—"

He cut her off. "Pull out your phone. I'm going to tell you to call Jack."

Her heart lurched. "Why?" Without her consent, her hand began to dig around in her purse, searching for her phone, following his command.

"You're going to ask him to meet you here as soon as possible. Alone."

"Kade, no. *Please* no. You don't need him."

He dropped the three Esri stones into her purse. "I do. He wears the draggon stone around his neck."

Her blood went cold. "Kade…" Autumn clutched at his hand. "You won't hurt him. *Please.* Deep down you're a good man. I know it."

His eyes turned bleak. "You're wrong, Autumn. So very, very wrong. Now, call Jack."

Autumn's hands were shaking, her mind screaming as her unwilling fingers punched Jack's speed-dial number. Kade paced the houseboat's small living room, his strides tense, his face as hard as granite.

"Kade, please tell me you're not going to hurt him." He was setting Jack up, forcing her to call him into his trap so he could take the draggon stone.

As he swung by the sofa where she sat, his hand snaked out to clamp around her wrist, forcing her to obey his will. "Don't talk to me. Tell Jack you're not sure anyone else should see this until he's had a chance to look at it. Keep your voice calm, even and friendly."

No. The denial screamed in her head as the phone rang in her ear.

"Hello?"

"Hi, Jack. It's Autumn." It was as if she'd been locked away while another soul took over her body. While everything inside her cried out in warning, her voice was just as Kade demanded. Calm and friendly as she relayed Kade's words.

"I'll swing by within the hour," Jack said. "See you then." The phone went silent with a click.

He was going to walk right into a trap that she'd help set!

A quaking started deep inside her, spreading through her body and down her limbs, driven by hopelessness and impotent fury. She wanted to beg him to reconsider. She needed to yell at him and rail at him for his betrayal and cruelty. And she couldn't say a word because of his order.

Kade took the phone from her hand and closed it, even as he kept a grip on her hand. "You won't leave this boat until I tell you to." His voice was hard, without inflection. "Go pack a suitcase with clothes and whatever else you'll need for the rest of the week. Then sit on the bed and don't make a sound until I come to get you."

When he released her hand, she rose as if pulled by a string, and moved to the small guest cabin on feet driven by a will not her own. Though her mind fought every move, she packed without thinking, without choice.

As she tossed clothes into her duffel, fear for Jack rode her, twisting her insides until she thought she was going to be sick. If only she knew the Esri death chant, all she'd need to do was get her hands on a matchbook and Kade would be history.

The thought chilled her. She was suddenly glad she didn't have the chant, didn't have to make that choice. Because as much as she hated what he was, hated what he was doing, she wasn't sure she could destroy the man who'd stolen her heart.

God, she was such a fool.

When her bag was packed, she sat on the bed and listened for Jack, unable to do anything else. A plane sounded overhead, following the Potomac in its descent into Reagan National Airport. The roar of a boat engine melded with the city sounds, filling her ears as she pressed her shaking hands together in her lap.

Tears trickled down her cheeks.

Kade, no. Please, no.

The seconds felt like minutes. The minutes like hours as dread formed a rock in her stomach the size of her fist. Footsteps on the dock shook her out of her trance of misery. Moments later, the boat gave a lurch that told her someone had come aboard.

No.

The rap of knuckles on the glass sliding door turned her blood to ice.

No, Jack! Don't come in. Run!

She pressed her palms to the bed, pushing against the unnatural bonds that held her there with every scrap of power in her mind. If only she could get up! If only she could run out there and warn him herself. As she fought Kade's terrible control, her hands began to vibrate and warm.

Then, like a spark catching flame, the warmth turned hot and shot up her arms in a scalding spray, just as it had last night. Her mouth opened on a silent scream as the vicious flame tore through her chest, carving spirals of color through her vision. She arched her back against the pain, gasping for air as tears sliced down her cheeks.

Voices penetrated her agony.

"Hi, Kade. Autumn asked me to stop by."

"Come in, Jack."

Autumn heard the faint squeak of the sliding door closing. And a single, heavy thud.

Then silence.

Autumn's tears slowly turned to sobs. *Larsen, I'm so sorry. I'm so very sorry. It's my fault. All my fault.*

So many mistakes. So many stupid moves. How could she have been so wrong about Kade? So wrong.

By the time Kade finally opened the door, her body had cooled, but her eyes ached, her head was throbbing and her heart lay in a broken heap in the middle of her chest. She blinked back the tears that blurred her vision and wished she hadn't when she saw the savage twist of his mouth.

He picked up her suitcase then grabbed her wrist with fingers vibrating with tension. "Come." The command was quick and harsh.

He yanked her after him and through the living room so quickly, she almost didn't see Jack. But as they reached the door, there he was, sprawled face down, the bandages to his head and arm gone. Myrtle had probably healed him once she'd recovered from healing Larsen, but it was all for nothing. Jack's healed arm lay at an awkward angle against his unmoving, lifeless body.

Bitter tears rolled down her cheeks as Kade pulled her through the door. Sobs broke over her with silent pain.

"Put your arm around me and lean into me as if you're seeking comfort." Though his words were brittle, Kade's arm slid around her shoulders in a mockery of the closeness they'd once shared. They walked slowly to the car, her suitcase by Kade's side. He'd told her to pack enough clothes to last until the next full moon and the opening of the dark gate between the worlds. As she'd packed that suitcase, the thought had gone through her head that he wouldn't hurt her. He clearly didn't intend to kill her.

Now, with a terrible clarity, she understood why.

She was his weapon. His lure.

One by one, he'd order her to call her friends and ask them to meet her. One by one he'd kill them.

When that gate opened, there would be no Sitheen left to stop Kade from leaping through with the seven stones of Esri. Their dark purpose, whatever it was, would be fulfilled.

All she'd wanted was to matter in some way. To help the Sitheen in this fight. Now, through her foolish, romantic gullibility, she was helping to destroy them. Through her, Kade had the means to lure the Sitheen to their deaths.

There was only one certain way to stop him.

With bleak determination, she knew what she had to do.

Chapter 13

"Next!"

After returning from the marina, Kaderil had locked Autumn in his apartment and now strode into the deli on the ground floor, the events of the past hour flaying him like a whip. His betrayal of Jack. The anguish in Autumn's eyes. His betrayal of himself and everything he was.

His hands clenched into fists at his sides as barely controlled fury lent a menace to his every step, his every glance.

He pushed past the long line of patrons, shoving his way to the front of the line.

"Hey!" A middle-aged human male in construction clothes tried to hold his ground against Kaderil's aggression. "Who do you think you are?"

With lightning speed, Kaderil grabbed the front of

the man's coveralls and lifted him until he was eye level, letting the full force of his fury blaze in his eyes. "Back off."

Fear leaped in the human's eyes, his hands raising in quick surrender. "Yeah. Sure. Go right ahead."

The line behind him disappeared. Even people sitting at the tables grabbed their food and left, watching him with a fear he'd never attracted from humans. Then again, he was a seven-foot monster capable of snapping necks with ease. They had reason to be afraid.

He shouldn't be around others in this mood. He wouldn't be if he hadn't felt the need to bring food to Autumn. Though Esri enjoyed and thrived best on food, they didn't need it to live the way humans did, and he had little in the apartment. She was his captive, bound to him until he went back through the gate. As such, he had to provide for her. Protect her. And, maybe, dim the anguish in her eyes.

"C-can I h-help you?" The youth behind the counter forced himself to meet Kadcril's ferocious gaze, earning a small measure of his respect.

"Fix me four sandwiches."

"Wh-what kind, sir?"

"I don't care!"

The kid grabbed two small loaves of bread, cut each in half, and began slapping various kinds of meat on the four rolls with surprising dexterity. As Kaderil watched, an odd buzz began to tingle along his skin. So faint, at first, that he thought it just a memory of the power he'd raised with Autumn last night, the first time by accident when he'd inadvertently taken her virginity, the second time when he'd cruelly forced her to raise the power with him, then realized her mortal body wasn't built to withstand such force.

As he stood there, watching the kid toss cheese on the meat, the buzz grew steadily more insistent until he was certain he was feeling true power. Power he and Autumn alone could raise. He turned, searching the now-empty deli for sign of her even as he knew she was locked in the apartment four stories above, where he'd left her.

The buzz grew worse. The power was rising.

Kaderil's pulse tripped. He'd felt the power buzz over him like this in the houseboat as Jack had arrived. He'd suspected Autumn was fighting her prison, but the power had only lasted a few seconds before dying. Was she once more fighting to escape the control he'd placed over her? And what if she succeeded? He wasn't sure how long his control over her would last when he wasn't close by.

"Hurry," he growled at the youth.

The buzzing continued and he started to sweat. What was she doing? If she didn't stop soon, she was going to injure herself. Her mortal body was too fragile.

He felt the tingling on his skin slowly ebb and he expelled the breath he hadn't realized he'd been holding. She'd given up at last. But no sooner was the thought in his head, than the buzzing returned, but not as strong as before. Wavering, as if the one raising the power were growing weak.

She was going to injure herself!

He turned and fled the deli, knocking aside a young couple trying to enter as he pushed through the door. He ignored the elevator and ran for the stairwell, taking the stairs five at a time. That wavering buzz continued, his pulse jumping another notch with every passing second. Had she somehow become trapped in the power?

He burst through the door into the empty living room and ran to the bedroom. His heart lodged in his throat at the sight of her on the floor, her arms and legs flung wide from a back arched in agony. Tears ran from her eyes into the hair tumbling around her face.

Her head swivelled toward him with painful difficulty, her eyes filling with a frantic desperation as she pressed her palms to the floor and once more engaged the energy. Her face contorted as a torturous moan escaped her throat.

She'd done this to herself.

"Autumn, no!" He fell at her side and pulled her hands from the floor. "What are you doing? You're going to kill yourself."

But her eyes rolled back, her expression one of utter defeat. "I'm...trying. Dear God, I'm trying, but...I can't. I don't have the courage."

Understanding hit him like a fist to the gut. She was *trying* to kill herself. Because of him. Because of Jack. *What had he done?*

"It wasn't your fault." He shook her hands lightly, not wanting to cause her more pain even as he struggled with his own desperate anger that she'd nearly ended her own all-too-short life. "You couldn't have stopped me."

"I meant to stop you...from killing the others. Larsen. Charlie." Her silent tears turned to choking sobs. "But I can't...keep it up. I can't...make myself."

Sudden understanding crashed into him, nearly driving him to his knees. She wasn't punishing herself. She was trying to *kill* herself. In drawing the power when she knew it would harm her, she had been attempting to sacrifice herself so that he couldn't use her to trap the others.

Just when he thought he was beginning to understand these humans, they astounded him anew.

Yet her sacrifice was for nothing.

He held her hands lightly as he stared down into that pale, bejeweled face that was becoming far too precious to him. "You will not try to kill yourself again." He released one of her hands and laid it gently at her side while he rubbed the back of her other hand with his thumb. "Feel no pain."

Her expression eased, but not enough. Her back remained arched and rigid, filling him with a remorse as deep and bitter as the Forest of Nightmares. With his finger, he brushed a loose tendril of hair from her damp cheek.

"Is it any better?"

"I'm so hot. As if I'm burning from the inside out."

Real fear raked claws down his heart. What damage had she done to herself in her wayward attempt to end her life? Her mortal's body was too weak.

He squeezed her hand. "Be cool, Autumn. Cool the fire inside you." If this didn't work, he was going to have to get help, though he doubted human doctors would know how to save her.

His anxious gaze roamed her face, watching for sign that his commands were helping. Slowly, he felt the heat and tension recede from her hands and body. Her back relaxed and she sank to the floor.

"Better?"

"Yes. N-no." With a violent shudder, she turned onto her side and curled into a shivering ball, taking his hand with her. "So c-cold."

His command to be cool was taking her too far. "I release you from my commands, Autumn. All of them." With his free hand, he brushed the hair back from her face. He'd vowed to leave her unharmed, yet from the moment they'd become one, he had done little but hurt her.

Despite his freeing of her body, she continued to shake. He had to find a way to help her.

"I'm going to lift you, Autumn. Tell me if I hurt you."

Her head nodded jerkily.

He scooped her up and stood, her quaking body tight in his arms. Then he carried her the few feet to the bed and laid her down as gently as he could. The moment he released her, she tightened once more into a ball. With aching uncertainty, he watched her.

"Are you still in pain?"

"N-no. Just c-cold."

Cold he could do something about.

Kaderil kicked off his shoes and lay beside her, pulling her against him and wrapping his arm tightly around her. She stiffened at the contact, but didn't pull away.

A shudder went through him as he held her shivering body against his and buried his nose in the fragrant scent of her hair. Though he hated the weakness, he knew he needed this closeness, this contact, probably more than she did.

As he held her, her shivering slowly ebbed, to be replaced by a shaking of a different kind. A shaking that tore his heart to shreds as he recognized the sounds of her crying.

"Autumn...don't. I won't hurt you."

"I d-didn't want to die. I tried to be strong, but I d-didn't have the courage."

With a sigh so deep it burned his eyes, he said, "I should have told you the truth."

"What truth?"

He pulled her closer. "You weren't the coward. I was."

"B-because you killed Jack?"

Her anguished confusion twisted like a cold ball deep in his gut. "Because I didn't."

She stilled in his arms. "I saw him."

"I knocked him out and took the draggon stone, then I stood over him for more than ten minutes trying to find the strength to do what I was sent here to do. To kill the Sitheen. The enemy."

"Don't lie to me about this, Kade. *Please.*" Her words showed him her vulnerability as much as any he'd ever heard from her.

"I'm not lying."

A great, hard shudder tore through his body as his mind flayed him with accusations of failure. Not only hadn't he had the strength to carry out the mission he'd been sent to do, a mission that should have been simple for the Punisher. But once he'd failed, he hadn't the courage to admit his failure to Autumn so that she might have been spared her own darkest hour.

What if she'd succeeded? What if he'd been too late to save her? She could have died because of him.

The tension slowly left her body. The quaking ceased

and her breathing turned deep and even. Kaderil held her close as she slept, feeling a deep welling of regret for what he'd put her through, even as he drank of this false closeness like a man too long without water.

For a few short days, she'd been his. Warm and loving, touching him freely and gifting him with her trust and her smiles. For a few short days, he'd understood, for the first time in his life, that the root of true happiness was closeness. Trust. *Love.*

Things he could never have with her now that she knew what he was. Things the Punisher could never have with any woman. But it would be infinitely harder living his solitary life now that he'd seen a glimpse of what he'd been missing.

How had he so lost himself? He was the Punisher. The dark blood. The one feared by all, and had been for centuries. A man without conscience, fulfilling his duties without qualms.

But here, in this place, with this woman, he felt only regret at the things his mission called for him to do. Only relief that he'd failed.

With a fierceness that startled him, he wished the pretense could be the truth. He wished he could be the human, Kade Smith, with Autumn at his side. With Jack and the others, his friends. He'd never had friends before. He'd never realized what pleasure there was in the smiles and simple touches of that kind of acceptance. How hard would it be to go back to fear, now that he knew that warmth?

He was the monster to them now, too. The monster they must try to slay. He never could, nor would, be anything else. Lost in his misery, he clung to Autumn as she slept, storing these moments, these last vestiges of warmth, for the endless loneliness ahead. When she finally stirred, he feared she'd pull away, casting him to the cold. Instead, to his amazed relief, she rolled over and laid her head on his shoulder.

Kaderil lifted a hand to stroke her soft hair that looked like flame, yet felt as cool as water beneath his touch. "You're awake."

"Mmm-hmm. Have you enchanted me?" she asked sleepily.

"No more than you've enchanted me. Why?"

"Because I'm not afraid of you anymore."

Her simple words brought a sweet pressure to his chest. "I've hurt you so many times, yet never once did I mean to. I would never hurt you intentionally."

"I know." Her head tilted until she could see his face. Eyes grave, she asked, "Did you really not kill Jack?"

"No, I didn't kill him."

"Did you mean to?" she asked softly.

"Yes." He tucked her head back against his shoulder, unable to watch her eyes as he explained. "What I told you last night was the truth. I was sent to retrieve the draggon stone and kill the Sitheen who knew of it. When Larsen was shot, I saw the stone hanging around Jack's neck. Last night, at Myrtle's, I knew the time was right to attack."

"You were going to kill him then? When they'd just been reunited?"

He felt a rueful smile tug at his lips. "Would waiting a day or two have been kinder?"

"No." He could almost hear her thinking. "Why didn't you do it?"

"Because of you."

Her arm wrapped around his waist, filling him with such tender affection he feared there would be no room left in his chest for his heart to beat.

"Why?"

He stared at the ceiling, wondering that question himself. "I don't know. I looked in your eyes and I couldn't do it."

"You were struggling with it before you looked at me. That's why you had that terrifying look on your face."

He couldn't deny it. The war inside him had been terrible, his Punisher's mind railing at him to move, but he'd hesitated, unable to bring himself to kill.

"I've never before had difficulty fulfilling my duties."

"Do you kill people a lot?"

"No. Never." He blinked at the simple answer.

"But they sent you here to do that, anyway. To kill the Sitheen."

"Yes. In Esria, they call me the Punisher. When one of the king's subjects fails him in any way, King Rith sends me to mete out the punishment. I break bones— arms, backs, necks—causing as much pain as I can."

"They heal quickly, though, don't they?"

"Within seconds."

"Still, that must be awful for you."

Kaderil grunted. "It's worse for my victims." But her softly spoken words burrowed deep beneath his shields, deep beneath the armor he hadn't even realized he wore. Because it *had* been awful for him. He'd hated the terrified eyes, the screams of fear as he'd grabbed his victims, the feel of bones snapping beneath his hands. Hated the terror his arrival sparked at any gathering.

He hated being the Punisher.

But, as he stared at the bleak expanse of white ceiling above his head, he knew it didn't matter. There was nothing else for him in his world and no place for him in this one.

Autumn's hand slid over his chest and back again in a move that both comforted and aroused. "What's going to happen if you don't kill the Sitheen as you're supposed to? Will you be the one punished?"

"Yes." He lifted her hand and raised the soft underside of her wrist to his lips. The future held no interest for him. Punishment, banishment, remaining the Punisher. They all suddenly felt the same—the same wide expanse of nothing that he'd lived with for fifteen hundred years. Only with Autumn had he ever felt alive.

The difference was, before he met her, he hadn't realized how barren his life had been. He'd been content. But no longer. When he returned without her, he would miss her warmth and her sweetness every day of his excruciatingly long existence.

As his lips moved over her wrist, he felt her shiver.

"Are you cold again?" he asked sharply.

"No." The word held a hint of laughter.

He unbuttoned the cuff of her flannel shirt, pushed it out of his way, and moved his mouth slowly up her inner arm, one lingering kiss at a time, drawing delightful shivers from her with each and every one. When he reached the tender underside of her elbow, he traced its line with his tongue.

"Kade…" She said his name with half a laugh, half a groan, filling him with joy.

He rolled toward her until he hovered over her, searching her gaze for a sign of welcome. The quick dart of her tongue on her lips told him all he needed to know. As his mouth covered hers, that tongue traced his lips and his heart swelled until he thought it was going to explode. The emotion struggling to get out went beyond joy, beyond caring, far beyond anything he'd ever known or ever imagined. It filled all the hollows, drove out the dark, sang in places that had only ever known silence.

Was this what the humans called love? Was this the reason some few Esri were willing to forsake all others for an eternity? He hadn't believed anyone could feel such depth of emotion for another. He hadn't believed such feeling existed. Yet it surged through his blood, transforming him.

Love. After fifteen hundred years, he'd fallen in love. With a human, Autumn McGinn. A woman who could never be his.

The bittersweetness of the moment filled him with such desolate longing that his eyes turned hot. The ache in his heart went almost beyond bearing. With everything he was, everything he would ever be, he wanted her.

Autumn pulled back, turning her face from his kiss. "Kade. I can't. I'm sorry. I just…can't."

She didn't have to explain. He understood all too well.

He rolled away from her, covering his eyes with his arm.

She couldn't forget what he was. *Esri.* A monster.

He had to let her go. As soon as the last of the power

stones arrived in her mail, he would release her into
Jack's protection. But not before. If he let her go now,
he'd never get that last stone. And he had to have it. That
much he could do for his king and his world. That much
he *must* do. Or he would truly have no place at all.

The ring of the doorbell made him stiffen, then bolt
upright.

Autumn rose more slowly. "Who do you think it is?"
Their gazes met, eyes wide.

"I don't know, but it can't be good." He looked into
the face that would haunt his dreams for thousands of
years and felt his heart clutch with fear. He grabbed her
chin and kissed her hard, then released her. "Hide,
Autumn. Don't come out, no matter what."

She grabbed his arm as he pulled away. "Be careful."

Her tender concern sang through his veins. "Hide."

Kaderil strode through the living room, his pulse
hammering in his chest. Either the Sitheen had found
him or Zander had decided to check up on him. Zander
worried him more. His hatred of the humans was spin-
ning out of control. If he found Autumn...

Kaderil took a deep breath and wrenched open the door.

Zander stood in the doorway, his white hair brushing
the top of his silver tunic, his face hard. He pushed past
Kaderil and strode into the apartment.

"Ustanis says you have the draggon stone. He felt the
transfer of possession. He also traced three of the lesser
stones to you."

Zander's nose lifted, his eyes narrowing with suspi-
cion. "I smell power. Other than yours. An oddly weak
power, yet something."

Kaderil's pulse leaped. Clearly Autumn had acquired enough power during their lovemaking for Zander to sense. She was in grave danger.

As Zander started toward the bedroom, Kaderil stepped in front of him, blocking his path. "Leave her alone."

Zander cocked his head, his eyes widening. He started to laugh. "You dipped a virgin well with your heart open and leaked power to her, didn't you?" His eyes glittered with a triumph Kaderil didn't understand. "The dark blood has fallen at last."

Zander thrust out a hand as he moved to step around him. Kaderil grabbed his wrist, keeping that deadly palm away from him and immobilized.

"I'll break it."

"Your breaking my bones won't stop me, Punisher. It never has. I'll have what I want and we both know it."

Zander tried to catch him with his other hand, but Kaderil caught the second wrist, as well. "She's nothing to do with you."

"There you're wrong, dark blood." Zander struggled against his hold. "She's the means to my revenge."

Kaderil stared at his captain, uncomprehending as he fought to keep those vicious hands controlled. "What revenge?" They'd been enemies for as long as he could remember, but the true hatred was Zander's and had always been. Bigotry, as the humans called it, toward Kaderil's dark blood. At least he'd always thought that the cause of Zander's hatred.

Zander's mouth curved in a grimace as he fought to free his hands. "Her life is mine to destroy."

The words were followed by the sound of someone

stumbling in the bedroom, then a crash as something breakable hit the floor.

Autumn.

That moment's distraction cost him his edge. Zander's fingers brushed his flesh, sending pain shooting through his arm.

"Give me the stones, Kaderil."

The draggon stone was around his neck, but the other three were in Autumn's purse in the bedroom and he wasn't letting Zander near her. He must get the upper hand. Using every ounce of strength he possessed, he pushed the man's wrists together, grabbed them with one hand, then broke both Zander's arms over his knee.

Zander cried out, but Kaderil kept hold of him as he felt the bones reknit beneath his palms.

"I'm not giving you the stones, Zander. Rith tasked me with bringing the draggon stone to him, and I've already told Ustanis I'll bring the lesser stones to the gate."

"That's not…good enough," Zander hissed between clenched teeth. "I want them now. All of them."

"You still question my loyalty?"

A strange light leaped in Zander's eyes even as he laughed. "You break the arms of your captain, dark blood. What kind of loyalty is that?"

"You threaten a woman who is not Sitheen."

"A woman who is *human.* Of no account except that she has somehow caught your lust. But she is of less import to me than the stones. I will have them, Punisher, make no mistake. And I'll have them now."

"No. They're of no use to you."

"That's where you're wrong. I have great use for them."

Kaderil stared at him, watching the light of excitement in his captain's eyes. "What do you mean?"

"Scenters often possess some small ability to call the power from the stones. Ustanis is such a one."

"So do you intend to use them to kill more humans?"

Zander smiled, the pain gone from his eyes, no longer struggling in Kaderil's hold. "Killing humans is always a worthy goal."

"You're wasting life, Zander. King Rith would not condone such slaughter, even of humans."

Zander's smile turned ugly. "You know Rith so well, do you? Do you think he covets the seven stones so that he can renew the natural power of Esria? Don't be a fool, dark blood. Rith is a Caller."

A chill slid down Kaderil's spine. "The Callers are no more." Only a Caller could raise the true power of the seven stones, a terrible and destructive power in the wrong hands, but the last was destroyed eons ago after a brief reign of terror that had left half of Esria dead.

"Wrong again, Punisher. Rith is a Caller and one of the strongest ever to rise. He has kept his gift a secret. But now that the stones have been found and are all but reclaimed, he will rise as the true ruler."

Kaderil stared at him with confusion and a deep sense of foreboding. "He already rules Esria. What more can he do?"

Zander's smile was vicious. "With the power he raises from the stones, he'll break down the very walls between these two realms. Gates will no longer be needed, for the Esri will move freely from our world to this without fear. The entire human race will be enchanted—or dead—and completely at our command. King Rith shall reign supreme. In both worlds."

The wrongness shook Kaderil. "He has no right to this world."

"Don't be a fool, dark blood. Our vast superiority gives us every right." With a quick, sudden move, Zander twisted his hands and grasped Kaderil's wrists, catching Kaderil off guard.

Fire poured through his body. Kaderil tried to yank his arms out of his captain's grip, but the pain debilitated him.

"Every right to seek out humans and destroy them where they stand," Zander continued. "Beginning with your female."

Kaderil's vision began to swim. He had to protect Autumn. He had to protect her world.

Terrible thoughts rolled and crashed in his brain. He'd known King Rith was not the most benevolent ruler Esria had ever seen, but he'd not suspected the man capable of such greed, such destruction. Yet he couldn't deny the avarice he'd seen in his ruler's eyes at the talk of the lost gate's discovery. Deep in his gut, he knew Zander spoke the truth. King Rith would use the seven stones to destroy the human world.

For centuries he'd been ashamed of the human blood that ran through his veins. In a shift that shook the very foundations of his existence, he realized it wasn't his human blood he was ashamed of, it wasn't his human side that didn't fit.

It was his Esri side.

With a massive surge of determined strength, he

wrenched free of Zander's grasp and clamped on to his captain's wrists, immobilizing him.

"You'll not get the stones." Kaderil's voice sounded raw and winded to his ears, but fury burned through his muscles, lending him strength. He whipped around, lifting Zander off his feet until he was flying in an arc around him. Then he released his foe, sending Zander crashing through the window in an explosion of shattering glass.

The Esri was gone.

As he stared at the destroyed window, he heard Autumn behind him. He turned to find her standing in the bedroom doorway, her eyes as wide as the full Earth moon.

"We're on the fifth floor," she gasped.

Kaderil sucked air into his lungs, reeling from the onslaught of terrible understanding. With an effort, he shook off the debilitating shock. He had to get Autumn to safety.

"That gives us about five minutes before he's completely healed. Get your keys and your purse. We've got to get out of here."

Autumn disappeared into the bedroom to emerge a moment later with her purse. "You threw your own man out the window? Is he going to forgive you for that?"

"No. He'll know what it means."

"What's that?"

"That I've turned traitor."

Chapter 14

"The stairs," Kade gasped. "Faster."

Autumn stared at him, at the way he was nearly bent over with pain after whatever that Esri colleague of his had done to him. "Not the way you're feeling."

"I'll...be fine. Soon."

"We're taking the elevator. You said we have five minutes before he heals from that five-story fall and comes after us. Hopefully the elevator won't take *that* long."

Inch by inch, Kade straightened, the look of pain sliding from his face. "I'm healed well enough. The elevator takes too long." He took her hand. "Come on."

"Kade...I'm in flip-flops!"

But he tugged her to the stairwell without breaking stride. He ushered her through the door, then bent over, pushing his butt into her hips.

She looked at him in disbelief. "*Excuse* me?"

"Climb on."

"Oh. You're kidding."

"Autumn."

"Okay, okay." Feeling suddenly like a little girl again, she climbed onto his back and flung her arms around his neck. "Are you sure about this?"

"I've got speed and strength. They've got to be good for something."

"Yeah, but you're injured."

As he leaped down the entire first flight, Autumn squealed, locked her legs around his waist and ducked her head. He was going to kill them. But the landing wasn't nearly as bad as she'd expected.

"I heard what he said about the walls between the worlds being torn down," she said into his shoulder. "Can they do that? Take us over like that?"

"Unfortunately, yes. But not without the stones. And I'm going to get them first."

Her chin hit his shoulder blade at the next landing, clacking her teeth together. "What do you mean?" she asked, when she could get the words out.

"I'm not going to let it happen. Princess Ilaria was right to give the stones to the humans. She may have known Rith was dangerous."

"So you're going to try to get the two stones your guys already have?"

"Yes. And they're not my guys. Not anymore."

"Do we need them all? We have four of the seven and there's one more coming in the mail if we can get it first."

"For Rith to take over this world, he needs all seven stones. But to cause other damage, no. A power wielder with a streak of greed or malice is the most dangerous creature in either world. If it suited him, he could call enough power from a single stone to make the entire population of this city walk into the Potomac River and drown themselves. Imagine how long the Sitheen will last against that kind of power. How long *any* of us will last."

Autumn shuddered. "Not long."

"No. And once the resistance is eliminated, he'll have his seven stones."

Finally, Kade landed for the last time and Autumn slipped off his back. He pushed her behind him and eased out into the lobby.

"Any sign of him?" she asked.

"No. Let's go."

Autumn slipped off her flip-flops, picked them up and ran for the car she'd had to park in the public parking garage down the street. She remembered driving up to this building last night when she still believed in fairy-tale princes and love-at-almost-first-sight. As she ran down the street at a speed too fast to credit, Kade grabbed her hand and pulled her closer. And she wondered if maybe she still believed.

They ducked into the dimly lit garage and ran up the first ramp to where she'd parked her car.

"Autumn!" The shout came from behind. "Run! Get away from him!"

Jack. They were here to rescue her.

They were here to kill Kade.

She pressed the button on her key fob to unlock the car.

"Go with them, Autumn," Kade said as she wrenched open the driver's door. "You'll be safer."

"No. Get in the car."

"I'll run. I can escape them easily."

"They're blocking the exit. Get in the car!" Slowly Kade joined her.

She started the ignition and threw the car into Reverse.

"I could make you go with them."

Autumn slammed on the brakes and turned on him. "If you ever use your power on me like that again, it's over, Kade."

"Autumn!" Jack's voice rang out, nearer.

"Hells bells. They probably think you've enchanted me." She hit the gas, shooting the car backward, out of the space, then headed for the exit, praying Jack didn't have cops following him with cruisers to block the exit.

"Autumn, you need to go with them. I'll run."

"And what if they catch you? What if Zander catches you?"

"I'm faster than all of them. I'm probably safer on foot than in this car that can be stopped and surrounded."

"Oh…stop it! You're right. I know you're right, but I'm not losing you again." She squealed the tires around the corner.

"You've never lost me. You'll never lose me unless you want to."

Her heart swelled at his words, her eyes burning even as she saw Jack and Harrison blocking her escape. If she stopped, Kade was dead. She honked the horn and stepped on the gas.

"Autumn, you'll kill them!"

"No chance. They're not expecting me to stop. They think I'm enchanted, remember?"

Harrison moved, but Jack held his ground. "Dammit." She laid on the horn. Finally, at the last second, Jack dove out of the way. "He expected me to stop."

"He doesn't know I'm Esri."

Kade's words startled her as she crashed through the gate arm. The midday sun blinded her as she roared onto the street, nearly sideswiping a trash truck.

"You attacked him."

"I hit him from behind. I used no magic. He doesn't know I'm Esri."

"He thinks you're just a thief?"

"Yes."

"I don't know if that's a good thing or a bad thing."

"Nor do I."

But her mind kept moving. "It's a bad thing. He's going to send the cops after us. If he knew you were Esri, he'd keep them away. Cops and Esri have proven to be a dangerous combination." She brushed a lock of hair out of her eyes. "We need to tell him."

"He won't believe you. The voices that advise him told him I'm Sitheen."

"And if he thinks you're Esri, he'll be coming after you with fire and a death chant instead of a gun. We can't win, can we?"

"There's another problem."

She glanced at him. His voice was so calm, so reasonable, she wanted to hit him.

"What?"

"Zander may go after them."

"Do you think he's seen them before?"

"It doesn't matter. He can sense power in others. He'll know there are Sitheen in the area and will go after them."

Chills raced over her skin. "We've got to call Jack. Quick. Get my phone out of my purse."

She hit the speed dial and put the phone to her ear.

"Autumn?" Jack snapped. "What in the hell are you doing?"

"Jack, listen to me. There's an Esri nearby. Kade threw him out a fifth-story window, but they heal fast."

"Autumn, Kade stole the draggon stone. Get away from him. He's dangerous."

"Jack, *listen.* You're in grave danger. That Esri can sense power, even the little bit that a Sitheen has. He hunts Sitheen. He probably already knows you're there. Get out of there!"

"Autumn…"

"'Bye, Jack." She snapped the phone closed and glanced at Kade. "We've got to get out of here before someone comes after us." She made a right turn but got caught behind half a dozen cars at the light at the end of the block. If someone did come after them, what was she going to do? She couldn't run a red light. She couldn't even reach the red light through all the traffic to run it!

"Where are we going?" Autumn asked.

"The marina. We need to get that last stone before Ustanis does and get your lead box so maybe he won't be able to sense them."

"But Zander can follow us, right? He can sense your power?"

"*Our* power. Apparently you've acquired some of your

own. And, yes, he can sense it, but only if he's close. He can't follow the scent the way Ustanis can the stones."

"Okay. The marina it is." But a flash of light in her rearview mirror caught her eye, sending her stomach into spasms. Two police cars a couple of blocks back.

"Cops. Oh, Jack, you didn't."

"Go faster."

"I can't outrun cops! I can't even figure out how to run a red light!"

"Autumn, I can't allow them to catch me. If they're wearing holly, I won't be able to control them and I'm not that much stronger than humans. I'll get stuck in one of your jails with no ability to escape. The full moon is tomorrow night. I must get those stones from Ustanis before then."

She knew he was right. And if the cops called Jack and he had finally figured out Kade was Esri, he'd kill him. "Okay, I'll try to lose the cops." But even as she was wondering how in the heck she was supposed to do that, the sound of sirens ahead made the question moot. The light turned green and no one moved as two more patrol cars, lights flashing, sirens wailing, blocked the intersection in front of them.

"We're trapped." Autumn's heart sank as she turned to Kade. "You've got to get away. *Now,* while you still have a chance."

His expression grim, he shook his head. "I'm not leaving you here alone. Zander's still nearby. We're going to have to run." Tension radiated through Kade's muscles. He thought of himself as Kade, now. If only he'd run in the parking garage and sent Autumn to pick up Jack and Charlie. She wouldn't be trapped with him now, surrounded by police. With guns.

The thought of the damage one of those weapons could do to her made his blood run cold. He couldn't allow her to get harmed, but neither could he risk getting captured himself, or her world was doomed.

He wrenched the door open. "Grab your purse. We've got to get out of here." He took her hand and they ran between the stopped cars for the curb as the cars behind them set up a wild honking.

"Police! Freeze!" The shouts came from the cops in front. The sirens continued to wail behind them. Escape in either direction was cut off and there were no breaks between buildings along the entire block. They were going to have to go through one of the shops. He ran for the closest one, an antique store.

"Hi!" Autumn called as the proprietor stared. "Just passing through!" They ran through the back and out the door into an alley. The alley opened onto a side street that led straight back, away from the cops chasing them from either side.

"We're faster. They won't be able to catch us on foot." Autumn's voice rang with an excited tension that had him looking at her with surprise and admiration.

"Yes, but they're in cars. We've got to get off the street."

The sirens were indeed getting closer again. They entered another alley behind a row of stores. One door, from which wafted the smells of food, stood open.

"This way!" They ducked into the back of a Chinese restaurant, nearly knocking over a small, dark-haired human. Kade grabbed the man's neck and said in Mandarin, "You will hide us and tell no one we're here."

He let go and the man bowed and motioned him to follow. Unfortunately, he led them right through the middle of a busy kitchen full of steaming pots and curious workers. He might have controlled the one, but he could not control them all. He had to touch them to control them and the minute he started grabbing for them, others would escape. No, he would have to hope the first held sway with the others. If not, they were in trouble.

The smaller man opened the door to a small, crowded, unlit storage closet and ushered them inside. Kade again touched his neck. "You will command the others to tell no one we're here. Not even the police. The fate of the world is at stake."

Again, the man bowed and backed out of the closet, closing the door.

Kade tried to move and kicked a large heavy can.

"It's a little tight," Autumn whispered at his back. "What did you tell him? And how did you learn Chinese? For that matter, how did you learn English?"

He blinked, having to think about it as he turned and pulled her against him. "I don't learn language. I understand the words spoken and use the language of the speaker. Or in this case, of the one I'm controlling. It's not intentional. It just happens."

"Another of your Esri gifts?"

"It would seem so. I believe all Esri have the ability."

She slid her arms around his waist and pressed her head to his shoulder. "What are we going to do?"

"If we're not captured?" He'd actually been giving

this some thought as he ran, terrified a bullet would find her. "We'll go back to the houseboat, get your lead-lined box and see if that last stone arrived in your mail. Then I'm taking you and the stones to Jack."

She stiffened in his arms. "Why?" He heard the well of hurt in that single word.

"Because I have to go after Ustanis to get the stones, and Ustanis is often with Zander. I've put you in too much danger already. I won't take you into a situation where you will almost certainly die."

He felt her sigh and heard the soft expelling of air. "I guess. But what if we need to raise our power again?"

"Raising the power hurts you. No, you'll be safest with Jack." And she'd stay that way only if he could get the stones from Ustanis and keep them out of King Rith's hands. Unfortunately, Ustanis now knew the Punisher could be bested. If he fought him—and he almost certainly would—Kade feared he, himself, would lose.

The sounds outside the door changed. A shout. A command. Autumn turned rigid within his arms.

"Cops," she whispered.

He released her and turned toward the door, pushing her behind him, his pulse leaping. But the Chinese-restaurant owner protected them and the door never opened. His pulse began to slow and the tension drained from his muscles.

"How long do you think we should wait?" Autumn asked. "No, this is my world. I'm the one who should know the answer to questions like that. The cops will be searching for us all up and down this block. We'd better stay put for a while. Maybe until dark."

Kade nodded. "I was thinking the same thing."

They stood in silence for what seemed like hours. Behind him, Autumn began to fidget.

"Tell me about your world, Kade. Is it so different from this one?"

"Yes." She slid her arms around him from behind and he covered her hands, holding her even as she held him. Whatever came of his life, he would never forget these moments, chased by those from both worlds, yet less alone than he'd ever been in his life. They were in the most dire of circumstances, yet never had he felt happier. Autumn believed in him. She trusted him, even knowing what he was. This was the greatest gift anyone had ever given him.

He stroked her hand. "Yes, my world is different. There's no sun in the sky, no clouds that fill with rain, no wind."

"Is it *underground?*"

"No. We have trees and grass, animals and people, as you do. Small creeks and streams, though no great bodies of water. I'd heard legends of the human realm, of the sun and the moon, the rain and snow, and they seemed too fantastic to be real."

She chuckled silently against his back. "It sounds so funny to hear you put it like that. Tell me more."

He thought of the land he knew so well and what he could share of it that might make it a little more real to her. "Our world is far smaller than yours, though I've never seen all of it. Some parts are forbidden. Others are to be avoided."

"Like that place where the princess is held?"

"The Forest of Nightmares. Definitely that place."

She lifted her fingers, sliding them between his in a sensual move that made him wish he could be certain they wouldn't be interrupted.

"Do you have family in Esria?"

"No."

"But...you're immortal. Don't immortals have parents?"

He chuckled, but there was no humor in it. "I had parents. I just never knew them or knew what happened to them."

"They abandoned you?"

"I don't know. Babies are rare in my world and are usually met with great joy. Why I wasn't, I can guess readily enough."

"Why?" Her tone was soft and kind.

"My dark blood made me something of an outcast. No mother would have welcomed such a son."

"You don't have the same magic they have, do you?"

"No. I have little true power. I quickly learned to use my size, my looks and my physical strength to keep others at bay. I taught them to fear me. Those who fear me give me a wide berth."

"So making them fear you kept you safe."

"Yes. But Zander knows the truth. He doesn't fear me. He has, in fact, always hated me. His mate was killed by humans in the days before the gates were sealed. He's never forgiven the humans. I think he's waited fifteen centuries for his revenge."

"That's why he's killing so many."

"Yes."

He felt her cheek press against his shoulder. "I'm sorry. Your life must have been very hard."

"I found a place. And a reason." And then lost them here, in this world. He could not go back to being the Punisher, even if King Rith allowed him to. He could not go back to driving fear into other's eyes after knowing such warmth.

Her cheek rubbed back and forth against his leather jacket. "Can I ask you something?"

"Anything."

"How old *are* you?"

He chuckled for real this time. "Older than you."

He knew she smiled. "Is that a terribly rude question?"

"No. I just hesitate to tell you when I know it'll only make me seem more strange."

"I know you're immortal. I know Zander and Princess Ilaria are more than fifteen hundred years old. Are you, too?"

He pressed his lips together, knowing how different it would make him seem to her. But he knew, somehow, it would be okay. She would accept it as she accepted him—a thought he wasn't sure he'd ever get used to.

"Yes. I was born shortly before the sealing of the gates."

"Wow. Was Tarrys right, then? Do you still have thousands of years left to go?"

"Yes." But the thought brought no happiness. Thousands of years to remember these few days, these few moments. Thousands of years to miss the one light in his life.

His one love.

* * *

Autumn shifted from foot to foot within the small, dark closet. She was afraid to move out of her tiny space for fear she'd knock something down or fall over one of the myriad cans of food. She rifled through her purse in the dark and found her phone, checking the time.

"It's been almost two hours, Kade. It should be dark by now. Even if they're still out there, we can lose them in the dark."

He said nothing, but after shielding her for two hours he turned and pulled her into his arms, kissing her with a restless passion that instantly heated her blood. Their mouths opened as one, their tongues colliding and sliding over one another as desire flowed thick and hot through her stiff body. Even after standing against him for two hours, the feel of his hands on her shoulders and the taste of his kiss overpowered her senses.

She would never get enough of him and realized, in that instant, that she still loved him. Human or Esri didn't seem to matter. He was Kade.

As they pulled apart, she stopped him from turning back to the door. "When you said you'd turned traitor… does that mean you'll stay here?" The hope filled her so completely she was afraid to hear his answer.

His hands found her face and he kissed her again, a sweet, sad kiss. "No, I can't stay here. I may not approve of my king's plans for your world, but Esria is my home and I must return there tomorrow night, no matter what happens."

Her heart ached at his words. "I wish you'd stay."

"We couldn't be together even if I did. The Sitheen can't

allow an Esri to remain in this world, Autumn. You understand that. And I won't condemn you to a life of running."

"But you're not like the other Esri."

He kissed her again, slowly and thoroughly. "I can't stay."

Her heart ached, tears stinging her eyes, but she refused to beg. He was right. This wasn't his world, as much as she wished it were.

"I suppose we'd better get going," she said, sighing. "Let's go out through the front. If we sneak out the back, we'll look like fugitives."

"And if they're waiting for us in front?"

"They we'll run." The prospect made her pulse skitter.

Kade nodded. "Let me go first. We'll attract less attention apart than together. If the police catch me, don't try to escape them. Go with them and have them call Jack."

The knot of tension in her stomach was making her nauseous. "I don't like this."

"I know. If you don't hear a commotion, come on out. Walk to the Metro station. I'll be a short distance behind you, protecting you."

Autumn felt the warmth of that knowledge ease the edges of her fear. "Okay. We'll head for the Metro." A sudden thought had her digging through her purse. "I've got half a dozen fare cards in here somewhere and I think they all have enough money on them for this trip." She came up with one and handed it to him.

Kade kissed her one more time, then turned and eased the door open a crack. Apparently satisfied, he took her hand and pulled her after him.

"Wait here," he said, just inside the kitchen door.

The restaurant workers ignored her as if they didn't even see her. When no commotion erupted, she left the restaurant, feigning a calm unhurriedness at total odds with the chaos of her pulse. The sun had set while they waited in the closet and, if there were any cops looking for them, she never saw them as she strolled down the busy sidewalk to the Metro station. With a sigh of relief, she ducked inside to take the long escalator ride down.

She'd always attracted attention for the wrong reasons. Now, she tried her best to appear small and forgettable as she watched for police. There was an odd comfort in knowing she was being followed, her every move tracked by the man who'd stolen her heart. Her mind shied from the knowledge that a little over a day from now he'd be gone where she could never follow.

How could she have fallen in love so quickly? So thoroughly? And to the one person she could never, *ever* spend her life with?

She switched trains in L'Enfant Plaza, then took the green line down to the waterfront. Kade got on the same train, but sat in the back of her car, lending her the strength and comfort of his presence.

When they reached their destination, they left the train from different doors, then moved separately through the crowd along the platform in the cavernous, space-age-like tunnel. The crush of people remained thick as business travelers headed home for the night.

Autumn took the escalator to the main floor, but as she shoved her fare card into the turnstile slot, Kade caught her eye as he silently passed her in an adjacent line. He wanted to go first this time. She knew why.

Everyone after them—cops, Esri and Sitheen—knew she'd been staying at the houseboat. Anyone could be waiting for them here.

With each foot the escalator rose, her pulse pounded harder. Fear tasted dry in her mouth. She had a sudden and overwhelming desire to tell Kade he was right. This was all too dangerous and all she wanted to do was head to the airport to catch the next flight to nowhere.

Her hand clenched the escalator's rail as her heart thudded in her chest. If she left now, she'd never see Kade again. And that scared her most of all.

The chill air raked at her face as the escalator climbed to street level. Ahead of her, Kade stepped off and walked briskly toward the entrance as if his only concern were getting home in time for dinner.

Autumn forced herself to breath as the escalator neared the top of its ascent. Two steps left. One.

"Police! Put your hands up!"

Autumn froze, her blood turning to ice as she stumbled off the escalator. People scattered, giving her a clear view of the two uniformed cops approaching Kade from either side, guns drawn. They couldn't hurt him. Bullets couldn't hurt him. But even as her mind chanted the words, her throat closed with fear.

Kade calmly raised his hands.

Autumn eased to the exit with the surging crowd trying to escape before they caught sight of the red beacon of her hair. Kade would get away. She had to do the same.

She hunched over, trying to minimize her height. Nearly to the entrance, she hazarded a glance up and caught the gaze of yet another cop. She knew the moment he recognized her.

His gun raised to her face. "Hands up! I've got her!"

Hells bells.

Autumn raised her hands, staring down the barrel of the gun as cold sweat broke out on her scalp. *Get away, Kade.* He was the one that was important. Not her.

"Turn around and put your hands against the wall."

She did, quaking with fear as she waited for her arms to be handcuffed.

"Release her." A man's voice. Not Kade's.

Autumn turned her head to glance over her shoulder...and froze. The cop was standing as still as stone while another man reached for her—a man as white as snow. Terror raked sharp claws through her heart as she recognized the Esri who'd tried to attack her in the houseboat. Kade's nemesis.

Zander.

Chapter 15

Kade watched in cold terror as Zander reached for Autumn. He'd thought to submit to the two police, luring them close enough for him to touch and control. But at the sight of Zander, all he could think of was getting to Autumn before Zander stole her life. He struggled to escape the cops' hold, but one shot him with a Taser that roared through his body like Zander's hand of fire. When his head cleared, he was on his knees, the cuffs snapping behind his back, his wrists bound.

With a roar of rage born of fear for Autumn, he surged to his feet and flexed his arms to rip the cuffs apart. But nothing happened. He wasn't strong enough.

As his gaze wrenched to Autumn, he saw Zander's hand land on the head of the cop who was getting ready to cuff her. The cop pulled out his gun.

"The draggon stone for your lady, Kaderil!"

Kade again tried to lunge but felt an answering blow to the back of his head that nearly drove him to his knees, but he stayed standing and grabbed the arm of one of the cops. "Release me."

The second blow did drive him to his knees.

Sweet Esria. His power was gone. The virgin's power had already waned.

He had to get to Autumn.

The sound of gunfire exploded in the escalator tunnel. Screams rent the air. One of the bullets pierced his forehead, burning, but he barely noticed it as he struggled to escape the cops' hold and go after Autumn. She wasn't on the floor, thank the spirits. She wasn't there at all. And he could only feel relief that Zander hadn't already killed her, though he knew if he didn't reach her soon, she was as good as dead.

He felt the bullet ease out of his forehead and watched as it fell past his eyes.

"Holy shit!" The cop who'd hit him stared at him in horror.

The second cop fell at his feet, shot, drawing the other's attention from him. Kade ran for the exit. He had to reach Autumn before Zander destroyed her.

Outside was chaos as humans scattered into the night, running from the violence. Though he ran, his speed was hampered by his hands being cuffed behind his back. He ducked into the shadows and bent over, sliding his bound hands behind his hips and knees. He had to roll on the ground to ease his feet through the circle of his arms, but he finally succeeded in moving his bound hands to the front, and lunged to his feet.

As he ran, Kade tried over and over to break the cuffs, to no avail. His newfound power was truly gone. Just when Autumn needed him most. Fear for her pounded through his body.

By the time he reached the marina, he was sweating and terrified he was already too late. Terrified he wouldn't find them on the boat at all. But as he raced down the dock, he knew he'd guessed right.

A sight met his eyes at once glorious and terrible. Autumn stood in perfect balance upon the back rail of the houseboat, silhouetted against the nearly full moon, in nothing but her sweatpants and a lacey bra, her unbound hair lifting in the breeze. The woman herself was glorious, but her perch, a hair's breadth from the water, terrified him. Clearly, she was enchanted. His sweet Autumn could never maintain such a balance on her own.

He lunged onto the boat. "What have you done to her?"

Zander blocked his path. "What do you think?"

Ustanis had never fully lost his fear of the Punisher. He ducked his white head then looked up. "She's not been touched, Punisher, by either of us. There wasn't time."

Zander waved Ustanis to silence, his face in shadows. "One word from me and she falls into the river, Malcolm. To sink. To drown."

Kade's eyes narrowed. "Why do you call me Malcolm?"

"Malcolm was the human who killed my mate, my Pensia. In the moonlight, you could be him again. I never killed him. I've rued that fact for fifteen hundred years." Zander thrust out his pale white hand. "Give me the draggon stone, Punisher, or she dies."

Kade's palms began to sweat at the impossible choice before him. Handing over the draggon stone to King Rith's man could destroy her world. Not handing it over would destroy the woman herself. The woman he loved.

"Call her down, Zander. I'm not giving it to you until you do."

"No, Punisher. I would enjoy nothing more than to end her as my Pensia was ended. But I won't. Unless you refuse to give me the draggon stone."

"I had nothing to do with the death of your mate, Zander. I was an infant."

"Give me the draggon stone!"

He didn't trust Zander. As soon as he handed him the stone, he had little doubt Zander would push her into the water. But he would go after her. He'd find a way to save her. He must.

Kade lifted the draggon stone from around his neck and tossed it to Zander. He rushed for Autumn, terrified she would fall into that dark water before he caught her. But Zander was surprisingly true to his word. With hands still cuffed, Kade pulled her toward him. Her skin was cold to the touch. She collapsed against him in a dead faint and he lowered her to the ground.

Behind him, Ustanis began to chant. A sudden snap of magic burned over Kade's skin. In a perfect circle around him, six green stones began to glow.

Dread balled in his gut. "You found the last stone."

"Ustanis found it in the marina office."

"What are you doing? What magic is this?"

Zander smiled, his white teeth glowing in the moonlight. "One of the black chants, Punisher. The black magic accessible only through the seven stones." His expression turned hard. "For a millennia and a half you've wondered why I didn't reveal your secret. It was because if I had, others would have challenged you. Destroyed your reputation, Punisher. Eventually, you'd have been banished and lost to me and I couldn't have that. I have been waiting for the perfect revenge. And for that, you had to fall in love, Malcolm."

"I'm not Malcolm!" Kade laid Autumn on the deck and lunged for Zander, but he hit a wall as solid as any he'd ever encountered. "What have you done?"

"Have you never heard of a shadow cage?"

Kade's blood went cold.

"I said I wouldn't take her from you, Punisher and I won't. Ever. She will be with you for all eternity. It's nearly complete, is it not, Ustanis?"

"Aye, my captain. Forgive me, Punisher. This was not my choice."

Kade pounded at the invisible walls. "Zander, no." Shadow cages were once used as prisons in Esria. Horrific prisons. "She won't survive without food and water."

Zander ignored his plea. "When it's done, we'll drop it into the water to settle on the bottom of the river. You will spend eternity alone with your lady."

"She'll *die*," he growled.

"Of course. And when we're through here, we'll take the stones to the gate and open it. At midnight tonight."

Kade stared at him. "The full moon is not until tomorrow."

"Another power of the seven stones in the hands of one who can use it. By opening the gate tonight, there will be no Sitheen to stop us. King Rith will have his stones and, when next we return to this world, 'twill be as conquerors."

"It is done, Zander," Ustanis said. He placed his hands against the cage.

Zander stepped forward until he was nearly nose to nose with Kade, and placed his hands against the cage's walls. "Goodbye, dark blood."

And suddenly the cage was levitating. Kade turned and dove for Autumn, laying atop her to brace her as the cage magically lifted over the boat's rail and dropped into the cold river. They hit the water with a jarring thud, then sank slowly, rocking from side to side until they settled on the river bottom.

The dark forms of fish moved past as the dock lights and the moon glowed distantly from above. He held Autumn's sleeping form against him and knew the darkest despair of his life. They were trapped, doomed to spend the rest of their respective lives in this dark abyss. Autumn's would end quickly without sustenance. A few days and she would be gone, while he would linger here for thousands of years, his only company the remains of his one brief love.

A magic cage could not be breached except by the most powerful of magic. A magic he'd never possessed even when he and Autumn were at their strongest.

He'd risked all to save Autumn and her world.

And failed.

* * *

Kade held Autumn's shivering, unconscious body tightly against him, within the circle of his bound arms, as the fury that rode him slowly turned to desolation. Autumn was doomed. He couldn't save her. Yet how was he supposed to watch her die? His heart twisted with a regret so deep he feared his soul would begin to bleed.

Time was impossible to guess, but he suspected a couple of hours had passed when he finally felt her begin to stir.

"Kade?" Autumn's voice was tight with cold and she gave a hard shiver. "Where are we?"

He wasn't sure how he could tell her. Instead, he pulled her closer, wrapping his open jacket around her shoulders as far as it would go. "How are you feeling?"

"I'm...*freezing*." She wiggled her bottom against his groin as she tried to press herself closer to his warmth. Her arms moved, and she gasped, clearly realizing her upper body was nearly bare. "My clothes..."

Kade rubbed his cheek against her hair, his misery sharp enough to cut. "Zander stole them while you were enchanted."

She went rigid against him.

"He didn't hurt you, sweet one. Ustanis told me as much, and he had no reason to lie. Besides, they had no time for such mischief. It was a ploy to make you appear more vulnerable. A ploy to get the draggon stone from me."

"Did it work?"

"Too well. I'm sorry you're cold. I would have given you my clothes, but I can't get out of the shirt and jacket.

I'm still wearing the handcuffs. The best I could do was open my coat and pull you inside with me."

"What happened?" She looked up at the ceiling of the cage as if trying to make sense of where they were. He followed her gaze to the dock lights flickering high above. As he watched, the dark shape of a fish obscured first one light then another.

"We're underwater!" she gasped.

"Yes."

"But...I'm breathing. And it's dry. I don't understand."

"Magic." He spat the word with all the hatred he'd ever held for Zander and those who used, and abused, that fine power.

"Are we stuck?"

He didn't answer, *couldn't* answer. Instead, he pulled her tighter against him.

"Kade, tell me what's happened."

"I couldn't let him harm you." He shuddered, but knew he couldn't keep the truth from her. He owed her that much. His palm stroked the chilled flesh of her bare arm. "It's called a shadow cage. One of the dark magics the power stones are capable of."

"Are we really underwater?"

"Yes, but you don't have to worry about breathing. We can't run out of air."

"Oh. I hadn't thought about that. How do we get out?"

He couldn't bring himself to utter the words, but he didn't need to. She understood.

"We don't, do we?" There was no fear in her words. No panic. And he suspected it was too soon for her to fully comprehend the utter bleakness of their situation.

That was just as well. He understood their situation all too well and wished he didn't.

"How did we get in the water?"

"Zander. He has the stones."

"*All* of them?"

"Yes. Ustanis used them to build this cage." He would use them to open the gate tonight. But she didn't need to know that. Let her think her friends would stop the Esri during tomorrow's full moon. Let her think her world would survive. If only…

A harsh breath escaped his lungs. "I shouldn't have let you come with me. I should have sent you away, far from this city where you couldn't be touched by Zander's hatred."

He felt her pull away, then twist in his arms until her soft breasts pressed against his chest. Her arms wrapped tightly around him, at once easing and intensifying his pain.

"This isn't your fault, Kade. I saw Zander in the Metro station. I knew we were in trouble." She rubbed his back with her palm. "He won't leave you behind, will he? Won't people come looking for you?"

There would be no one to seek him out even if it were possible. "A shadow cage deflects magic. No one would find it unless they specifically looked for it. And, yes, Zander will most happily leave me behind. He's somehow convinced himself that I'm the human who killed his mate. He can't kill me, or he could never go home. Ending the existence of another Esri is strictly forbidden. But he found the perfect revenge."

"You can live without food and water?"

"Not pleasantly. But, yes, I can live."

"But I can't." A hard shudder went through her. "There's got to be something we can do. What if we tried to raise the power again?"

"The power is gone, Autumn. I tried to control the cops who cuffed me, and I failed."

"They were probably wearing holly. Jack's got the whole force wearing it even though most of them don't know why."

"Even so, I'm not as strong. I can feel the difference."

"Can't we at least try? I mean, *really,* what else do we have to do?"

He stroked her soft hair, hearing the hope in her words and knowing it wouldn't last. His brave, determined girl.

"Yes. Of course we can try."

"Do we need to sit up?"

"I believe so, yes." Kade lifted his bound arms to his head to release her.

Autumn sat up and wrapped her arms around her chest. "I never thought I'd say this, but I'd welcome a shot of that power about now. Burning from that fire sounds better than freezing to death."

He reached for her and she unfolded her arms and put her hands in his. "How big is this cage?" she asked.

"I explored it briefly before you woke up. Not quite tall enough for me to stand up in, but long enough to lie down."

She shuddered. "You can't spend the rest of your life like this."

He squeezed her hands. "I'm more concerned about *your* life at the moment." He lifted their joined hands. "Now, concentrate. Fight me."

Autumn rose until she was kneeling, then took a deep breath and squeezed his hands. He could tell she was pushing, could feel the quivering begin in her muscles, but nothing happened.

Finally she sat back, panting. "It's not working."

He'd known it wouldn't. Despair lapped at his courage, but Autumn was not yet defeated.

"Kade, there has to be a way. There has to be something we can do. In the morning, when the sun comes up, one of the boaters will see us."

"No human can see within a shadow cage."

"You mean, we'll be able to see the boats overhead, but they won't see us?" For the first time, he heard real fear in her voice.

He pulled her against him, slipping the circle of his arms over her head and cradling her head against his shoulder. "I'm sorry, sweet one. There's no way out of this."

"Dear God. He's buried us alive." Shivering now as much from fear as cold, he suspected, she wrapped her arms around his neck and buried her face against the warm skin of his throat. "This can't be happening."

He pulled her against him, wrapping his open jacket as far around her as it would go. Her breasts flattened against his cotton shirt. His cheek rubbed against her hair, misery stinging his eyes. "I won't let you suffer. When it becomes too hard for you, I'll end it. All you have to do is tell me you've had all you can take and I'll end it for you quickly and without pain. I promise."

Then he'd hold her corpse until it fell apart in his

hands and hate himself for not protecting her. For not saving her from this fate.

"I'm sorry, Kade," she murmured against his throat. "I shouldn't have insisted on going with you."

He pulled back and kissed her. "No recriminations. No looking to the future. We have now. We have each other." He kissed her again, her lips soft and welcoming against his. "Until I met you, I realize now, I'd never lived at all. I'd gladly trade the rest of my existence for these few days with you. I love you, Autumn McGinn."

Her arms tightened around his neck. "I love you, too."

He held her, letting her words flow over him, but knowing they were born of the desperation of the moment and not true reflections of her heart. No one could love a monster.

He kissed her. "Thank you."

She unwrapped herself from him and put her hands on his cheeks. "You don't believe me. I can hear it in your voice. But I do love you, Kade. Honest-to-God, cross-my-heart."

The wish to believe her threatened to overwhelm him. Along with the certainty that she couldn't. Mustn't. His hands tightened at her back. "I'm not worthy of your love."

"Oh, Kade. Why? Because you're Esri?"

"Because I'm not a good man. I've done terrible things. Millions of them."

"You hurt people."

"Yes."

"But they healed right away."

"Yes, but you don't understand. The fear… The terror

in their eyes as they begged me for mercy…" He pulled her into his arms, needing her warmth to battle the cold tearing at his insides.

His hands fisted at her back as memories poured through him and the need to end the lies. She couldn't love him. And she deserved to understand why.

"There was one…" His voice broke as his mind shied away from memory. But he had to tell her. She had to understand why she couldn't love him. "There was one that haunts my sleep even though it's been centuries."

"Tell me," she murmured.

"Yes. Rith had just risen to power. The law in the land required girls to be twelve before their virginity was sold, but it was well known most were ripe younger. King Rith changed the law and demanded all ripe virgins be brought to him."

"He wanted to rape them himself?"

"He wanted their virgin's power, yes. There were only three. Two Esri and a Marceil slave. The Esri came willingly, but the little Marceil ran. She was ten years old. She'd just come into her ripeness, but was still little more than a child. And Marceils are so small anyway…" She'd been a wisp of a thing, barely reaching his waist. "I was sent to bring her in."

"Not to hurt her?"

"At that point, no. I caught her quickly enough. She begged me to hide her. To protect her. But a girl's virginity is a powerful weapon. Though she might have had a couple more years to get used to the idea, she would have had it taken from her eventually. No, I pitied her for her fear, but no girl keeps her virginity past twelve."

He shuddered with the memory of what came next. "What gives me nightmares was Rith's punishment for her disobedience. He took her brutally, then locked her in a room with me and told me he wanted to hear her screams until morning."

"You tortured her all night long?"

"No. She was already on the verge of hysterics. I broke a few of her bones while Rith watched. Her bones healed quickly enough. Once Rith left, all I had to do was look at her to get her screaming again. But her screams live in my nightmares. Not until today have I ever been so close to renouncing my loyalty to my king." He'd hated Rith that night.

"What happened to her?"

"I don't know. She was sold to a new master soon after and I never saw her again." He laid a gentle kiss on her head. "Don't love me, Autumn. I'm not worthy of so precious a gift."

"You're wrong."

Her words astounded him. Hadn't she heard his confession?

"You hurt people because you had to, Kade. Not because you enjoyed it. There's a huge difference. It was Rith's cruelty that hurt that girl, not yours."

"But it was me she feared and would have continued to fear if she'd remained at court."

"Another bit of Rith's cruelty." Her sweet lips touched his cheek. "You don't enjoy hurting others. When you were sent to kill innocent people, you couldn't do it." Her mouth brushed against his temple in a touch so gentle, he could swear he felt the kiss caress his heart. "And when you realized the evil your king meant for this world, you turned against him."

She kissed him full on the lips this time, stirring his senses. He was so tempted to capture that mouth in a thorough kiss, but he sensed her words weren't finished. And her words were like light filling the darkness of his soul.

"You're a good man, Kade. A wonderful man. I knew you were the one for me within an hour of meeting you, though I think I fell in love with you on the roof that night." Her eyes went wide. "Dear God, they could have killed you up there."

"I thought they were going to."

"But you never acted like it. You threatened to sue them!"

"I had to make them think I was human."

"It worked." She planted another gentle kiss on his cheek. "Afterward, you were standing there in the middle of that circle, surrounded by the Sitheen and you looked up at me, where I was standing by the rail. I can't even explain what happened. I felt as if you saw me. *Really* saw me. And I knew you were the one I'd been waiting for."

"And then you discovered I was Esri."

"Yes, well, that threw me for a bit. But even while my mind was screaming, *He's Esri!* my heart was saying, *He's Kade.*"

Her words seeped into the cold chambers of his heart, filling them with warmth and light and a love beyond bearing.

"I knew I loved you after you hit me in the head with

that pole, then pushed me into the chair to find the injury. You were so concerned. No one had ever shown me such concern."

"I was afraid I was going to have to call an ambulance. I've been a klutz all my life, but that was the first time I nearly killed someone. I could have done some real damage to you with that thing if you'd been human."

"You changed me." He kissed her soft cheek.

"No." Her slender hands cupped his jaw. "You were always in there. You were always a good man, Kade. I'm convinced of that. I'm just the first one you ever let see it."

Chapter 16

Love for Kade poured through Autumn as she sensed he was finally starting to believe the truth. To believe she loved him.

His mouth covered hers in a deep, drugging kiss, his tongue sweeping inside, ending the conversation. She could feel the need in this kiss as she had his others, but something had changed. There was a gentleness beneath the passion this time. Almost a reverence. And she *felt* the miracle of his love.

Slowly their kiss deepened. Kade slid his hands down her back and into the waist of her sweatpants, his fingers cupping her buttocks, sending heat of an entirely different kind flooding through her system.

While his hands kneaded her bottom, he kissed her cheek, then trailed kisses down her neck, making her shudder again with a feeling that had nothing to do with cold or fear. And while her mind was abuzz with questions and fears of what might be happening on the outside of their cage, she understood what he was asking for. Understood what he was offering.

Paradise. For a few hours. Maybe a day. Before she became too thirsty, too hungry, too cold to give him anything more.

Could she forget and give herself up to him for those hours?

Kade kissed her forehead, then her temple, sending shivers racing through her. "Let me love you as you've never been loved. I can make you forget everything but me, everything but us. If you'll let me."

And this would be the last joy he might have for centuries. The last memory. The last love.

She slid her arms around his neck and kissed his mouth. "Love me, Kade," she whispered against his lips. "Love me as no one ever has before nor ever will again."

He kissed her, his mouth covering hers, his lips brushing over hers with tenderness, his kisses growing harder, more urgent with every brush of his lips. But the fire erupted between them and the tenderness turned to need and want. A shiver went through her, part cold, part pure heat as he slid one hand lower, stroking the dampness between her legs.

She gasped and rocked with pleasure against his hands. "I want you. I want to feel you beneath my hands. I want to feel you against me. Over me. *In me.*"

Kade groaned. "If only I could get out of these damned handcuffs."

He would be wearing them until they disintegrated and fell off him. The thought was too terrible to contemplate. She pulled her mind back from the abyss and embraced the moment, refusing to look ahead even a few hours. They had now. And now would have to be enough.

He pulled his arms from around her and pressed her back to the floor. She could see his dark form moving across the wavering moon, then felt his hands at her waist. Her sweatpants and panties slid down her thighs and legs. She heard the soft whisper of fabric on skin and knew he was probably removing his jeans and boxers. The thought made her moist and hot.

He stretched out beside her, his hands moving over her in tandem, the cool chain of the handcuffs between them. One strong hand traced the contours of her body, setting her aflame with each touch, with each kneading of her breast, with each stroke of her hip.

She leaned up and kissed his shoulder and his chest, then grew bold in this desperate hour and reached for him, wanting to feel him in her hands. Her fingers slid over the soft head to the hard, silken shaft. It filled her hand, moving against her palm.

A groan escaped Kade's throat and his lips fastened on her shoulder. "So beautiful," he murmured, his kisses trailing to her neck.

"You can't even see me."

"You feel beautiful. And my hands feel what my eyes have seen before, remembering the contours, raising the pictures in my head. You are the most beautiful woman I've ever seen, ever known."

She gasped, excitement shivering through her body as his tongue trailed beneath her ear.

"Lie down for me."

She did and reached for him, but he didn't cover her body as she expected. She felt him rise onto his elbow a moment before his mouth grazed the top of her breast. His kisses moved lower until his hot mouth covered her breast, sucking the fullness into his mouth right through her bra. She dug her fingers into his hair, holding his face against her, never wanting the wonderful sensations to end.

Her breath caught in her throat as his mouth left her breast. She felt him shift onto his knees. Her stomach quivered as his kisses resumed, leaving damp shivers down her abdomen. His hand hooked beneath her thigh and lifted, opening her to his seeking mouth. Even as the chilled chain dragged across her tender flesh, the heat inside her exploded to fire.

"Kade!" She feared she would come out of her skin at the exquisiteness of the feeling. His tongue slid over her, inside her, sending sensations shooting through her body and spiraling down her limbs, melting her from the inside out. She gasped and arched against his mouth, rocking her hips, desperate for completion.

Just when she thought she would come undone, he lifted his face and kissed her belly. He moved back up her body, kissing the top of her breast.

"I've dreamed of this," he murmured, his voice rich with satisfaction. He covered her mouth with a deep, drugging kiss, and her body with his as he cradled her head in his bound hands.

She opened her legs, welcoming his weight and his

warmth, and the full, hard length of him as he pressed that great fullness against her most sensitive flesh. He entered her slowly, stretching her with ease, sending shafts of brilliant joy arcing through her body. She was ready for him, incredibly in need of this closeness, this completeness.

He filled her, the feeling so intense, so perfect, that on that first stroke he sent her tumbling over the edge in an explosion of passion, finishing what he'd started with his mouth.

He pulled partway out, then thrust into her again and again, every slide of his thickness sending more wondrous contractions cascading through her. Slowly, the heat began to build all over again, her body rising toward another crest.

Kade's body melded with hers in a perfect symmetry. Higher and higher she rose this time. Love for the man in her arms nearly overwhelmed her and tears trickled down her cheeks.

"I love you, Kade," she gasped against his cheek as she neared that final crest.

"I love you, Autumn McGinn."

With the next thrust, she was gasping, swept away by the intensity of the explosion that went through her, an explosion that banished the cold and sent strength barreling through her body. She felt Kade tumbling with her on a groan of pure pleasure, thrusting hard. Again.

"Autumn."

"Hmm?" She opened her eyes, then froze as she stared into a pair of blue nightlights. *Kade's eyes.* In the glow from his eyes, she could see his hair flying above his head.

The stab of fear left over from before, dissipated in a wave of confusion. "But…I'm not a virgin anymore. How did we raise the power again?"

"I don't know."

Against her back, she felt an icy wetness and jerked. "It's cold! Get up! I think we've sprung a leak."

Kade pulled out of her in a last, shivering pleasure, then rolled away and pulled her up. As he looked toward the floor, his blazing eyes shone blue on what was definitely a growing puddle of water.

"We've punched a hole in the cage." A triumphant grin lit his face.

Autumn stared at him. "Does that mean…? Do we have an escape? Or are we…am I…going to drown?"

He swung those blue beacons toward her. If anything they grew brighter. "You're not going to drown. If we raised enough power to do this, we can enlarge it." He moved away from her, screwing up his face as he yanked his hands apart. With a satisfying snap, the chains of the handcuffs broke.

He shrugged out of his coat and swirled it over her shoulders. "If we get out of here, we'll be swimming. The fewer clothes the better." He tore off his shirt and knelt before her, magnificently naked, his hair flying, his blue eyes aglow. As wild and magnificent a malc as was ever made.

He held out his hands to her, the cuff chains dangling from his wrists. She took his hands and he led her to the puddle.

"Sorry, this is going to be cold, but we need to focus all our energy on this one spot."

Autumn nodded, looking into those glowing orbs with amazement. And love. "Let's do it."

"If calling our power hurts, tell me." The smile that lit his mouth was nothing less than feral. "We'll try raising it through more lovemaking."

"Could you do it again so soon?" She hated being such an innocent.

His thumb stroked her cheek. "All I have to do is touch you and I want you all over again." Lowering his hand, he tugged on hers. "Let's try this first. I have an idea."

He knelt in the puddle. "Come around behind me and put your hands on my shoulders."

Autumn rose and went to kneel behind him, her knees sliding between his. She wrapped her arms around his neck and he reached for her hands.

"I want you to hold on to my shoulders and envision your power going through me, sweet one. Do you understand? Don't push against me. Push through me."

"Okay. If this works, will the hole get bigger, or will the cage disappear?"

"I don't know." He squeezed her hands. "I hope we find out."

He released her and she kissed his cheek. "Let's blow this Popsicle stand."

"Let's...what?"

"Don't ask." Autumn laughed, something she never thought she'd do again. But hope was a heady emotion.

"Ready?"

"Do it." Autumn cupped Kade's bare shoulders with her hands and imagined the power surging through her, into him and through his hands.

The water was rising, covering her ankles. Her pulse pounded in her ears. "Is it working?"

"Something's happening. Are you okay?"

"Yes. My hands are warm, but the power doesn't hurt."

"Keep doing whatever you're doing. The hole's getting bigger."

Autumn concentrated hard, pouring everything into Kade on a river of love. Her hands grew warmer as power tingled through her, rising and growing, her mind and body clawing toward an unseen pinnacle. She almost felt as if she were racing for an orgasm, except this release, if it worked, would be literal.

The freezing water lapped at her calves. It *was* working. The water was rising quickly now.

Hope soared as she pushed harder, willing the power into Kade's body.

More. *More.*

The power exploded in a rush, pain shooting through her body on a river of fire and joy.

"That's it!" Kade shouted. "Hold your breath!"

She took one quick, gasping breath and the cage imploded.

Autumn struggled toward the surface, Kade holding tightly to her hand, pulling her up with him. Her head broke the surface and she expelled her caught breath in a gasp, her body still hot with pain. Icy water ran into her eyes and she pushed her hair back, blinking hard.

Kade caught her and pulled her to the ladder on the dock. "Are you okay?"

"Yes."

"The power hurt you. I felt it attack you as it surged."

"It only hurt for a moment. That surge was what we needed."

"Yes." He helped her, half carrying her up the ladder, until they stood, dripping and all but naked on the docks beneath an almost full moon.

"Anyone who sees us is going to think we're crazy."

"Anyone who sees us is going to think they're hallucinating."

Autumn tried to laugh, but the effort was too painful. "We've got to call Jack. Tell him Zander has the stones."

"We've got to get you dry and clothed before you get sick." He swept her into his arms and headed for the houseboat.

Autumn laid her head against his shoulder. "Clothes are good. Maybe they left my purse on the deck with the house keys."

Kade rushed onto the boat. "Can you stand?"

"I think so."

He set her on her feet, propped against the side of the cabin. His eyes had stopped glowing, but the docks were relatively well lit.

"Do you see my purse?"

"No. Zander may have taken it to keep the stones in."

"Cute. Unfortunately, that's where my keys were."

"I'm more concerned about the lack of a phone." He took the sliding door in his hands and wrenched it off its track, removing it from its frame. "What time is it?"

"Why?"

"Because Zander's opening that gate tonight."

Autumn gaped at him. "But…it's not the full moon."

"He means to use the power of the stones. Apparently, Ustanis has the ability to manipulate them in that way."

"But...the Sitheen won't know. They won't be there to stop him."

"Exactly his plan."

The direness of the situation washed over her anew as she stumbled into the dark houseboat and flipped on a light. Her anxious gaze flew to the clock on the microwave. "It's almost eleven-thirty! We don't have much time."

"I need something to wear."

Autumn grabbed a couple of towels and tossed Kade one, then ran back to her small bedroom. She'd taken most of her clothes, but had left a couple of things. She flipped on the light and pulled out a pair of sweatpants that might fit an extra large man. She looked up to find Kade standing in the doorway, towel drying his hair, his hard body gorgeous and still fully aroused. Her gaze moved up to his face and she found his eyes on her, thoroughly hot.

"Mmm-hmm." She tossed him the sweatpants then dug a pair of panties out of her drawer.

"My body has a mind of its own where you're concerned," Kade said, pulling on the pants. "But it's going to have to wait." As she pulled on her jeans, he came to stand in front of her and cupped her bare shoulders with his hands. "Once you're dressed, I want you to leave here. Leave the city so Zander will never find you."

Autumn stared at him. "Kade...no way. I'm coming with you."

He shook his head. "I'm not risking you again."

"I love that you're trying to protect me, but if those

stones fall into the hands of your king, I'm doomed. You said so yourself. Let me help you. If my life is over, let me go out trying to win."

His eyes bored into her, ablaze with emotion and fear…for her. "If Zander gets his hands on you, he'll kill you."

"I know that. But maybe I can help you. I helped you get out of that cage, didn't I?"

He didn't look convinced.

"Kade, please. All my life I've wanted to do something important. This is my chance to make a difference. To actually help instead of always screwing things up."

He grabbed her. "I can't lose you."

"I can't lose you, either. Which is why I refuse to send you there alone. Don't take this from me, Kade. Let me help. Let me be part of this."

She could see the struggle written across his face. And knew the moment she'd won. "This really means that much to you?"

"You know it does."

He kissed her hard. "You have more courage than anyone I've ever known."

"Is that a yes?"

"Against my better judgment."

Autumn grinned and finished dressing in record time. She grabbed a jacket and hurried after him through the open door. "Are we going to run all the way to Dupont Circle?"

"No, it's too far. And we need to get a phone." He grabbed her hand and they ran through the marina and up to the street, which was lined with bars and restaurants.

"What are you going to do?"

"I'm hoping I'm able to control others again."

Autumn squeezed his hand. "A cop!"

"Perfect." He started running toward the police cruiser as it pulled into a parking lot half a block down.

"Kade, are you crazy? They'll try to arrest us, again!"

He released her hand. "Wait here. They can't harm me."

"No." She sighed as he took off. "And you'll make such a great impression with those broken handcuffs around your wrists."

She watched as he started running, moving so fast, she could hardly see him. He reached the police officer as he was getting out of his cruiser, probably without the man ever knowing he was there. The cop got back into the car and Kade jumped in behind him. A minute later, the car pulled up in front of Autumn. She opened the back door and jumped in.

Kade touched the officer's neck. "You will put on your sirens and drive to Dupont Circle as quickly as you would in the direst emergency. First give me your phone."

"Personal phone," Autumn said hurriedly, not wanting to be handed some high tech cop thing.

"Personal phone."

The cop pulled something from his back pocket and handed it to Kade, then started the sirens and took off.

Kade handed Autumn the phone. "Is there a problem?" he asked as she stared at it in consternation.

"I'm trying to decide the best way to go about this. I don't know anyone's numbers. They're all programmed into my speed dial. Let me try 4-1-1."

She called information, got nothing for Jack, but finally got a number for Larsen.

"Autumn?" Larsen asked sleepily.

"Larsen! The Esri have all seven stones and they're opening the gate tonight."

"What?"

"At midnight. Listen to me. Kade's not what Jack thinks."

"He's Esri. Autumn, Kade is Esri! One of the cops shot him in the forehead and the bullet popped out."

"I know he's Esri. But he's on our side. We're heading to Dupont Circle right now to try to stop the other Esri from taking those stones through. We'll meet you guys there."

And hopefully one of them would get there in time to stop the Esri from taking those stones into Esria. *Someone* had to save the world.

Chapter 17

Kade held Autumn against him, relief flooding through him, as the cop tore through the relatively empty streets, sirens blaring. Against all odds, they'd escaped the shadow cage.

She loved him.

Never had his spirit soared so high. His heart still ached from the sweetness of her declaration, though he doubted he'd ever feel he deserved her love. But he would cherish it for all the long, dark years ahead of him. If he survived this night.

The car careened around a corner and he braced himself, holding her tightly. "Are you feeling better?"

"Yes. I'm fine." She looked up at him with such happiness, such *hope* in her eyes. "It was worth a little discomfort to escape that cage, believe me."

He kissed her, pouring his love into her, wishing with everything he was that they could have a future together. That she could be his mate. But it could never be.

The police officer pulled the cruiser to a jarring stop in front of Dupont Circle Park, blocking traffic in the circle. In the middle of the park rose the huge marble fountain the humans had built upon the gate to Esria.

In front of the fountain, Zander and Ustanis worked to open the gate. Kade could see the green stones lying in a circle around the fountain, already glowing. Ustanis was standing on the fountain's base, his hands raised to the sky, his orange eyes bright, his hair whipping around his face.

Kade jumped out of the car, pulling Autumn with him, then ordered the policeman back to the waterfront. When the cruiser drove off, Kade pulled Autumn close, his heart in his throat. "Stay here. You *must*. I'm going to try to get those stones, but I don't want you coming near Zander. Once the Sitheen arrive, they'll take over.

"Autumn…" He grabbed her shoulders and pulled her around to face him. "If that gate opens, I'm leaving tonight." And if it didn't, if he managed to stop Zander and Ustanis and hold them until the Sitheen arrived, Jack and the others would sing their death chant for all three of them. Either way, his time in this world was at an end. "This has to be goodbye."

He saw the shock in her eyes and was sorry for it. He kissed her hard. "I love you."

"Kade…" He released her and took off running, but not before he heard her say, "I love you, too."

Living without her was going to be the hardest thing he'd ever done. But living without her, *knowing* Rith was destroying her world, would be unbearable. He must not fail.

Kade ran for Ustanis, using his increased speed to cover the distance in a handful of seconds. First, he must keep that gate from opening. Second, he had to get the draggon stone. He knew better than to think he could take the two Esri alone. The help of the Sitheen was critical even though it would likely mean his death. If that was what it took to save this world—Autumn's world—then it was a sacrifice he was prepared to make.

His speed allowed him to reach Ustanis before either of the two Esri realized he was there. He grabbed Ustanis. The power Ustanis was raising singed Kade's hands, but he pushed through the discomfort, and with the Punisher's growl, threw the Esri far from the gate. He landed in the grass a good twenty feet away. Kade ran for him, determined to get that draggon stone.

Ustanis leaped to his feet and faced him, holding his ground. He now knew, as Zander always had, that Kade's strength was all in his muscles.

"I don't approve of Zander's plan, Punisher. Nor my king's."

"Then give me the stone, Ustanis."

His eyes darted with fear. "I cannot. It is my duty…"

Kade lunged for him and Ustanis met him head-on, his hands outstretched, his orange eyes still glowing. But Kade was too fast. He grabbed the other Esri's wrists and hauled him forward.

"The draggon stone isn't your duty. It's mine."

The stone was within reach. But before he could take it, something hit his head and stuck. Pain exploded.

Zander.

He couldn't release Ustanis or he'd lose the stone and he had to get that stone. As he reached for Ustanis's neck, a second hand slammed into his arm, searing it with agony.

"How did you escape?" Zander hissed in his ear.

Kade struggled to reach Ustanis, but the power ripping through his head was stealing his balance, disorienting him.

"You should not have been able to escape! That was my revenge, dark blood. I will end you here. Now."

"If you end me," Kade gasped, "you forfeit your life." Autumn would die. Her entire world would die.

"Nay!" Zander spat. "You're a traitor. A murderer. You should have been ended centuries ago for destroying my Pensia, Malcolm. You'll not live another day."

"I'm not Malcolm!"

But Zander didn't seem to hear him.

His vision wavered. The pain in his head was intolerable. Unendurable for much longer. His mind was fogging. *No.* He couldn't die. He must save the stones. He must save Autumn's world.

Kade struggled to reach the hand against his head, the pain destroying his sense of direction. His fingers closed around the wrist and he yanked, tearing the hand loose from his head. But the pain remained. And Zander still had hold of his other arm and was pouring pain into his body, a hundred times worse than he'd ever done before. Never before had Zander meant to kill him. Tonight, he did.

Belatedly, he realized he no longer had Ustanis. His blurred vision tried to focus on the spot where the glowing-eyed Esri had stood a moment before. He was gone.

Kade fought the pain, focusing on Autumn. Lurching around, he grabbed Zander's leg and pulled, unbalancing the white Esri for a moment. He snapped the leg in three places before the pain slammed into his arm again. Kade turned, grabbing Zander's arms, but not quickly enough. The pain was making him slow. Zander caught Kade's arms in the same grip. It was too much. Despite the renewed power, it was too much. He couldn't beat Zander. And if Zander killed him, all was lost.

A blast of power hit him from the fountain and he would have stumbled if he'd not been holding on to Zander.

Ustanis had done it. He'd opened the gate.

As he watched, Ustanis jumped into the fountain and disappeared, the draggon stone still glowing around his neck. If Zander picked up the six green stones and followed, the human realm was doomed.

Kade struggled against the pain of Zander's fiery touch.

"I will end you, dark blood. I have hated you for an eternity. I have waited for the perfect revenge. Now, you've stolen it from me. No more! I will end you now. Here!"

Zander's words swirled in his head, blending with the pain that fired his body as they struggled, locked in combat. Thanks to the renewal of the strength he'd found with Autumn, he was strong enough to fight this superior foe. But fighting wasn't enough. He must win.

Something tugged at his shirt behind him. He barely felt it, had no time to worry about it. Then cold hands pressed against the heated flesh of his back.

Autumn.

"Autumn...no! Run! Get...away." If he lost this battle, Zander would kill her. Or worse.

"No." The soft word exploded in his ear. "You're going to beat him. I'm going to help you beat him. I love you, Kaderil."

She'd never called him Kaderil. Kaderil was a monster. The thought penetrated the fog of pain. She loved the monster. The knowledge filled his heart and his mind with a fresh and desperate determination.

As she held on to him, as she pushed her strength into him as she had in the shadow cage, he felt the stirrings of power buzzing along his flesh.

"Too...dangerous," he ground between teeth clenched tight with pain.

"I love you." Her words, and the depth of emotion behind them, poured into him. "We'll do this together."

His skin had to be burning her hands, yet she held on. Such determination. Such courage.

Already, he was starting to feel stronger. Her power renewed his. Her love made him feel reborn, mighty in ways he'd never been before.

But Zander did not back down. Hatred flowed out of him in waves. "You don't deserve to live, dark blood. You've never deserved to live!"

The intensity of Zander's hatred was astounding. It became suddenly, brutally clear that only one of them would survive this night. The survivor must not be Zander.

The power surged suddenly, racing through him as it had in the shadow cage. He heard Autumn gasp behind him.

"Autumn! Let go."

"No."

"It's going to damage you."

"Doesn't matter. You must win."

He could feel the energy building, growing stronger moment by moment. Heat built in his body, in the hands he pressed against Zander's arms. Nose to nose, they battled, hatred arcing between them, fury seething in their eyes.

The power roared through Kade's body, building in a cresting wave, strength beyond anything he'd ever known. He struggled, using every ounce of power, muscle and will in his body. He must stop Zander.

"I will end you, dark blood." Zander's eyes began to smoke. His skin beneath Kade's hands turned scorching. "I will end you!"

With a cry, Zander arched back, his body sparking. Kade released him a second before Zander burst into flame.

The death chant. Kade hesitated only a second before whispering the words that would end this deadly foe.

As it flamed, Zander's body began to sparkle with the lights of death, a million iridescent colors. The lights rose to hover above him before exploding in a brilliant arc, turning Zander's body to ash.

The full import of what he'd done slowly sank in. He'd killed a fellow Esri and was now marked for death. He couldn't go back. Couldn't stay here. But Autumn was safe.

He turned to her and froze as he saw her on the ground, unconscious…or dead. His heart stopped in his chest. He fell to his knees beside her, his hands frantically touching her, feeling for life. She was on fire, but breath still struggled within her.

"Get away from her, Kade...or whatever your real name is!" Charlie was bearing down on him with a flamethrower, his face tight with hatred, but the only thing that mattered was Autumn.

Kade scooped her into his arms, his chest so tight with fear, he thought his own heart would stop beating. "Cool your body, Autumn. Cool the fire." *Please let my words be enough to save her. If they're not, I don't know what to do.*

He looked up at the Sitheen who had once looked at him with welcome and friendship. The man whose eyes now blazed hatred.

"She's dying, Charlie. I have to try to save her."

"Autumn!" Larsen came running, Jack and Harrison close behind her.

"What did you do to her, you bastard?" Jack roared.

Kade shook his head, his senses focused on Autumn. Her body wasn't cooling. It wasn't working! "She helped me defeat Zander, but it was too much for her. I must help her or she'll die."

Desperation fueled his anger as he rose to his full height, holding Autumn tightly against himself. "Back off!" he growled, the full force of the Punisher in his voice. "I must save her!"

Larsen stepped forward and grabbed Charlie's arm. "Guard the gate, Charlie. You, too, Jack. Let him do what he can for her."

Jack stared at her. "He's Esri!"

"Look at him! He's a man protecting his mate. He loves her, Jack. Let him help her."

Jack scowled, but he backed down. "Son of a bitch."

Larsen met Kade's gaze. "Save her, Kade. I love her, too."

Kade nodded, but as he laid Autumn on the grass, the fury drained away, replaced by cold fear that he was already too late. He'd demanded they let him save her, but he didn't know how! Before, when she'd been full of pain, she'd been awake. She'd told him how she hurt or that she was too cold, and he'd helped her. He didn't know what to do!

Power. He still had power. But the power was hot. It went into her and harmed her. Maybe, if he could reverse the process...

He knelt beside her and took her limp burning hands in his. He closed his eyes and pulled the heat back into his own body. "Autumn, hear me. Cool your body. I'm trying to pull the heat out of you. Help me. Purge yourself of the fire. Give it to me instead."

Little by little, he felt his body heating. Little by little, her hands cooled. But she wasn't stirring. It wasn't enough.

He gripped her hands tighter. "Don't leave me, sweet one. Don't leave me." He felt the heat go into his eyes and felt his eyes bleed tears. "I love you, Autumn McGinn. You can't die!"

"Pour your love into her, Kaderil."

Kade's eyes snapped open. Through the moisture that fogged his vision he saw Jack squatting on the other side of Autumn, his hands on his knees. "Not your power. She can't handle the power. Just your love."

Kade blinked, then nodded. He squeezed his eyes closed, feeling the moisture track down his cheeks. His love for her filled him so completely it threatened to absorb his entire being. With everything inside him, every ounce of strength he possessed, he pushed his heart and soul into her through his hands.

Still, it wasn't enough.

He lay down beside her, lifting their joined hands to her head and pressed his fingers against her temples. Then he lowered his head and covered her warm, still lips with his mouth.

Live, Autumn. You. Must. Live. I love you more than life. Beyond measure.

Against her mouth, he whispered, "Live for me. I love you. *I love you.*"

He kissed her, willing her to live as the tears flowed freely down his cheeks.

A slight movement against his mouth made him freeze. Had he imagined it?

No. Autumn's mouth moved ever so slightly against his. Joy exploded through him. "Autumn…"

He kissed her, pouring his love into her. Her lips moved again, stronger moment by moment until she was kissing him back thoroughly, her tongue sliding into his mouth, her arms sliding around his neck to pull him close.

He wanted to shout and laugh and rejoice.

He pulled back from her kiss to gaze into her eyes, searching for assurance that he wasn't imagining her recovery. Gray eyes shining with love stared back at him.

He brushed a loose tendril of hair from her face. "Are you okay?"

"Yes. Did we win?"

"Zander is no more. But Ustanis has the draggon. And he's gone through the gate." In his peripheral vision he saw the flamethrowers in the hands of the Sitheen. With a jolt, his desire to laugh died. He kissed her one more time, a brief outpouring of his love, then he stood and helped her to her feet.

Autumn at his side, he faced the Sitheen. "I believe the six lesser stones of power are still here. The pale green stones lying in a circle around the fountain. But the draggon stone has gone through the gate. If Ustanis is still close by, I may be able to get it back. I'm your only chance."

Charlie raised his flamethrower. "You're not going anywhere."

The other three Sitheen moved around him until he and Autumn stood at the center of the deadly circle. And he knew it was over. These were the people who must fight this war, not him. Chances were slim he'd make it through the gate and back with the draggon stone before it closed. And once in Esria, he would soon be destroyed for having ended Zander. His life was over either way.

He pulled Autumn against him and kissed her hard, one last time, feeling her warm body pressed against his, wishing he could stop time right this moment. He gazed down into her gray eyes and felt his heart break at the loss, at the knowledge he would never touch her again. "I love you, Autumn McGinn. Now, go." Releasing her, he gave her a gentle push toward Larsen.

But she held her ground stubbornly. "No way. They're not going to hurt you."

She didn't understand. "Autumn…this is the way it must be." He looked to Jack for help. "I won't fight you. But I don't want her to watch."

Autumn whirled to him, then back to the others. "You're not going to kill him. My God, after all you've seen, after all he's done, you've got to see he's not evil. He's a good man. He risked his life…he *forfeited* his life in his world in order to help us."

"He's Esri," Harrison spat.

"Actually…he's only half Esri," Jack said, his tone strangely conversational. He was the only one of the Sitheen whose flamethrower remained at his side. "And if we kill him, I'm going to have a riot erupting in my head."

"What do you mean?" Larsen asked.

Kade's pulse raced with tension. He'd accepted his fate. What was this game?

Jack shrugged, an almost-smile forming on his mouth as he met Kade's gaze. "It seems we're related, Kaderil."

"Why are you calling me Kaderil?" Kade stared at the man…the human. "Related?"

Jack cocked his head. "Have you ever heard the name Malcolm?"

"Yes." Zander had said the name often enough. "Who is he?"

"You don't know?"

"I know only that Zander blamed a human named Malcolm for the death of his mate."

Jack stood as if listening to a voice only he could hear. Slowly he started to nod. "Malcolm killed several Esri when they attacked his village fifteen hundred years ago. Zander's mate might well have been one of them."

Kade stared at him. "Isn't Malcolm the name of one of the ancestors who talks to you in your head?"

Jack nodded. "My oldest Sitheen ancestor and the one who's best able to answer my questions."

"But what does this have to do with me?"

Jack did smile now. "He was your father, Kaderil."

Kade stared at him, his jaw dropping. "I had no father."

"Yeah, he's sorry about that. Your mother was also half Esri, but immortality passes along the maternal side and she was immortal. She had to return to Esria to birth you. While there, she learned of Zander's plot to attack your father's village. She left you behind, where you'd be safe, and returned to warn your father. But she was captured by a Sitheen who didn't know her and destroyed her before your father could save her. Your father tried to find a way to get to you, but humans can't travel through the gates unescorted, and the Esri and humans were at war in that place. Soon after, the gates were sealed and you were lost to him. He never forgot you, never stopped worrying about you."

Jack moved toward him, his tension gone. "Apparently, when I shook your hand on the roof that first time, your father recognized you. He lied and told me you were Sitheen, fearing I'd kill you if I knew you were immortal." His expression turned grave. "I would have."

Kade shook his head, his mind reeling from this revelation. "He took a terrible risk. I was sent to kill you. To kill all of you."

"He suspected that." Jack laughed and shrugged. "He hoped we'd work it out."

"And have we?"

"I think maybe we have." Jack's gaze went to Autumn. "You trust him?"

She slid her arms around Kade's waist, filling him with overwhelming gratitude. Never in his life had he had someone stand beside him. Believe in him.

"I trust him. More than that, I *know* him. I've seen inside him, Jack. He's as fine an ally as humans could ever hope to have."

Jack pursed his lips and nodded slowly. "Your father says you've made him proud, Kaderil. He's glad, after all this time, you're finally home."

"Home." The word felt alien to his tongue and yet the hope that blossomed inside him was unbearably fragile. He was half human. As human as he was Esri.

"It's up to you, of course," Jack said. "But I'm thinking Autumn would be very happy if you stayed."

"Hot damn," Charlie said. "We've got us our very own Esri."

Kade shook his head. "I would stay. There is nothing I wish more. But Ustanis took the draggon stone through the gate, and I must try to retrieve it before he gives it to King Rith. Rith will cause great destruction to your world with those stones."

Autumn looked up at him, her eyes filling with misery. "But they'll kill you. You said yourself it's forbidden to kill another Esri."

"Esri!" Larsen yelled. "They're coming through again."

Kade swung toward the gate as the Sitheen raised their flamethrowers. But standing ghostlike in the fountain was only one Esri, Ustanis's young son. He stood half in this world and half in the other, out of danger from the Sitheen's fire.

"It's the kid," Autumn gasped. Charlie started forward and Autumn yelled, "Charlie, no!" The youth's image dimmed until Charlie stopped, then grew more solid again. The boy's wary gaze slowly moved from the warrior to Autumn.

"My lady. I gave you my vow to repay your kindness. My father, Ustanis, gave me leave to give you this." He threw something out of the fountain, a chain that glittered in the moonlight and landed on the pavement with a soft clatter. A moment later, he disappeared.

Charlie rushed forward. "It's the draggon stone! The Esri gave back the draggon stone."

Autumn whirled to Kade, laughing, her face a mask of surprised delight. Love for her welled to overflowing and he lifted her high and swung her around. When he set her on her feet, she hugged him tightly.

"I owe you an apology, Autumn." Jack's tone was full of wry appreciation. "I thought you'd made a mistake by letting that kid go. But I think you may have just saved us all."

"Thanks, Jack." Autumn's joy shimmered over her in waves.

"Uh…that draggon stone went through the gate." Charlie strolled back to join them. "Wasn't that thing the key that was supposed to open all twelve gates if it ever again entered Esria?"

They all looked at one another with dismay.

"I guess we'll know soon enough," Jack said. His

gaze swung to Kade and Autumn. "Are you two on board? We're going to need you. Both of you."

Autumn looked up, meeting Kade's gaze with laughter in her eyes. "They need us."

He nodded, love misting his vision. "No one will ever need you as much as I. Come." He took her hand and pulled her a short distance from the others. "For the first time in my life, I have a place and a people. And a purpose I believe in. But none of that means anything without you. Will you be my mate, my wife, Autumn McGinn?"

Love shone from her eyes. "There's nothing I want more. I would be honored, Kaderil, to be your wife."

He smiled. "Kade. Kaderil was Esri. Kade is human. And while we both love you, Kade is the one who belongs here, in this world." He kissed her. "By your side."

Autumn grinned, tears overflowing her eyes. "I love you, Kade."

And he knew he'd found his true place at last.

* * * * *

The editors at Harlequin Blaze have never been afraid to push the limits—tempting readers with the forbidden, whetting their appetites with a wide variety of story lines. But now we're breaking the final barrier—the time barrier.

In July, watch for BOUND TO PLEASE by fan favorite Hope Tarr, Harlequin Blaze's first ever historical romance—a story that's truly Blaze-worthy in every sense.

Here's a sneak peek....

BRIANNA stretched out beside Ewan, languid as a cat, and promptly fell asleep. Midday sunshine streamed into the chamber, bathing her lovely, long-limbed body in golden light, the sea-scented breeze wafting inside to dry the damp red-gold tendrils curling about her flushed face. Propping himself up on one elbow, Ewan slid his gaze over her. She looked beautiful and whole, satisfied and sated and altogether happier than he had so far seen her. A slight smile curved her beautiful lips as though she must be in the midst of a lovely dream. She'd molded her lush, lovely body to his and laid her head in the curve of his shoulder and settled in to sleep beside him. For the longest while he lay there turned toward her, content to watch her sleep, at near perfect peace.

Not wholly perfect, for she had yet to answer his marriage proposal. Still, she wanted to make a baby with him, and Ewan no longer viewed her plan as the travesty he once had. He wanted children—sons to carry on after him, though a bonny little daughter with flame-colored hair would be nice, too. But he also wanted more than to simply plant his seed and be on his way. He wanted to lie beside Brianna night upon night as she increased, rub soothing unguents into the swell of her belly, knead the ache from her back and make slow, gentle love to her. He wanted to hold his newly born child in his arms and look down into Brianna's tired but radiant face and blot the perspiration from her brow and be a husband to her in every way.

He gave her a gentle nudge. "Brie?"

"Hmm?"

She rolled onto her side and he captured her against his chest. One arm wrapped about her waist, he bent to her ear and asked, "Do you think we might have just made a baby?"

Her eyes remained closed, but he felt her tense against him. "I don't know. We'll have to wait and see."

He stroked his hand over the flat plane of her belly. "You're so small and tight it's hard to imagine you increasing."

"All women increase no matter how large or small they start out. I may not grow big as a croft, but I'll be big enough, though I have hopes I may not waddle like a duck, at least not too badly."

The reference to his fair-day teasing was not lost on him. He grinned. "Brianna MacLeod grown so large she must sit still for once in her life. I'll need the proof of my own eyes to believe it."

Despite their banter, he felt his spirits dip. Assuming they were so blessed, he wouldn't have the chance to see her thus. By then he would be long gone, restored to his clan according to the sad bargain they'd struck. He opened his mouth to ask her to marry him again and then clamped it closed, not wanting to spoil the moment, but the unspoken words weighed like a millstone on his heart.

The damnable bargain they'd struck was proving to be a devil's pact indeed.

* * * * *

*Will these two star-crossed lovers find
their sexily-ever-after?
Find out in BOUND TO PLEASE by Hope Tarr,
available in July wherever Harlequin® Blaze™
books are sold.*

USA TODAY Bestselling Author

JENNIFER ARMINTROUT

I have reached my breaking point. And now I will not, cannot be stopped.

With the Soul Eater on the verge of God status, it's time for me to take a final stand, even if it means losing everything. Even my life.

I've got plenty of power on my side. But it's nothing compared to the army the Soul Eater is building up. And time is running out.

They say that good always triumphs over evil. I hope that's true. Because the odds aren't in our favor, and the fate of the world is in our hands.

blood ties book four: all SOULS' NIGHT

"This fast, furious novel is a squirm-inducing treat."
—*Publishers Weekly* on *Blood Ties Book One: The Turning*

MIRA®

Available the first week of June 2008 wherever books are sold!

www.MIRABooks.com   MJA2537

REQUEST YOUR FREE BOOKS!

2 FREE NOVELS PLUS 2 FREE GIFTS!

Silhouette®

nocturne™

Dramatic and Sensual Tales of Paranormal Romance.

SN08R

Silhouette® Desire

HIGH-SOCIETY SECRET PREGNANCY

Park Avenue Scandals

Self-made millionaire Max Rolland had given up on love until he meets socialite fundraiser Julia Prentice. After their encounter Julia finds herself pregnant, but a mysterious blackmailer threatens to use this surprise pregnancy and ruin his reputation. Max must decide whether to turn his back on the woman carrying his child or risk everything, including his heart....

Don't miss the next installment of the Park Avenue Scandals series—
Front Page Engagement
**by Laura Wright—
coming in August 2008
from Silhouette Desire!**

Always Powerful, Passionate and Provocative.

Romantic
SUSPENSE

Sparked by Danger, Fueled by Passion.

Conard County: The Next Generation

When he learns the truth about his father, military man Ethan Parish is determined to reunite with his long-lost family in Wyoming. On his way into town, he clashes with policewoman Connie Halloran, whose captivating beauty entices him. When Connie's daughter is threatened, Ethan must use his military skills to keep her safe. Together they race against time to find the little girl and confront the dangers inherent in family secrets.

Look for

A Soldier's Homecoming

by *New York Times* bestselling author
Rachel Lee

Available in July wherever you buy books.

Thoroughbred Legacy

The purse is set and the stakes are high...

Romance, scandal and glamour set in the exhilarating world of horse racing!

Follow the 12-book continuity, starting in July with:

Flirting with Trouble, Book #1
by New York Times bestselling author
ELIZABETH BEVARLY

Biding Her Time, Book #2
by **WENDY WARREN**

Picture of Perfection, Book #3
by **KRISTIN GABRIEL**

Something To Talk About, Book #4
by **JOANNE ROCK**

*Available wherever books are sold,
including most bookstores, supermarkets,
discount stores and drugstores.*

Silhouette

nocturne™

COMING NEXT MONTH

#43 BEAST OF DARKNESS • Lisa Renee Jones
The Knights of White

After breaking the order's most sacred rule, Max needs only to pass a test to regain his knighthood. But is his humanity too far gone, or can Sarah—who communes with the spirit world—bind the beast that lurks within?

#44 HIS FORGOTTEN FOREVER • Michele Hauf
Bewitching the Dark

A war between the vampires and witches had been brewing for centuries before Truvin Stone stirred it to a boil. Now, with no memory of his former life, Truvin can right his many wrongs, but only if he doesn't use the love of Lucy Morgan's pure soul to nefarious ends.